DATE			

AUG 3 0 1984

THE
CAPTIVE SOUL
OF THE MESSIAH

BY HOWARD SCHWARTZ

Poetry
Vessels
Gathering the Sparks

Fiction
A Blessing Over Ashes
Lilith's Cave
Midrashim: Collected Jewish Parables
The Captive Soul of the Messiah

Editor
Imperial Messages: One Hundred Modern Parables
Voices Within the Ark: The Modern Jewish Poets
Gates to the New City: A Treasury of Modern Jewish Tales
Elijah's Violin & Other Jewish Fairy Tales

THE
CAPTIVE SOUL
OF THE MESSIAH

New Tales About Reb Nachman

by Howard Schwartz
Illustrated by Mark Podwal

SCHOCKEN BOOKS • NEW YORK

First published by Schocken Books 1983
10 9 8 7 6 5 4 3 2 1   83 84 85 86

Library of Congress Cataloging in Publication Data
Schwartz, Howard, 1945–
   The captive soul of the messiah.
   1. Parables, Hasidic.   2. Messiah—Legends.
3. Nachman, of Bratslav, 1772–1811—Legends.   4. Hasidim
—Legends.   5. Legends, Jewish.   I. Nachman, of Bratslav,
1772–1811.   II. Title.
BM532.S37   1983   296.8'33   83–42710

Designed by Nancy Dale Muldoon
Manufactured in the United States of America
ISBN 0–8052–3873–5

Acknowledgments

Some of these tales have previously been published in the following journals: *Agada,
The Aquarian Minyan Newsletter, Conservative Judaism, Contemporary Literature in
Translation, Corona, Four Worlds Journal, Genesis 2, The Jewish Post, Judaica Book News,
Judaism, The Melton Journal, Merkava, Midstream, New Traditions, Parabola, The Recon-
structionist, Response, River Styx, The St. Louis Jewish Light,* and *Tales.*

Some tales have also been published in the following anthologies: *A Big Jewish Book,
Gates to the New City: A Treasury of Modern Jewish Tales, Imperial Messages: One Hundred
Modern Parables,* and *Wandering Stars II.*

"The Golden Bird" is reprinted from *Elijah's Violin & Other Jewish Fairy Tales* by
Howard Schwartz. Text copyright © 1982 by Howard Schwartz. Reprinted by
permission of Harper & Row, Publishers, Inc..

FOR BONNY FETTERMAN

If a man could pass through Paradise in a dream, and have a flower presented to him as a pledge that his soul had really been there, and if he found that flower in his hand when he awoke—Ay!—and what then?

SAMUEL TAYLOR COLERIDGE

Contents

Three THE GOLDEN DOVE

Preface

In his tales, teachings, and the few dreams that have come down to us, Rabbi Nachman of Bratslav emerges as a figure drawing from the wellspring of inspiration. The world as he saw it was filled with signs, omens, and premonitions. Every act, no matter how small, held potentially great significance.

On his deathbed Rabbi Nachman told his Hasidim it was not necessary for them to appoint a successor—he would always be their Rebbe. His Hasidim obeyed and still regard Nachman as their master. Nor have the Bratslavers withered away in the absence of a Rebbe, but have flourished as if Nachman's hidden hand provided all the guidance they required.

But it is not only the Bratslavers who have encountered Rabbi Nachman's wandering spirit. There are an astonishing number of reports of those who have experienced Nachman's benevolent presence, reports not unlike those about Elijah the Prophet which are so common in Jewish folklore. Some of these reports come from respectable sources, such as the Israeli writer Yehuda Yaari. Yaari told me that while he was working on a Hebrew edition of Nachman's tales, he did not refer to the originals, but worked from memory. And as he wrote he swore he heard Nachman's voice reciting the tales, and like Rabbi Nussan of Nemerov before him, he wrote down what he heard. I may be gullible, but I believe Yaari, whose retellings of Nachman's tales are among the most inspired.

As for the tales collected here, they are not, for the most part, retellings of Nachman's tales, but tales inspired by Nachman's own, by his world vision, and by his powerful spirit. They were written in the awareness that the springs of inspiration are eternal, and that while Nachman drew from those springs far more than most, there still are many untold tales left to tell.

Howard Schwartz

One

THE BOOK OF REB ADAM

The Book of Reb Adam

Now there was a Book that contained all of the celestial mysteries, but it had been lost for many centuries, and was presumed to have been burned when the Temple in Jerusalem was destroyed. So believed all of mankind, but Samael, the Evil One, knew otherwise. He knew that the Book still existed, and even where it had been hidden. For the Lord had commanded the angel Hadarniel to conceal the Book in a cave in the wilderness, and there, at God's command, the angel had pronounced a spell which made it possible for only the pure souls who were born among men to take it from that place. After they had read it, and made its knowledge their own, they had returned the Book to that cave. In this way it had come into the possession of great sages, such as Simeon bar Yohai and Rabbi Isaac Luria, known as the Ari, who revealed some of its infinite truths in their teachings, but only those which they were permitted to reveal. And how did these sages discover the secret of where the Book of Mysteries was hidden? Some, such as Enoch, learned of it in a dream, while to others, such as Abraham, its hiding place was revealed by an angel.

By reading in this Book it was possible to penetrate great secrets of knowledge, hierarchies of understanding, and ideas of wisdom; to know the way of life and the way of death, the way of good and the way of evil; and to forsee the concerns of each and every year, whether for peace or for war, for plenty or for hunger, for harvest or for drought. By gazing there the destinies of the stars were revealed, as well as the course of the sun and the names of the overseers of each and every firmament. Revealed as well were the secrets of how to interpret dreams and visions, and how to rule over all of a man's desires, as well as how to drive away evil spirits and demons. Happy was the eye that beheld that Book, and happy the ear that listened to its wisdom, for in it were revealed all the secrets of heaven and earth.

There once was a holy man whose name was Reb Adam. He lived alone in a small hut in the forest, where he studied the Torah day and night. In this way he had gained knowledge of many mysteries, and thus he had attained great powers. But he only used these powers to serve the ways of righteousness, for his soul was very pure.

Now there was also an evil sorcerer in league with Samael, who discovered through his knowledge of the stars the existence of the Book of Mysteries, and even the location of it. But because of the spell that the angel Hadarniel had cast, it was impossible for him to enter the cave in order to bring the Book out. For only one of the pure souls could remove the Book from that place, and in every generation there was only one such soul to be found. So it was that the evil sorcerer searched in the stars and discovered that the pure soul in that generation was Reb Adam. And the sorcerer tried to think of a way to trick Reb Adam into turning over the sacred Book to him. For once the sorcerer had it in his possession, he could become ruler of the world, since the Book would give him almost infinite power.

The sorcerer thought long and hard about how he could make Reb Adam perform this deed for him. At last he decided to cause an illness to fall upon him, a contagious disease. This he accomplished by casting a spell that only he knew how to break. And this was the first step in his plan.

Reb Adam was very surprised when he became ill, for he had never been sick a day in his life. But now he found himself with a serious disease, and since he did not know its cause, he decided that he had better see a doctor. So he walked into town, and went to visit the finest doctor there, as the evil sorcerer had known he would. Meanwhile, the sorcerer, who could make himself resemble anyone else through his magical powers, had kidnapped the doctor and taken his place. And when Reb Adam came to him, he warned him that the disease was quite contagious, and that he must therefore depart to a very remote place, so as not to endanger others. Naturally Reb Adam did not want to bring harm to anyone else, so he obeyed the order and went to the distant place the sorcerer had suggested. And the sorcerer saw to it that this was near the cave where the Book of Mysteries had been hidden.

Now Reb Adam vowed to remain in that desolate place until he had been cured of his illness. Yet despite all the remedies he tried and all the prayers he offered up, he remained as sick as ever. Then one day a wanderer came to the hut where Reb Adam lived. Reb Adam covered his face and told the man to depart because of his illness, but the man, who was the evil sorcerer in another disguise, said he had heard of Reb Adam's illness from his doctor and that he knew of a cure for it.

Now Reb Adam was very encouraged to learn that there might be a cure for his illness. And so he listened to what the wanderer had to say. Thus he learned that in a nearby cave there was a certain manuscript, preserved in a golden casket, and if Reb Adam agreed to retrieve this Book for him, the wanderer would cure him of his disease. Reb Adam vowed to do as the man had asked, and the evil sorcerer passed his hand over Reb Adam's body, and he was healed. Now Reb Adam wondered greatly at the powers of this man, but at the same time he was very grateful the disease had been cured. Then the wanderer led him to the cave in which the Book was hidden. But before Reb Adam entered it the wanderer said, "Remember, you have vowed to give this Book to me, and a holy man such as yourself would never break a vow. Also, you must not open the Book at all, nor read from it, for it does not belong to you, but to me."

Then Reb Adam crawled into the entrance of the cave, to search for the Book where the wanderer had told him to. At last he found it, concealed in a crevice, and when he held it in his hands he sensed it was very sacred and wondered what Book it could be. At first he did not open the Book, since the wanderer had forbidden it, but then he thought about the strange acts of this man, who had the power to cure him with a wave of his hand but had not been able to enter the cave to retrieve the Book. And he began to suspect that the man might serve the powers of evil rather than the powers of good.

So it was that Reb Adam decided to examine that Book, and

to his amazement soon discovered it was the fabled Book of Mysteries. On the first page it was stated that the Book was not to be given to anyone else, for only one who had a pure soul could gain admittance there. Furthermore, it was written that any vow that might have been made to give the Book to another had been made in error, extracted by deceit, and was therefore null and void. And there too, Reb Adam found, were certain holy names for protection against such a man, who would surely be a powerful sorcerer, if not the Evil One himself.

Then, while still in that cave, Reb Adam turned the pages of the Book of Mysteries, and read there the history of the Book. In this way he learned that it had first been revealed to Adam while he was still in the Garden of Eden, to let him know the forms and features of his descendants, and all that was destined to take place among the generations of men. It was the angel Raziel who had been sent to read to Adam from the Book, inscribed in the angel's own hand from the words spoken by the Holy One, blessed be He. But when Adam heard the first words issue from the mouth of the angel, he had fallen down in fear. Therefore God permitted the angel to leave the Book with him so that he could read from it on his own, and in this way Adam came to know the future and was made wise in all things.

Contained in the Book was a secret writing explaining mysteries which had not been revealed even to the angels, except for Raziel, the angelic scribe, and whenever Adam opened the Book, angels gathered around him to read in it as well. Therefore the angel Hadarniel was secretly sent to him and said, "Adam, Adam, reveal not the glory of the Master, for to you alone and not to the angels is the privilege given to know these mysteries." After this Adam kept the Book by him secretly, studied it diligently, and utilized the gift of his Master until he discovered mysteries which were not known even to the celestial ministries. But at last the envy of the angels became so great that they stole the Book and threw it into the sea. Adam searched for it in vain, and then fasted for many days, until a celestial voice announced: "Fear not, Adam, I will give the Book back to you." Then the Holy One, blessed be

He, called upon Rahab, the Angel of the Sea, and ordered him to recover the Book from the depths of the sea and to give it to Adam, and so he did.

When Adam transgressed, the Book flew away from him. He then begged God for its return, and beat his breast, and entered the River Gihon up to his neck, until his body became wrinkled and his face haggard. God thereupon made a sign to Raziel to return the Book to Adam, so that its wisdom might not be lost among men. And this is the Book of the generations of Adam.

As Reb Adam continued to read, he learned that after the death of Adam the Book had disappeared; later the cave in which it was hidden was revealed to Enoch in a dream. It was from this Book that Enoch drew his vast knowledge of the mysteries of creation, and before he was taken up into heaven and transformed into the angel Metatron, Enoch entrusted the Book to Methuselah, who read the Book and transmitted it to Noah, who made use of its instructions in building the ark. Noah took the Book with him into the ark, preserved in a golden casket, and in this way it was successively revealed to Abraham, Isaac, Jacob, and Joseph, who consulted it to discover the true meanings of dreams. The Book was buried with Joseph and was therefore preserved when his coffin was raised by Moses from the Nile and carried beside the Tabernacle throughout the wanderings of the Israelites in the wilderness.

Thus the Book came into the possession of King Solomon, who made good use of its wisdom, and also sought its assistance in constructing the Temple. However, the Book again disappeared after the destruction of the Temple. It had not been destroyed, but instead had been carried by the angel Hadarniel to that cave in the wilderness, where it had been found by Simeon bar Yohai and the Ari, and others who possessed a pure soul. Reb Adam also read there the list of those who were destined to read in that Book, and he found his own name inscribed there; following it he found the name Israel ben Eliezer, and following him the name of Reb Nachman of Bratslav. And this was the last whose name appeared among those who were destined to share in the knowledge of that Book.

After he had read in the Book of Mysteries, Reb Adam understood it had been his destiny to acquire the Book in that cave. So
too was he quite certain that the wanderer who had brought him
there had known this, but had concealed it from him, in the hope
that he might take from him the Book that was rightfully his. And
as he emerged from the cave, Reb Adam thanked God that he had
decided to examine the Book, and had not brought it out without
opening it, as he had been told to do.

No sooner did Reb Adam emerge from the cave, with the
Book in one hand, than the man approached with his hand out-
stretched and said, "Why did it take you so long? Was it so hard to
find? Here, give it to me!" But Reb Adam refused to part with the
Book, and nothing the man said convinced him to change his mind.
He explained that his vow to give up the Book had been forced
upon him, due to his illness, and therefore had no effect. And
when the evil sorcerer saw that Reb Adam had recognized how
precious the Book was, and how sacred, he grew furious and
shouted, "If you refuse to give me the Book, I shall swallow you
alive!" And immediately he stretched himself until he reached the
sky. But Reb Adam quickly pronounced the holy names he had
read in the Book, and the evil sorcerer was restored to his actual
shape and soon discovered that he had lost all his powers. Then the
man ran away as fast as he could, and later found that all of his evil
knowledge had been erased. He never pronounced another spell.

So it was that Reb Adam returned to his home completely
healed. There he continued to study the Book of Mysteries all the
days of his life. And with the knowledge he obtained from it he
was able to perform extraordinary deeds, for the Book revealed the
celestial mysteries and how they could be applied in the most
wondrous ways. And before his death Reb Adam summoned his
only son and instructed him to transmit the holy writings to the
man whose name he had read in the Book, following his own.

By reading in the Book of Mysteries Reb Adam learned that
the next to receive the Book was Israel ben Eliezer of the town of

Okup. Before his death Reb Adam commanded his son to deliver the Book to him, and he warned his son that until this Israel had received the Book, Reb Adam's own soul would be forced to wander in exile. For the soul of a *Tzaddik* may not return to the celestial realms until the soul of another *Tzaddik* has taken its place among men. For the soul of one who is chosen in his generation to carry the candle that is lighted in heaven must continue to carry it until another takes it up. For the candle may never be put down.

Reb Adam also told his son not to open the Book, since it was only intended for Israel ben Eliezer. But his son could not resist the temptation to see what mysteries were concealed there. So it was that he stopped on his way to Okup to probe its secrets. Seating himself on the bank of a river, he opened the Book and saw to his amazement and dismay that it was blank. How was such a thing possible? The son of Reb Adam was unable to fathom this mystery and quickly closed the Book and resumed his journey.

But when Reb Adam's son reached Okup, and learned that Israel ben Eliezer was only a boy, he was even more confused by his father's request. Still, he intended to fulfill the wishes of his father, especially since his father's soul was at stake. Therefore he decided on a test: he left the Book of Mysteries on the prayer bench on which the boy Israel studied during the night, when everyone else was asleep. Then Reb Adam's son hid himself to see what would happen when the boy found the Book. Now when Israel found the Book lying there, he wondered greatly what Book it was, and where it had come from, and he had a strange sense that it was a gift from heaven. Then, with fear and trembling, he opened the Book and saw to his amazement that it was blank. Yet, strange to say, this fact did not distress him. Instead Israel left the blank pages open on the prayer bench and closed his eyes and began to pray out loud, and while he was praying he suddenly gasped and grew silent. For at that moment he had seen for the first time the words inscribed in that Book, which can only be read when the eyes are closed, except when the Book is read in the cave where the angel hid it. At that instant Israel took up the candle lighted in heaven, which the soul of Reb Adam had carried until then. And the words he read there contained such great truths that he found himself able to see from one end of the world to the other, as if the heavens were once again filled with primordial light.

Now the son of Reb Adam did not know what it was that the boy Israel saw when his eyes were closed. But he could not help but notice the aura that suddenly surrounded Israel's face, which was so bright that it illumined the room far more than the light of the candle with which he studied. And it was then that Reb Adam's son recognized that he was in the presence of a holy man, who was indeed worthy of receiving his father's precious Book.

When the son of Reb Adam recognized the holy nature of the Baal Shem, he hesitated no longer, but revealed himself to the boy Israel and told him the tale of how he had come to bring him the Book. Naturally the Baal Shem was deeply indebted to Reb Adam's son and readily acknowledged his gratitude. That is when Reb Adam's son was overcome with curiosity to know how it was that he had recognized the precious nature of the Book, even though its pages were blank. "Its pages are not blank," said the Baal Shem. "But I myself opened the Book," Reb Adam's son confessed in amazement, "and I saw nothing at all!" So it was that the Baal Shem understood that the secret of how to read the pages of the Book had not been revealed to the son of Reb Adam, and he perceived that Reb Adam's son was not destined to read in that Book.

But the son of Reb Adam could not bear that the boy Israel had penetrated the mystery of those blank pages. And he begged the Baal Shem to reveal this secret to him. He said: "Surely, you have discovered the secret of how to read this Book. Never have I been consumed with such a longing to know a secret. I am afraid that I might die of this longing!" And the Baal Shem, hearing this, hesitated no longer, and revealed the secret to him. Then the son of Reb Adam asked if he might be permitted, just once, to read a page of that Book. Again the Baal Shem sensed that this was not the will of heaven, but again the son of Reb Adam implored him until he saw that there was no hope in trying to dissuade him. So the son of

Reb Adam opened the Book and closed his eyes, and in that instant he glimpsed a hidden sun so bright that he was blinded, and when he opened his eyes the next instant all he saw was darkness.

From that time on the Baal Shem always consulted the Book of Mysteries in order to reach a proper decision. Yet it was not necessary for the Book to be present in order to read from it. For one of the secrets the Baal Shem had learned from reading there was a spell that made it possible, whenever his eyes were closed, to see its flaming letters inscribed in the darkness. And by reading in the Book he was able to see the future as clearly as he saw the past.

In this way the Baal Shem used the knowledge he gained by reading in the Book of Mysteries to serve good all of his days. And before his death he sealed the Book in the side of a mountain near Kamenetz, as he read in the Book that it was intended for him to do. And he sealed the Book so that it could not be reached unless the recondite and Ineffable Name of God were spoken, the secret of whose pronunciation is known to only one in each generation. And after the death of the Baal Shem it was believed that both the location of the Book and the secret of how to open the cavern in which this treasure was hidden had been lost. But this was not true. In fact, the location of the Book was well known within the family of the Baal Shem, for he had revealed it to his daughter Odel on his deathbed, and Odel had passed on this secret of the Book's location to her sons, Moshe Hayim Ephraim and Baruch of Medzhibozh, and also to her daughter, Feige. But the Baal Shem had taken with him the secret pronunciation of the Name that would cause the stone to release what it held within.

It happened during their lives that both of Odel's sons made their way to this secret place, and sought to find the key among the many secret formulas in the *Sefer Yetsirah*, the Book of Creation. But the rock remained closed, for neither of these brothers were destined to read in that sacred Book. In the next generation, however, there arose the one to whom the Baal Shem had intended the secret to be delivered. And this was the son of Feige, Reb Nachman of Bratslav, in whom the fire of the Baal Shem was reborn.

~~~

Sometimes it happens that a Torah scroll will require repair. A letter will become so worn it cannot be read, or the parchment will begin to tear. Then the services of a *sofer* are required, one who writes and repairs Torahs. Now there was no one in Medvedevka, where Reb Nachman made his home, who repaired Torahs. The nearest *sofer* was Reb Eliezer, who lived in the town of Volkovitz. And when it was discovered three days after *Tu B'shvat* that the *Sefer Torah* of Reb Nachman's *shule* was in need of repair, Reb Nachman decided at once that he himself would escort Reb Eliezer to town, for repairing the Torah is a great *mitzvah*. Reb Nachman then wasted no time, but prepared to depart at once for Volkovitz, much to the amazement of his Hasidim.

When Reb Nachman reached Volkovitz, he arrived at the home of Reb Eliezer just as he was about to depart. Reb Nachman told him the reason for his mission, and Reb Eliezer explained that he had been about to travel to Medzhibozh, where there was an artisan who fashioned the finest pens for writing the Torah. He was going there to obtain more of these pens, for the last one had broken that very day. Reb Nachman saw the hand of fate in this, and he offered to accompany Reb Eliezer to Medzhibozh. So it was that they traveled together, and when they reached Medzhibozh they remained at the house of this artisan, whose name was Reb Naftali.

That night Reb Nachman had a dream in which he was climbing up the side of a mountain. He climbed and climbed, and at last he reached a plateau far above the earth. There he met, to his complete amazement, another man, who greeted him as if he had been waiting for him a very long time. "Welcome, my son," he said. And although Reb Nachman had been born twelve years after the death of his great-grandfather, the Baal Shem Tov, he somehow recognized him at once, as if they had known each other all of their lives. And he and the Baal Shem embraced for what seemed a very long time. Then Reb Nachman remembered he had come to that remote place for a purpose, although he did not know what it was. And the Baal Shem did not wait for him to ask, but said,

"The time has come for you to retrieve the Book that I received from Reb Adam, which I closed in the side of this mountain before I departed from the world. This is the place you must come to, outside Kamenetz, which your mother has made certain that you know of."

Reb Nachman then realized that this Book had been waiting for him all of his life, and that the time had come for it to be revealed. But he remembered the failed efforts of his mother's brothers to recover the sacred Book, and he said, "Surely you know of the attempts of my uncles to set the Book free from where it is hidden. For they both knew the location of the Book, which was revealed to them by their mother, who was your daughter, Odel; but they were unable to discover the secret of how the Book can be reached." "That is because they were not destined to read in the Book, Nachman," said the Baal Shem Tov. "For it was revealed to me that the Book must remain hidden until the next generation, when you would retrieve it. Nor should you fear that you will not know how to break the spell. There is one word and only one word which can release the stone that conceals it, and that is the same word with which I closed the stone in the first place." "And what word is that?" asked Reb Nachman, with great curiosity to know such a secret. "It is the secret Name of the Holy One, blessed be He. If I told it to you now, while we are together in the Kingdom of Dreams, you would not be able to remember it when you awoke, for this secret cannot be taken beyond the Gate of Dreams. However, I have sent you to the only one in your generation who is familiar with this secret, and that is the *sofer*, Reb Eliezer, with whom you set out in the first place. Now Reb Eliezer does not realize that he knows this secret. Therefore do not reveal to him either why you are taking him with you to Kamenetz or why you want him to accompany you when you reach the mountain, until you arrive at this place where we are now. Simply ask him to come with you and he will surely not refuse, and when the time comes, he will recall the Name that has been entrusted to him. But be certain to reach the cave in the side of the mountain before dawn. When the cavern has been opened, you may both enter it. But only you, Nachman, may open the Book which lies within the golden chest. Know that in order to read it you must close your eyes." Then the Baal Shem embraced Reb Nachman once more, and it was at that moment that Reb Nachman awoke, with the sensation of the Baal Shem's embrace still clinging to him. And he took a deep breath, in the certainty that the quest had started to reveal itself, and in the confidence that he would proceed step by step. But at the same time he knew that he must go slowly, as though hesitant. For only such calm, steady progress, overleaping nothing, would lead to the goal.

The next morning Reb Nachman approached Reb Eliezer as they met going to pray *Shahareis*, the morning prayers. He said: "A great matter hangs in the balance. It is imperative that we travel together to Kamenetz today, and depart immediately after we have prayed." And Reb Eliezer took one look at Reb Nachman, and saw that an aura shone from his face and that his eyes were illumined. And he did not hesitate, but said, "Of course I will come."

After that Reb Nachman moved with a strange assurance, as if he had once before taken the steps he was about to go through. And perhaps that was so, since he had traveled to that mountain the previous night in the dream in which he had met the Baal Shem Tov. All obstacles seemed to fall away, and things proceeded with remarkable ease, so that he and Reb Eliezer reached the foot of the mountain on the third day.

It was dusk when they reached the mountain, and Reb Eliezer suggested they wait until dawn to begin the ascent. But since the Baal Shem had warned Reb Nachman to complete the ascent before dawn, he insisted that they begin climbing at once. "Then shall we climb in the dark?" asked Reb Eliezer. "There is no darkness which cannot be expelled by the light of the Holy One, blessed be He," said Reb Nachman. And Reb Eliezer nodded for Reb Nachman to begin the ascent.

As they climbed, their hands gripped the rocks with strength and surety, as if their hands had eyes with which to see. And when they reached the plateau wherein the Book had been sealed, there was only a short time left before the first wings of light would appear. It was then that Reb Nachman revealed to Reb Eliezer for the first time the true purpose of their quest, and explained Reb Eliezer's role to him. Naturally, Reb Eliezer was overwhelmed at the importance of their mission, since the spirit of the Baal Shem had returned to direct them to this goal. Nor could Reb Eliezer understand why he had been chosen. For how could he be expected to pronounce the Ineffable Name? He had never heard it spoken even once in his life.

Reb Nachman looked at him unwaveringly and said, "I have brought us to this place, and now it is for you to unseal the stone that conceals the Book." And just as Reb Nachman spoke these words the first rays of dawn struck them. And at that instant Reb Eliezer had a strange vision, for all at once he heard the sound of wings flapping, and when he looked up he saw four black birds flying in formation. And no sooner had he set eyes on them than each of the four birds suddenly resembled a Hebrew letter, and the four letters spelled out a word—the four letters of the Divine Name.

Reb Eliezer stared with disbelief, but the Name remained fluttering before his eyes, as the four birds remained in formation. And suddenly, out of nowhere, a word took form in the depths of Reb Eliezer's being. True, he had never heard that word spoken by another man, but somehow he recognized it from a great distance. And the word made its way upward within him and suddenly took wing from his lips, and that was the true pronunciation of the Name.

Just then there was a loud rumbling and a great stone began to move, revealing a cavern illumined by a light which seemed to glow from within. Reb Nachman motioned for Reb Eliezer to enter first, for it was he who had spoken the Name, making it possible for them to reach that sacred place. And Reb Nachman followed closely after him.

When Reb Nachman had stepped inside the cavern, the first thing he noticed was a golden chest, that lay in the center of a

circular chamber. And Reb Nachman knew at once that this must
be the chest in which the Book of Mysteries had been hidden.

When Reb Nachman came to the chest, he was able to open it
at once. (Had he not been destined to open it, however, the chest
would have remained hermetically sealed.) And as soon as it was
opened, Reb Nachman's eyes fell on the Book that lay inside it.
Then, as Reb Eliezer waited, Reb Nachman took the Book of
Mysteries out of the golden chest and opened it to the first page.
At the same time he closed his eyes, as the Baal Shem had told him
to do, and when he did he saw flaming letters take form in the
dark, as they did on the first day of Creation, when the Holy One
brought the world into being.

And there, in that cavern, with the Book of Mysteries opened
before him and his eyes closed, Reb Nachman read at last in those
flaming letters his true destiny, that which is revealed to so few.
For there he saw the history of his soul as it is inscribed in the
Pargod, the Curtain hanging before the Throne of Glory, from its
creation, to its presence at Mount Sinai during the Giving of the
Torah, to his own birth. And he read there as well the future
destiny of his spirit to wander in this world, so that he could
continue to bring down blessings from above even after his death.
And it was there that he learned that when the time approached for
him to depart this world he must inform his Hasidim not to appoint a successor, for in that way he could continue to be their
Rebbe for all time.

Such were the secrets that were revealed to him while he read
in that Book that it was as if all the veils of all the mysteries had
been torn away, and Reb Nachman was able to gaze upon even the
glory of the *Shekhinah* without averting his eyes. And all that he
saw there and all that he learned were imprinted upon his memory
and for the rest of his life he was able to envision it simply by
closing his eyes.

And the last words that Reb Nachman read there told him
that he must leave the Book of Mysteries in that golden chest,
concealed in that cavern. But that did not mean that he would be
apart from it, for so great was the blessing of the Book that anyone

who read there only once was able to read in the Book without its being present for the rest of his life, simply by closing his eyes and pronouncing the spell he had learned there. And thus the Book would remain sealed until the time arose for another *Tzaddik* to read in it, in a future generation.

Then Reb Nachman closed the Book, brought it to his lips, and replaced it in the golden chest with great care. And when he arose he saw that Reb Eliezer was waiting for him. He had seen Reb Nachman take the Book from the chest and open it, and he had glimpsed its blank pages. He had also seen how Reb Nachman seemed to read from it—with his eyes closed. And although he was greatly mystified, he did not doubt that a miracle had taken place, for the sacred aura of that cavern was quite apparent. Then Reb Nachman closed the chest and led Reb Eliezer to the entrance of the cavern, and they stepped outside. The moment they were outside the cavern they heard a loud rumbling, and the stone that had opened to admit them closed once more. And without further hesitation, they began their descent.

When Reb Nachman and Reb Eliezer at last arrived in Medvedevka, they expected to find the Hasidim there wondering greatly at their delay, for the journey that should have lasted three days had lasted ten days instead. And it is true that the Hasidim were surprised to see them, but that is because they believed them to be a day early—for only two days had passed in Medvedevka since Reb Nachman's departure.

At first Reb Nachman was very confused by this, but suddenly he understood that his journey beyond Volkovitz had taken place outside of time. Yet he had retained the ability to read in the Book of Mysteries whenever he closed his eyes and pronounced the spell, so he recognized that he must have entered the *Yenne Velt*, the Other World, where time does not exist.

All at once Reb Nachman remembered the initial reason he had traveled to Volkovitz—to bring back Reb Eliezer, the *sofer*, so that he could repair the Torah. And since the act of repairing the Torah is a great *mitzvah*, Reb Nachman took Reb Eliezer by the arm and said, "Let us waste no more time, but let us hurry to the

Torah which brought us together for our quest. For now it is time for the *tikkun* to begin."

So it was that Reb Nachman and Reb Eliezer and many of Reb Nachman's Hasidim hurried to the *Beit Knesset*, to take the Torah out of the Ark. There Reb Nachman took out the *Sefer Torah* and kissed its cover, and drew out the scroll of the Torah, and opened to the first *parasha* in Genesis, which is that of Creation; for it was there that the first letter, *Bet*, had become rubbed out, and the parchment had become torn. But when Reb Nachman looked, he saw that the letter *Bet* had been inscribed again—in fiery letters, black fire on white. And when he looked at that letter and saw as well that the parchment showed no sign of ever having been torn, he knew that the *tikkun* had already taken place, and that which had been broken had been repaired at last.

The Celestial Orchestra

ONCE it happened that Reb Nachman woke up in the middle of the night, and instead of the deep silence that usually pervaded, he heard something like a faint music. At first the sound was no more than that of an approaching wind, but soon he could make out that it actually was a kind of music. What could it be? He had no idea. But he continued to hear it, ever so faintly, sometimes present, sometimes about to disappear. And as it did not grow any louder, he had to strain to listen. One thing was certain, though: Reb Nachman felt drawn to this music, as if it were a message coming to him from a great distance, which he was trying to receive.

Then Reb Nachman got up and went into his study, and sat down by the window. And yes, from there the music seemed slightly louder, as if he were a little closer to its source, but it remained very faint. It did not seem to come from any instrument with which he was familiar, for it did not sound like a violin or a flute; not like a bass fiddle and not like a drum. Nor did it have the sound of a voice or voices. If only he were able to hear it better, he thought, he might be able to identify its source.

Then Reb Nachman left the house and walked outside. He walked out into the field beyond the gate, under a sky crowded with stars. There he had no memory, except for questions that concerned the origin of the mysterious music. And while his eyes were fixed on the heavens, the ground remained unknown beneath his feet. And for that time he did not impose patterns on distant stars or imagine the life they might sustain. Nor did he count the gift of the stars as riches. Instead he listened for a long, long time.

At first Reb Nachman thought that what he heard was seamless, and was coming from a single instrument. After a while he was almost able to separate the instruments that wove their music together so well. Yet this new knowledge did not satisfy his longing and curiosity; in fact, it only served to whet it. Where was this distant music coming from? Surely it was not drifting there from any orchestra in Bratslav, or from anywhere else in this world, of that Reb Nachman was certain. No, this was some kind of celestial music, music of the spheres.

It was then that Reb Nachman realized how much he wanted to follow that music and discover its source. And this longing grew so great that he became afraid his heart might break. Then, while he was staring up into the stars, he saw a very large star fall from its place in the heavens and blaze across the sky like a comet. He followed that star as it fell, and shared its last journey. And somehow it seemed to Reb Nachman that he was falling with that star and was caught up in that same motion, as if he had been swept away by an invisible current, and he closed his eyes and let himself be carried.

Now it happened that when Reb Nachman opened his eyes again he found himself seated inside a chariot of fire that blazed its way across the heavens. And he did not have time to wonder how this had happened, or what it meant, but merely to marvel in awe as the wonders of the heavens passed before his eyes. Before him he saw two kinds of luminaries: those which ascended above were luminaries of light; and those which descended below were luminaries of fire. And it was then, when his eyes had become adjusted to the sudden illuminations crossing his path, that Reb Nachman became aware of a presence beside him and began to perceive a dim body of light.

That is when the angel who drove the chariot first spoke to him, and said: "Reb Nachman, I am the angel Raziel. You should know that your calling and your prayers have not gone unheard in heaven. This chariot has been sent to bring you to the place you long for, the source you are seeking."

And with each word the angel Raziel spoke, the light surrounding his ethereal body grew brighter, until he appeared to Reb Nachman as a fully revealed being. This was the first time Reb Nachman had ever been face to face with an angel. And yet, strange to say, he did not feel the fear he would have expected, but rather felt as if he had been reunited with a long lost companion.

Just then the chariot approached some kind of parting of the heavens, which resembled a line drawn across the cosmos. As they drew closer, he saw it was actually an opening through which an ethereal light emerged. Raziel recognized the question taking form in Reb Nachman's mind, and he said: "We are approaching the place where the Upper Waters and the Lower Waters meet. This is where the Upper Worlds are separated from the Lower Worlds, and what belongs to the spheres above is divided from what belongs to the spheres below."

No sooner did the angel finish speaking than the chariot approached close enough to that place for Reb Nachman to catch a glimpse of what lay on the other side. And what he saw was a magnificent structure suspended in space. And from that one glimpse he knew that whatever it was, no human structure could begin to compare with it. But then, before he had time to question the angel, the chariot passed through that very aperture, to the complete astonishment of Reb Nachman, for it was no higher than a hand's breadth. It was at that moment that Reb Nachman grew afraid for the first time, for he realized he was flying through space at a great height and did not dare to look down. Then he said to the angel, "How is it possible that we have passed through that place which is no more than three finger-breadths?"

Raziel said, "In your world of men, Reb Nachman, it is possible to contain a garden in the world. But in this kingdom it is possible to contain the world in a garden. How can this be? Because here, whoever opens his heart to the Holy One, blessed be He, as much as the thickness of a needle, can pass through any portal."

Even as Raziel spoke these words Reb Nachman had already been captured by the radiant vision which loomed ahead. And again, without his having to ask, Raziel replied, "The place you are about to be taken to, Reb Nachman, is the very one you have been seeking. Yet since even this chariot is not permitted to approach much closer to that sacred place, you must soon depart from it and remain suspended in space, like the Sanctuary you see before you."

And without any other explanation, Reb Nachman realized that the wonderful structure he saw must be the Celestial Temple, after which the Temple in Jerusalem had been modeled, and with which it was identical in every aspect, except for the fire surrounding the heavenly Sanctuary. For the marble pillars of this heavenly miracle were illumined by red fire, the stones by green fire, the threshold by white fire, and the gates by blue fire. And angels entered and departed in a steady stream, intoning an unforgettable hymn to a melody Reb Nachman heard that day for the first time, but which he recognized as if it had been familiar to him all the days of his life.

It was then Reb Nachman realized he was no longer within the chariot but was suspended in space without support for his hands or feet. And it was then, with his eyes fixed on that shimmering vision, that Reb Nachman was able to distinguish for the first time the Divine Presence of the *Shekhinah* hovering above the walls and pillars of the Temple, illuminating them and wrapping them in a glowing light, which shone across all of heaven. It was this light he had seen from the other side of the aperture, before the chariot of fire had crossed into the Kingdom of Heaven. And so awestruck was Reb Nachman to witness the splendor of the *Shekhi-*

nah, he suddenly experienced an overwhelming impulse to hide his face and began to sway in that place, and almost lost his balance. Had it not been for the angel Raziel speaking to him at that instant he might have fallen from that great height. The angel said, "Take care, Reb Nachman, and know that the Temple remains suspended by decree of the Holy One, blessed be He. And you must remember above all to keep your eyes fixed on its glory, if you are not to become lost in this place. For should you look away from the Temple for as long as a single instant, you would risk the danger of falling from this height. Even a mere distraction would take you to places unintended, from which you might never return. So too should you know that no living man may enter into that holy dwelling place and still descend to the world of men. For no man could survive the pure fire burning there, through which only angels and purified souls can pass."

And it was then, when he had regained his balance, that Reb Nachman finally discovered the source of the celestial music which had lured him from his house in a world so far removed, and yet so close. For as he followed that music to its source in the Celestial Temple, his eyes came to rest on concentric circles of angels in the Temple courtyard. Then he realized that the music he had been hearing was being played by an orchestra of angels. And when he looked still closer he saw that each of the angels played a golden vessel cast in the shape of a letter of the Hebrew alphabet. And each one had a voice of its own, and one angel in the center of the circle played an instrument in the shape of the letter *Bet*.

And as he listened to the music, Reb Nachman realized it was the long note of the letter *Bet* that served as its foundation, and sustained all of the other instruments. He marveled at how long the angel was able to hold this note, drawing his breath back and forth like the Holy One Himself, who in this way brought the heavens and the earth into being. And at that moment Reb Nachman was willing to believe that the world only existed so that those secret harmonies could be heard. And he turned to the angel Raziel, who had never left his side, and once more the angel knew what he wished to know, and said, "The score of this symphony is the scroll of the Torah, which commences with the letter *Bet*, endless and eternal, and continues with each instrument playing in turn as it appears on the page, holding its note until the next letter has been sounded, and then breathing in and out a full breath."

And when Reb Nachman listened to that music he arrived at a new understanding of the Torah, and realized that among its many mysteries there was one level on which it existed only as pure music. He was also aware that of all the instruments in that orchestra it was only the letter *Bet* that spoke to him and pronounced his name. Then the angel Raziel turned to him and said, "The souls of all men draw their strength from one of the instruments in this orchestra, and thus from one of the letters of the alphabet. And that letter serves as the vessel through which the soul of a man may reveal itself. Your soul, Reb Nachman, is one of the thirty-six souls that draw their strength from the vessel of the letter *Bet*, which serves as their Foundation Stone and holds back the waters of the Abyss."

Then it happened that when the angel Raziel said the word "Abyss," Reb Nachman forgot all of his warnings for one instant, and glanced down at the world so far below. And the next thing he knew, he felt like a falling star. That is when he realized he was still standing in the field beyond the gate, where the star he had followed had now disappeared. And the celestial music, though faint once more, still echoed in his ears.

The Palace Beneath the Sea

On *Simhat Torah*, when the Torah is closed and then opened again, Reb Nussan brought his son Baruch with him to hear Reb Nachman's *D'var Torah*, for that year held his son's *bar mitzvah*. Reb Nachman began his *D'var Torah* with these words: "There is a light higher than a man's soul. This is the light of which it is written *And God said, 'Let there be light,' and there was light.* This is the light of the infinite." And as Reb Nachman spoke these words, a glowing smile came over the face of Baruch, and he continued to smile throughout the *D'var Torah*.

Afterwards Reb Nachman sought him out and said, "Tell me, Baruch, what was it that you smiled about, for in your smile I saw the radiance of the *Shekhinah*." And Baruch became pale, for he had not thought that Reb Nachman had noticed him. But then he found his courage and said, "With your first words you answered the first question about the Torah I ever had." And Reb Nachman said, "And what question was this?" Baruch replied, "I could not understand what the light was that God created on the first day, since the light of this world is that which was created on the fourth day, when the sun and moon were brought into being. You answered this when you said it was the light of the infinite."

Now Reb Nachman also smiled, and he said, "Yes, the rabbis called this light the primordial light, for when it was present it was possible to see from one end of the world to the other." Baruch was very curious to know more about this primordial light, and he said, "What happened to this light?" Reb Nachman replied, "Some say that God knew there would be evil people in the world, and therefore he hid the light. Others say that it was lost at the time of the Fall. But let me tell you a tale about this light." And this is the tale that was not recorded by Reb Nussan, Reb Nachman's scribe, but by Reb Nussan's son, Baruch:

There was once a king who possessed a priceless treasure.

This was a miraculous golden lamp, which shone with a wonderful light emitted from a stone that had been set inside the lamp. And what was the source of the light? It had no source—the light simply shone from within. And although the king did not know it, the stone had a wondrous history. For in that stone was preserved the last of the primordial light. When the Holy One, blessed be He, decided to withdraw the primordial light from the world, He preserved some of it inside that stone. That is why it still shone with such a radiant light. For many generations after the Fall the stone was hidden in one of the treasuries of heaven, and not even the angels shared in the blessing of its light. It was only when Enoch proved himself to be perfect in his righteousness that the Holy One permitted the stone to be displayed in the celestial realm, and to cast its light throughout the upper world. And when Enoch ascended into Paradise in a fiery chariot, this jewel was presented to him as a sign that his pure soul had been acknowledged on high.

When Enoch returned to earth for thirty days to share the secrets he had learned on high, he gave the wondrous stone to his son, Methuselah, who hung it above his bed and slept in its radiance every night, and thus lived longer than any other man. The stone, called the *Tzohar*, was inherited by Lamech, Methuselah's son, and thus it came into the possession of Noah, Lamech's son. Having been raised in the presence of the light cast from that stone, Noah was the most righteous man of his generation, and thus it was he who was chosen to preserve the human race at the time of the Flood. Noah hung the stone inside the ark, and thus illumined the deck during the long darkness brought on by the Flood.

But Noah proved to be a less than perfect man, and no sooner did the ark come to rest on Mount Ararat, than the *Tzohar* fell from where it was hung and sank into the sea. It was then carried by the currents until it became lodged in the crevice of a cave that was still underwater at that time, although the waters soon receded and the cave re-emerged in an Egyptian valley. As fate had it, it was to this cave that Emtelai brought her infant son Abraham. And although Abraham was left alone in that cave, the radiant glow of the *Tzohar* not only illumined the darkness but preserved the infant, and even caused him to flourish, so that in a short time he could walk and speak as well as a grown child. This was the miracle Emtelai discovered when she returned to that cave, and from then on she knew that her child bore a great blessing. Abraham took the stone with him when he left the cave and hung it around his neck and before long he discovered that it was an astrolabe, in which the secrets of the stars could be read, and a healing stone as well. For any sick person who came into the presence of that stone was healed. In fact, some say that the stone possessed the power of bringing the dead to life, and that Abraham discovered this when the stone touched a bird he was about to cook over a fire, which came to life and flew away.

Abraham bestowed the stone on his son Isaac, who gave it to his son Jacob at the time he was deceived into blessing him, rather than Esau, as the firstborn. Jacob secretly gave it to Joseph, whom he loved more than his eleven other sons. And so the stone, hanging around his neck, was the one possession Joseph retained when his brothers took his coat of many colors and cast him into the pit, and it illumined the darkness there until he was found by a passing caravan. When Joseph reached Egypt he set the stone inside a golden cup, and used it to divine the future and interpret dreams. Later, the cup was buried in Joseph's coffin, and the coffin was sunk to the bottom of the Nile. But before the children of Israel departed from Egypt, Moses came to the banks of the Nile and called out to Joseph for him to join them, and soon the coffin rose up from the bottom as if it consisted of the lightest wood, while in fact it was made of solid gold.

Moses recognized how precious was the stone, and he had Bezalel set it inside a golden lamp, which hung inside the Tabernacle the Children of Israel carried through the wilderness beside Joseph's coffin. This is how the *Ner Tamid*, or eternal light, came into being, which we still signify by maintaining a flame before the Ark at all times. The sacred lamp remained in the possession of the Jews for many generations, and eventually took its rightful place inside the Holy of Holies of the Temple in Jerusalem. When the Temple was destroyed, the lamp and the illuminating stone fell into the hands of pagans for many generations. Eventually it came into the possession of a king who ruled a great kingdom, who recognized at once that it was a priceless treasure.

Now since this king, who lived in a palace by the shore of the sea, did not know the true history of the golden lamp, he assumed it to be enchanted and wondered if it had any other powers. He showed the lamp to the palace soothsayer, who sought to discover its powers by reading in the stars. And because he was a master at this art, he was able to discern one very important truth about the lamp, although many other mysteries remained unrevealed to him. When he returned to the king he told him that the lamp endowed the king with great benefits merely by the fact of its presence. For as long as the king retained the golden lamp in the palace, and passed on the knowledge of its existence to his descendents, his kingdom would flourish. But if it fell from his possession, or if his heirs failed to acknowledge its importance, its powers would cease to protect them and the kingdom would be lost.

When the king heard this, he grew terrified that the golden lamp might somehow be stolen, and he made the soothsayer vow never to reveal even the existence of the lamp, much less its beneficial powers. But even after this the king did not feel secure. Therefore he decided to conceal the lamp in a place so well hidden no one would ever find it. Yet this place could not be beyond the palace, or the benefits of the lamp would be lost. Faced with this dilemma, the king decided to construct a labyrinthine cave beneath the palace, at the end of which the golden lamp would be hidden. In this way it would continue to protect him while remaining well concealed.

Now the king kept the purpose of the cave and labyrinth secret even from the builders, who did not know why it was being constructed and were even forbidden to reveal their work to their wives. And when the labyrinth was complete, the king had a heavy metal door placed at the opening of the cave, locked with seven locks and sealed with seven seals. After he had completed the labyrinth, the king called in the astrologer and told him to read in the stars to find out if he had hidden it well enough, and if his destiny was now secure. The soothsayer sought to discern these matters, and succeeded in both cases, for the replies were intertwined: If the king wished to remain safe, he had to have engraved on the metal door the secret of how to open the gate and pass through the labyrinth. Otherwise, the action of the king would be regarded by heaven as selfish, since no one would ever be able to enter there, and the blessings of the lamp would be withdrawn. But at the same time the king was free to conceal the key to the gate and labyrinth in a code, using any symbols he wished. For it was recognized that the king needed this much protection to prevent the lamp from being stolen during his lifetime.

When the king heard this, he commanded that the soothsayer create a code which none could penetrate. And the king told him that he would test it by giving it to ten of the wisest men in the kingdom. And if even one of them deciphered even a single symbol, the soothsayer's life would be lost. The soothsayer left the royal chamber terrified, for although he was skilled at deciphering codes himself, he had no experience in creating them. And he feared that there would be nothing he could create which one of the wisest could not decipher.

Now the soothsayer had been taught his skills by an old sorcerer, and he recalled that the old man had often consulted a book of signs and symbols whose meaning he had refused to reveal even to his apprentice. The soothsayer thought to himself that perhaps the old man could help him write this message in those obscure symbols, for surely no one else could decipher them.

When the old sorcerer heard the plea of his former student, he did not refuse him, but took down the secrets which were to be conveyed and expressed them in the mysterious symbols of the *Kabbalah*, in which he was well versed. For he suspected at once from the description of the golden lamp that it might be the eternal light of the Tabernacle, which had been lost for so long, and he discerned the hand of fate in the astrologer coming to him for help. By using those symbols and their powers he hoped to transmit the secret of how the lamp could be retrieved by one, like himself, steeped in those supernal mysteries. In that way the eternal light might come into the possession of the Jews once more. The old man did not consider taking the lamp for himself, using the knowledge he had of its location, for he knew that to do so would be to sign a death warrant for the king.

The soothsayer himself was greatly mystified by the signs and symbols the sorcerer wrote down, which were to be engraved on the cavern door. But that was all for the better as far as he was concerned; he hoped, above all, that the code remain unbroken. And it did. None of the ten wise men to whom the king showed the symbols could decipher even a single one. The king was greatly pleased at this, gave the order to engrave the symbols on the metal door, and considered the matter closed. The soothsayer was rewarded for his good work, and became the closest adviser to the king. Thus both their lives and the kingdom flourished, while the golden lamp continued to glow in the depths of the labyrinthine cave constructed beneath the palace.

This king ruled for many years, and he was succeeded by his son, and the dynasty lasted for many generations. But a time came when his descendents came to doubt not only the importance, but even the existence, of the hidden lamp. So it was that before long the waters of the sea rose up and covered the palace and the city beside it, and no trace of their existence remained. Meanwhile, as the generations passed, the underwater palace was covered over with fine particles of sand and earth, which mixed together until it became a pure, white clay. So it was that for hundreds of years the kingdom was covered with waters, and no record of it remained in the world. Yet the time also came when the waters began to recede, and little by little the land appeared; but still no trace of the palace or kingdom was to be seen, for they were buried beneath many layers of clay.

Now when that land emerged from under the waters, it became part of the kingdom of another king, who decided it should be settled and a city built there, for he did not know that there was a city buried beneath it. He had it announced that all of the Jews of his kingdom were commanded to leave their homes and resettle in that land, which had been underwater so long. Since the power of the king was very great, the Jews obeyed him, and traveled there to make their homes.

Among those who settled in that new city was a potter who was the Hasid of a great master. All who owned the pots and vessels made by this potter found them to be almost indestructible, even when heated on the fire, yet they were also unusually light. Now the secret of this potter's wonderful pots was the clay that he used, which came from a particular pit. The potter was aware of the remarkable qualities of this clay and he continued to dig far down in that one place rather than dig in another, for that clay was unique. After years of such digging he one day struck metal with his shovel, far down at the bottom of the pit. He could not imagine what could be buried there, for at that time the people still did not know of the city beneath them on which their own had been built.

The potter carefully scraped away the clay, and found himself confronted with the metal door that was the entranceway to the labyrinth in which the golden lamp had been hidden. The potter saw that the door was locked with seven locks and sealed with seven seals, and he tried to read the symbols engraved on it but he could not make out a single word. Nevertheless he suspected it might prove to be of great value and he thereupon went directly to his Rebbe, and told him about the discovery in the bottom of the clay pit. When the Rebbe had the potter draw some of the symbols he had seen on the door, he recognized them at once as symbols of the *Kabbalah*. Therefore he agreed to accompany the potter at once, and descended with him into the pit.

When the two Hasidim reached the metal door, the Rebbe studied the symbols and soon recognized that they had been written by a master of the *Kabbalah*. Because he was well-grounded in these symbols and knew how to read them, the Rebbe was confident he could decipher the secret of how to unlock and unseal the door. And he recognized that the potter had been guided to that place by the Holy One, blessed be He, so that he could accompany him there.

By deciphering those symbols, the Rebbe discovered that it was necessary to pronounce the Ineffable Name in order to release the locks and seals of that door. Now in every generation there is only one *Tzaddik* who knows how to pronounce the Name. Just as the sorcerer who had created the code had been the chosen *Tzaddik* of his generation, acquainted with the mystery of the Name, so too was this very Rebbe the one who knew the secret; even thus does fate make it possible for us to thread a needle while our eyes are closed. And no sooner had the *Tzaddik* spoken the sacred Name, than the locks fell away and dropped to the floor and the doors swung open. The entrance to an underground cave was revealed, but the Rebbe noticed right away that the cave was not pitch black like most caves, but was instead illumined with a crystalline light, which had the cast of a pale aura. And when the Rebbe stepped inside the entrance of that cave, he felt as if a change had taken place, as if he were standing upon sacred ground. The potter followed after him, rapt by all that had occurred, and wondering greatly at what was to be found.

Before they had walked more than a few steps, a sweet fragrance reached them, fresh and pregnant. It was the scent of fresh fruit, and the Hasidim both wondered how any such fruit could grow in that cave, which had been closed up for so long. It was then that they reached the first of the carob trees which flourished in that underground cave. The presence of these trees, filled with ripe fruit which no man saw or tasted, filled them with a strange sensation, for there had been no one to share their rich offering. The Rebbe broke off two carobs, and gave one of them to the potter. And when they tasted them, they were astonished at how sweet they were, and how ripe. They would have been even amazed had they known that the cave had been barren when it had been closed up by the earlier king, and that over the ages the primordial light which shone from the wondrous stone in the golden lamp had fertilized every passageway in that labyrinth, and carob trees had grown up, even though not a single carob seed had been left in that place!

Soon after they had tasted the carobs, both the Rebbe and the potter heard a low murmur, which sounded like the sea from a great distance, or a barely audible song. The Rebbe said, "Do you hear a distant song, like that of the sea?" And the potter nodded vigorously, for he had just been trying to make out what the sound was. And the Rebbe said, "I am certain that the taste of the carob has made it possible for this sound to reach our ears. Now we must follow that distant music, for it is the guide which will lead us through this labyrinth."

And that is what they did. They followed the voice of the waters, and if they made a wrong turn, the voice faded away, and thus they were guided through the labyrinth, the sound becoming clearer and clearer, the song more unearthly and intriguing, until at last they reached the source of the underground stream which ran through those passages (a stream which had also not existed when the king had the caves dug out beneath the palace). And the source of the wonderful music was a waterfall which cascaded down one side of the cave. The Hasidim listened to that voice, wrapped in the glowing light that emerged so strongly there, and it seemed as if they were in the presence of another being, its limbs woven by the tender waters as they poured down from the top of the rock from which they arose. For a while it seemed to hypnotize them, but then the Rebbe shook himself free and climbed behind that rock. There, in a deep crevice, he found the golden lamp from which had come the flowing light that filled every passageway. And he reached in and took out that lamp, and held it so that he could see the glowing stone. When he looked into the source of the light, a vision took form before the Rebbe's eyes, and he found himself in the presence of the *Shekhinah*, and saw that she was the true source of that light, which was the reflection of her robe, which was woven out of light. And in the presence of the *Shekhinah*, the Rebbe bowed his head, and the potter followed suit. Then the Rebbe wept tears of joy, for he knew that the miraculous light that had been lost for so long had been restored to his generation at last.

The Letters of the Torah

ALL his life Reb Nachman had recurrent dreams in which he was traveling to the Holy Land. In some of these dreams he was traveling through a cave, in some he was crossing a mountain, and in others he was riding in a caravan through a vast wilderness. Once Reb Nachman dreamed he was sailing on a ship. In that vivid dream he woke up inside a ship's cabin, and felt the rising and falling of the waves beneath him. He sat up and wondered how long he had been at sea—it seemed as if it had been many months. Then he noticed that the sky outside the port window was still black. He wondered about this and went to the window and looked out. There he saw flickers of light, like cracks in the darkness. So too did he hear a strange noise, like a great wind. At first he thought a storm might be approaching, but suddenly he saw that the darkness had been brought on not by rain clouds but by a great mass of birds, which covered the sky and blotted out the sun. Reb Nachman could not believe his eyes, for never in his life had he seen so many birds in one place.

Taking leave of the cabin, Reb Nachman hurried up to the deck. There he found that he was alone, for everyone else had remained in their cabins, either believing it was still night, or else expecting a storm. And it is true that the beating of those hundreds of thousands of wings did stir up quite a wind, enough to make Reb Nachman secure his *yarmulke* with his hand. But suddenly something happened that was so strange that Reb Nachman thought his eyes must have deceived him—for all at once he saw a word formed among the multitudes of birds, and that word was *Bereshith*, in the beginning. Reb Nachman blinked hard, for he did not understand how such a thing could be possible. And when he opened his eyes he saw that the word had indeed vanished, but in its place was another word, *bara*, created, which follows *Bereshith* as the second word of the Torah. And when he saw that word

before his eyes, Reb Nachman knew that he was witnessing a miracle. He closed his eyes again, and when he opened them he saw, as he had hoped, the Name of God written across the sky by a flock of birds among the multitude gathered there. And when Reb Nachman looked at the Ineffable Name he suddenly remembered how Reb Eliezer had pronunced it at the cavern where they had received the Book of Mysteries. That pronunciation had been erased from his memory until then, and when he recalled the great secret of how to pronounce it Reb Nachman also understood many other mysteries, among them the meaning of those words which took form in the sky before his eyes. For that was no flock of birds he saw—it was the letters of the Torah, swarming above him in the sky.

Now although Reb Nachman knew full well that the letters of the Torah were scattered in great profusion there, he was not certain of the meaning of this sign, or even if it were good or bad. There was such a great crowding, as far as the eye could see, that he understood that all six hundred thousand letters of the Torah must be present there. Yet those letters rarely formed full words, for what he saw primarily were the letters scattered chaotically everywhere, as if the earth were unformed and void and darkness was upon the face of the earth. Among those letters, however, the ones which formed the Divine Name still remained in focus in the heavens, burning in a black fire which set them apart from all the others. The Name filled Reb Nachman with its glory, and he felt it was on the tip of his tongue, when all at once he spoke it out loud for the first time. And in that instant there was a great beating of wings, and a great wind, which lifted up the waves and rocked the boat; and when Reb Nachman looked again he saw that the letters had ordered themselves and the heavens resembled a scroll on which the letters had been written. He saw the whole Torah written there from beginning to end, and when he read its words, they became imprinted in his memory, so that for the rest of his life, he was able to call up any *parashah* of the Torah and see it in his mind as if he were reading from the very scroll of the Torah itself, as it was received by Moses on Mount Sinai.

Suddenly the wind that had been formed by the beating of wings grew again, and there was the sound of distant thunder, which drew close. And in that moment of great intuition Reb Nachman recognized that thunder as the Thunder of Sinai, and that the letters gathered there also represented the six hundred thousand Israelites who had gathered at the foot of Mount Sinai, ready to receive the Torah at last. And he knew that because the vision had come to him then, he had at last been found ready to receive the whole Torah from on high, and that until that moment he had never realized the Torah's fullness and perfect unity. Then he knew not only that another shell had dropped away, but that one of the shattered vessels had been restored and was ready to receive once more.

As Reb Nachman stood there, his eyes were fixed upon a premundane world that took form before him. He saw how the letters of the Torah were garments of God's will and expressed so precisely the Word that was spoken, and how His will clothed the entire Torah. So too did it become apparent how it was that "God had looked in the Torah and created the universe," as it is written in the *Zohar*.

That is when Reb Nachman fully understood for the first time how the world must have appeared before the creation of the Torah, which was created two thousand years before this world was brought into being. For the Torah that existed then was not like the Torah as he now saw it, inscribed in the heavens before his eyes, since the letters of the Torah had not yet combined into words as they are written now. Instead they must have resembled the letters as they had appeared to him at first—a dense flock scattered across the sky. And when the world came into being and time began, the letters combined into words, and each word took its proper place, so that the whole Torah could be seen as he saw it there, from beginning to end.

Then it happened, as Reb Nachman gazed with newborn eyes upon the full span of the Torah, that he read the words in a new way, and saw in that instant how the entire Torah is actually God's Name. And as Reb Nachman fixed his gaze upon the Ineffable

Name, he saw it transformed until all of the letters of the Torah had been absorbed into God's most sacred Name, which consists of only four letters—YHVH. And that is when he first understood that all life in this world is a part of the hem of God's garment, a part of which has been entrusted to each man and woman to be preserved or destroyed. And it was above all the command of the Holy One, blessed be He, to repair that which has been torn until the garment had been fully restored, for then the Messiah can wrap himself in it and commence the End of Days.

It was then, as he looked closer, that Reb Nachman saw how much of that garment consisted of stories which had been woven together, and it was then that he became aware for the first time of his destiny as a teller of tales, tales which would eventually be stitched to those of the forefathers and become a part of them, as a sleeve stitched to a shoulder of a robe becomes fused into a single garment.

With this new understanding fresh in mind, Reb Nachman peered into the white flames surrounding the black letters, and saw glowing there a multitude of tales, like golden birds, hovering within reach. And he knew that when he returned from the Holy Land he would not hesitate to draw them down from on high and bring them to the world below, where they could continue to exist as tales that would be retold until the end of time. And then Reb Nachman awoke in his room in Bratslav, and felt as if he had returned from a long journey, though at the same time he also felt as if his soul were somehow continuing that voyage to the Holy Land. And all that day Reb Nachman felt like a man living in two worlds, as if he were walking on both sides of a river at the same time.

A Garment for the Moon

ONE day, after Reb Nachman had spoken to his Hasidim about how the shattered vessels could be restored only through their efforts, he saw that Reb Shimon seemed downcast and asked him why. Shimon replied, "I have been thinking about the heavy responsibility that lies on our shoulders, Rebbe, to restore the world to its pristine state. For it seems to me a much greater responsibility than could be handled by any man." Reb Nachman smiled when he heard this and said, "The most important thing, Shimon, is never to abandon hope, for a little man can accomplish far more than you might think possible. Listen to this tale and take heart." And this is the tale he told:

Once upon a time the moon came to the sun with a complaint: the sun was able to serve during the warmth of day, especially during the summer, while the moon had to serve during the cool of night. The sun saw that the moon felt unhappy with her lot, particularly in the wintertime, so he told the moon he would have a garment sewed for her, to keep her warm. Then he called upon all the big tailors to make a garment for the moon. The little tailors also wanted to help, but they weren't invited, so they said among themselves, "We're not going to go."

After talking about the matter for some time, the big tailors concluded it was simply impossible to sew such a garment, because the moon is sometimes little and sometimes big. Therefore it was impossible to take its measurements or to sew a garment which would always fit.

But after the big tailors gave up the task, the little tailors decided to try. When the big tailors heard about this, they said, "If we couldn't do it, how can you expect to succeed?" But the little tailors refused to give up. They met among themselves to discuss how this garment might be made. Many suggestions were given, but none of them could solve the problem of the moon's changing size.

Just when the little tailors were at a loss as to how they should proceed, one poor tailor among them stood up and said, "I have heard of a faraway kingdom where there is found a fabric which has the substance of light. This fabric stretches to whatever size is required if the object to be fitted is large, and shrinks as much as necessary if the object is small." Then the little tailors cried out at the same time and said, "Why that is just what we need to sew a garment for the moon!" And all agreed that they must obtain that wonderful material so that the sun could fulfill its promise and the moon could keep warm on cold nights. But how were they to obtain it? They discussed this among themselves, and decided that the little tailor who had heard of this fabric must set out on a quest to retrieve it. Then they collected a few kopeks among themselves with which to purchase the fabric, and they each wished the little tailor good luck.

After that the little tailor, whose name was Yankel, was sent to search for that faraway kingdom in which the material woven out of light was to be found. He packed a few clothes in a sack and took along a few loaves of bread, and set out on his journey. And how did he begin to search for that distant land? He stopped wherever he went and asked the people if they knew where that kingdom was located. But when the people heard that Yankel was searching for a cloth made out of light so that the little tailors could sew a garment for the moon, they always broke out laughing and assumed Yankel was a fool.

In this way Yankel traveled for many months, sleeping under the stars, until the nights began to grow colder. And as he lay on the ground at night and looked up at the moon, Yankel thought he saw the moon shiver, and he was determined to keep going until he obtained that material so that the moon could have a garment of its own.

Then it happened one day that Yankel arrived at a great river, and took the ferry across to the other side. And since the river was so wide, and it took quite a while to get across, Yankel decided to ask the old ferryman if he knew the location of the kingdom in which the miraculous fabric could be found. The ferryman did not laugh as had so many others, but told him he would find what he was seeking on the other side of that river. And when Yankel heard this, he could hardly believe his ears, for in his heart of hearts he too had begun to wonder if that kingdom truly existed.

Then Yankel asked the ferryman if this fabric was easy to come by, or if it was very dear. And the ferryman told him that it was very dear indeed, for only the queen of that land possessed a gown woven of that wonderful substance. And when Yankel heard this his heart sank, for how was he, a poor man, to obtain this material if only a queen could afford to own it? Still, he had traveled that far, and he did not intend to abandon his quest just when he had finally reached that faraway kingdom. And he consoled himself by hoping that the queen might decide to assist him when she heard why he was seeking that fabric.

Now when he entered that city, Yankel was surprised to see everyone walking around with a sad face. He wondered about this, and at last he stopped someone and asked why this was. The man replied, "You must be a stranger here, for every inhabitant knows the reason. We are sad because our beloved queen is sad." Now Yankel was sorry to hear this, since he had hoped the queen might come to his assistance, but what chance would there be if she were so unhappy? Then Yankel himself began to grow sad, so that his face resembled the faces of the inhabitants of that city. At last he said to the man, "And why is it that the queen is so sad?" The man replied, "Because her royal garment, which is woven out of light, has become unraveled. And now she has nothing to wear to the wedding of her daughter, the princess. And since she has nothing to wear, the wedding has been delayed, who knows for how long?"

When Yankel heard this, his heart leaped. For after all, was he not a tailor? And did he not make his living—a poor one, it is true—by repairing garments, as well as by sewing new ones? In fact, Yankel spent most of his time restoring old garments, for his customers were the poor folk who could not afford new ones. And besides, it was the big tailors who sewed most of the new clothes, while the little tailors, like Yankel, had to make do with the repairs. But Yankel wondered if there were no tailors in that land who might repair the queen's gown themselves. He asked the man about this, and the man said, "Of course we have tailors here. But none of them know a thing about working with cloth woven out of light. Therefore they are helpless to assist. For the royal garment was made long ago, and handed down from one generation to the next. And since the material stretched or shrank as needed, it has fit every queen to perfection. But now that the garment has become unwoven, there is no one who knows how to repair it, for this secret was lost long ago."

Now when Yankel heard this, he remained hopeful, but he was also afraid, for if none of the tailors of that kingdom knew what to do, how would he? Still, he had not given up hope when the big tailors of his own kingdom had, nor would he give up hope now.

Then Yankel told the stranger he was a tailor, and that he was willing to try to repair the garment for the queen. The stranger was delighted to hear this, and told Yankel that the queen had announced some time ago that any tailors who entered that kingdom were to be brought to the palace, to attempt to repair the royal gown, since all of the tailors of that kingdom had already tried and failed. So he led Yankel to the palace, and when the guards heard he was a tailor, they quickly gave him an audience with the queen.

Now when Yankel found himself, a poor tailor, standing in the splendor of that court, before a great and powerful queen, he was overcome with fear, for it was only then that he realized he had forgotten to ask what would happen if he failed. Now, though, it was too late, and with a quivering voice Yankel told the queen he was willing to try to repair her royal gown.

The queen nodded sadly and said, "I wish that repairing it was all that was needed. But the problem is more serious than that. You see, the fabric of the gown has begun to unravel, and because it is woven out of light, when it unravels it simply turns to light again and disappears. Therefore it is not only a matter of repair, for it is first necessary to create some new material. But the secret of how to weave cloth out of light has long been lost."

Now Yankel realized that if he could rediscover that secret, he would be able to produce the fabric needed to weave a garment for the moon. Therefore he told the queen that although he did not know how such miraculous material could be made, he was willing to search for the secret, no matter how long it would take him to find it. The queen was very impressed with his determination, for the tailors of that kingdom had quickly abandoned all hope of accomplishing this task. And she told him she would gladly assist him any way she could and certainly wished him luck, for she longed to attend the wedding of her daughter, the princess, but could not until she was able to wear the royal gown woven out of light as had been the custom in that kingdom for so many centuries.

Then Yankel asked the queen to see the garment that had become unraveled, for that seemed like a reasonable way to start. And the queen had the garment brought at once, and gave Yankel a room in which to examine it.

And when he sat down to study that royal gown he was amazed at its beauty, for the fabric was like moonlight, exquisitely woven and without any sign of stitches or seams. Yankel also marveled at its flexibility—it would stretch as far as he pulled it, but when released would resume its original shape. So too did the sleeve shrink to the size of his hand when he placed it inside there. And the more he studied it, the more Yankel thought it would make a fine garment for the moon.

Then Yankel examined the hem of the garment, which had begun to unravel. He searched for the loose end of the thread of light, and when at last he found it, he saw that as soon as the thread unraveled it turned to light and disappeared, just as the queen had said. Meanwhile Yankel had become so absorbed in the task of studying that wonderful garment he did not notice that many hours had passed, and now it was night. And while he worked, the full moon rose up in the sky until it was framed in the window of the chamber in which Yankel sat, and cast its light inside. And when the light of the moon struck that garment, a remarkable change took place—the gown became illumined, and began to glow with a wonderful, pale light. This change startled Yankel, and he jumped back, as if the garment had come to life. And indeed it did seem transformed, as if it had longed to bask in the moonlight. Then a miracle took place, right before Yankel's eyes—the hem of the garment, which had been unraveling and growing shorter, began to grow larger again in the light of the moon. Yankel could not believe his eyes, for the restoration which had seemed so unlikely was actually taking place. And suddenly, in a moment of true inspiration, Yankel snipped off a tiny piece of the garment and held it up in the moonlight. And as he watched the tiny piece began to grow, little by little, as if it were being woven in the light, until it was ten times larger than it had been at first. And Yankel knew that he had stumbled upon the secret of how to create that precious material, woven out of moonlight.

Meanwhile the light of the moon had continued to restore the queen's gown, and by the time the sun came up, the dress had been completely repaired. Yankel proudly showed it to the queen, who was amazed at his success, for the garment was as good as new. Then the queen tried it on, and the garment shrank until it fit her perfectly. And when she looked into the mirror and saw how beautiful she looked in it, her sadness turned to joy, and she hurried to make plans for the wedding of the princess. But before she did, she asked Yankel what reward he wanted, and told him he could have anything his heart desired. Then Yankel took out the tiny piece of cloth he had snipped from the hem of the garment, and asked the queen if he might keep it as a momento. The queen readily agreed to this request, and saw to it that Yankel received a bag of gold coins as well. Then she thanked him once more from the bottom of her heart and hurried off to make preparations for the wedding. And Yankel took his leave and slowly made his way back to the city from which he had come.

Now since Yankel had traveled very far to reach that kingdom, it took him many months to return. And during that time there were many full moons, and while the full moon shone in the sky, Yankel would take out the small piece of material and expose it to the light of the moon. And on each night of the full moon the cloth would multiply in size ten times, until by the time Yankel returned it was of immense size, large enough to fit the moon.

When Yankel finally reached his town and all the little tailors saw the magnificent fabric he had brought with him, woven out of light, their hearts leaped for joy, and they all joined together to sew a garment for the moon. So it was that the sun was finally able to keep its promise, and the moon received a wonderful garment to keep it warm on cold nights. And that garment fit perfectly, expanding when the moon grew larger and shrinking when it grew small. And the moon has kept that garment to this very day, wearing it with pride and joy since, after all, it was created out of its own light.

The Golden Bird

Now it was the custom of Reb Nachman of Bratslav to take long walks in the forest alone, as did his great-grandfather the Baal Shem Tov. One day Reb Nachman was walking among the majestic trees, deep in thought, when he heard the trill of a bird in the distance. And that melody was so sweet and resonant that Reb Nachman hurried further into the forest, in the hope that he might catch a glimpse of the bird which had such a beautiful song. He traveled an untold distance, ignoring the way as he went, so great was his curiosity. But although his ears sought out the slightest sound, the forest was strangely silent, and Reb Nachman did not hear as much as a rustling leaf, for even the wind seemed to be holding its breath.

At last Reb Nachman concluded that he had set off in the wrong direction, and in despair he sat down at the base of one of those towering trees, whose upper branches seemed to reach into heaven. Perhaps because he was leaning there, a verse from Proverbs suddenly came into his mind: *The Torah is a Tree of Life to those who cling to it,* and at that moment a feather fluttered down through the branches of that tree, and fell beside Reb Nachman where he sat, and at the same instant he heard clearly the haunting trill of the bird which had lured him to that place. Then Reb Nachman jumped up and searched in the branches, in the certainty that the bird must be in that tree, but nothing was to be seen. He contin-

ued to look long after it was apparent the bird had eluded him
once more, and then he sat down and picked up the feather. He
was amazed to discover that it was golden, and shone in the sun
like a mirror. And when he saw that golden feather he knew it
must have come from the bird with the enchanting song, and once
again he was overwhelmed with longing to seek it out. But then
Reb Nachman noticed that the rays of the sun were slanting
through the trees and realized the afternoon was coming to an end.
He knew very well how dangerous it would be to be caught in the
forest after dark, and with great reluctance he left that place and
made his way back. Then, to his amazement, he seemed led as if
by an unseen guide, for he flew through the forest as if he had
made his home there all of his days, and before the sun reached the
horizon he emerged from it, with the golden feather in his hand.
And with one look backward, he returned to his home in Bratslav.
Nor did he reveal the events of that day to anyone and that night,
before he went to sleep, he placed the golden feather beneath his
pillow.

So it was that no sooner did Reb Nachman fall asleep than he
found himself in the forest once again, the golden feather still in his
possession. In the distance he saw a circular pool and realized he
was very thirsty. He went to the pool, bent down, and drank from
the clear water, which satisfied him to his soul, and when he stood
up he saw in the water the reflection of the golden bird, flying
overhead, more wonderful than anything he had ever imagined.
But when he raised his eyes, it had already disappeared. And once
again Reb Nachman knew he could not rest until he had seen that
bird with his own eyes. And then he woke up.

All the next day Reb Nachman wondered if he would be
permitted to continue that night the quest for the golden bird
which had so far evaded him. For he sensed that nothing would be
served by searching for it in the forest outside Bratslav, that it was
his destiny to seek the bird in the Kingdom of Dreams. And that
night, as he slept, a garden in the distance that, no matter whence
he tried to approach it, would vanish before he was able to find an
entrance. And each time the garden reappeared, Reb Nachman

heard the haunting song of the golden bird, which pierced him to his soul. And he knew that if he could only find a way to enter that garden, he might well find the golden bird, for no other could have such an unearthly song. Although he continued to glimpse the garden from time to time he was never able to find an entrance, no matter how many times he circled the area in which it appeared.

It was then Reb Nachman remembered the golden feather, and how it had shone like a mirror in the sun. He took it out, holding it so that it faced the direction in which he had glimpsed the garden, and saw at once that in the mirror of the golden feather the garden did not disappear from his sight, but remained clearly in view. Then he circled the garden once more, this time viewing it from the mirror of the feather, and in this way he was able to discern the gate, previously invisible. And he saw how that gate opened and closed in the blink of an eyelash. So he made his way there, and stood before the gate and closed his eyes, but when he opened them he found to his dismay that he had awakened. Once more the dream had ended before he had achieved his goal. But this time he was confident the quest had not come to its end, and that he might still find his way into the garden of the golden bird.

So it was that when Reb Nachman closed his eyes to sleep on the third night, he opened them to find himself standing inside that glorious garden, where he heard the haunting song of the golden bird clearly once more. And in the distance he saw a tree so wide he estimated it would take five hundred years' journey to travel around it. Beneath the tree flowed four streams, which spread throughout the garden, one in each direction. And high in that tree Reb Nachman saw the golden bird, glowing in the branches like a golden star. And when the bird started to sing, its song carried his soul to the heights.

It was then Reb Nachman saw a man walking in the garden whose face was glowing, and whose eyes cast such a great light they seemed to illumine the path on which he walked. This man approached Reb Nachman, who lowered his eyes, knowing he was in the presence of a holy man. And the man said, "Welcome to this garden, Reb Nachman. I have been waiting for you to arrive ever since you found the golden feather, for I knew you would not rest until you found the bird from which it came. As for me, I am the gardener here; it is my blessing to tend the sacred fruits and flowers and to see that they grow ripe."

And Reb Nachman said, "Peace be with you. I had longed to find one who could guide me in this enchanted place, and who knows the ways of the garden better than the gardener? But tell me, what is your name, and how is it that you have come to tend this garden?"

The man said: "I am the Ari. Just as I was a gardener of the Torah, and found the hidden meanings buried beneath the surface, and understood how scattered sparks can take root and bring forth a harvest of abundance, so it is that I have been rewarded by being made gardener of this garden, in which the golden bird makes its home."

Reb Nachman was overwhelmed to find himself in the presence of the Ari, as Rabbi Isaac Luria, of blessed memory, was known. At first Reb Nachman was silent, but then he found the courage to speak, for at last he had the opportunity to discover the secret of the golden bird, whose golden feathers reflected in the sunlight like the facets of a jewel, and whose melody had lured him the way a flame attracts a moth. And he asked if the Ari could share this secret, and the Ari said in reply, "That golden bird, Reb Nachman, is the beloved bird of the Messiah. For the song of that bird translates the prayers of Israel into a haunting music that fills the heavens."

It was then that Reb Nachman suddenly remembered something which had completely slipped his mind until that moment. It was a tale about his great-grandfather, the Baal Shem Tov, who once was praying with his Hasidim when he prolonged the Eighteen Benedictions for such a long time that his Hasidim grew impatient, and one by one departed from the House of Prayer. Later the Baal Shem told them that by leaving they had brought about a great separation. For while the Baal Shem had prayed he had ascended the ladder of their prayers to reach a place where he had seen a vision of a golden bird, whose song could not but bring

peace of mind to all who heard it. And he was certain that if such a
song were brought to the world of men, it would surely bring
peace everywhere it was heard. And the Baal Shem told them that
by stretching forth his hand he had come within reach of taking the
bird from that tree. But just then the ladder of their prayers had
broken, and he had fallen back to this world as the bird flew away.

Then the Ari, who could read Reb Nachman's thoughts,
spoke and said, "Yes, this is the same golden bird that the Baal
Shem saw. Nor was it any accident that his Hasidim grew impatient, for heaven made certain of this, so that the Baal Shem would
not succeed in taking the bird before the time had come for the
Messiah to be born among men. For it is in this garden that the
Messiah makes his home, and that is why his palace is known as
the Bird's Nest, for it is the song of that bird which sustains the
worlds above and below. The Messiah enters that hidden abode on
New Moons and holy days, and on the Sabbath, for that is when
the bird leaves this enchanted tree and returns to its nest. And all
the while the bird sits in its nest it sings, and the Messiah glories in
its song, which contains the essence of a hundred thousand
prayers. Had the Baal Shem succeeded in bringing back even one
golden feather, peace would have followed for many generations.
Had he brought back the golden bird itself the Messiah would
surely have followed, so little can he bear being separated from its
song."

Now Reb Nachman was startled when he heard this and
became very solemn, for like the Baal Shem he longed for nothing
more than that the Messiah should usher in the End of Days. At
last he said to the Ari, "What if I should attempt to bring the
golden bird out of this garden?" But no sooner had he spoken
these words than a sudden wind arose, and plucked the golden
feather from his hand, and carried it off, so that Reb Nachman
knew it was gone. Nor was that warning lost on him, for he
recognized he might be expelled from the garden as swiftly as that
feather in the wind. Then the Ari replied, "You, Reb Nachman,
have entered this kingdom as a dreamer, while the Baal Shem

came here as one awake. Therefore that path is closed to you, for even if you succeeded in capturing the golden bird, you could not carry it beyond the gate of the Kingdom of Dreams. At the very instant you touched its feathers, you would find yourself alone and empty-handed in the world of men, and all that has transpired so far would be lost to you, like a dream lost between sleeping and waking."

Now Reb Nachman was not surprised to hear these words, for he had not forgotten that he had entered the Kingdom of Dreams. And the last thing he wanted was to be expelled from there. He said to the Ari, "But tell me, if I am permitted to know—how may I make my way back to this garden in order to hear the sacred song of the golden bird, as it translates the prayers which ascend from the world below? Nor does it matter to me if I come here as a dreamer or as one awake, as long as I am permitted to be in its presence and to hear that haunting melody."

The Ari smiled and said, "For you that will be very simple, Reb Nachman. You need only turn to the verse in which it is written that *The Torah is a Tree of Life*, and it will serve as your key to this kingdom. For on that night you will travel to this world in a dream, and share in the presence of the golden bird and the song that tranforms the prayers of men, which, as you see, are themselves the keys of heaven."

And no sooner did the Ari finish speaking than Reb Nachman awoke and found himself in the world of men once more. But this time he did not feel the quest was incomplete; on the contrary, he understood that his roots among the living were just as deep as those which drew him to the world above, where the song of the golden bird filled the heavens. And from that time on his Hasidim noticed that Reb Nachman left the Holy Scriptures by his bed every night, opened to the Psalms. And from then on they also noticed a divine smile which could be seen on his lips and in his eyes when he awoke. And all who knew him marveled at how peaceful he was every morning, as if he had returned from a journey to a faraway kingdom of peace.

Two

THE CAPTIVE SOUL
OF THE MESSIAH

The Captive Soul of the Messiah

> It is a part of man's condition that he must
> endure time and change; seas, rivers,
> deeps, deserts and wildernesses filled with
> serpents and scorpions. Only thus can he
> be worthy of entering the gates of holiness.
>
> Rabbi Nachman of Bratslav
> *Likutey Halachot*

SOME Rebbes were always waiting for the coming of the Messiah. Before sleep they would lay out their Sabbath clothes near the bed and lean a pilgrim's staff against them, leaving strict orders to be awakened at the very first sign. Other Rebbes often complained because the Messiah had not yet come. On their deathbeds they swore to shake all the worlds in Paradise in order to bring the Messiah down to earth. But Reb Nachman of Bratslav had grown impatient with waiting, and one year, during the long night of the Seder, Reb Nachman was overwhelmed by longing and almost fainted at the table. That night, before sleeping, Reb Nachman sent up a dream question with his prayers—to know why the Messiah had not yet come. And in reply he received a dream that lasted for four nights.

The first night Reb Nachman dreamed he was *davening Maariv*, the evening prayer, when he received a clear message in his mind. The message was to leave the House of Prayer, and to follow the path that ran outside its door until he arrived at a house with four stories known as the House of Pardes. He should enter there and perform the tasks assigned to him as quickly as possible. And if he completed them in time, he would find his great-grandfather, the Baal Shem Tov, waiting for him on the fourth floor.

In the dream Reb Nachman finished praying and then hurried down the path, clinging to the hope that he might fulfill his lifelong dream of meeting the Baal Shem, who had died only twelve years before he was born. As he walked, Reb Nachman noticed that the

path seemed somehow transformed, for it was like and yet unlike the one he knew so well. And when he had walked for one mile he came to a house that he had never seen before in that place, although the house itself was vaguely familiar, as if he had seen it before somewhere else. At first Reb Nachman thought this house had only three stories, for that is all he could see from where he was standing. But as he came closer, the fourth story manifested itself in his sight. Then Reb Nachman knew this must be the house in which he might meet the Baal Shem.

When he came to the front door, Reb Nachman saw the letters of the word *Pardes* inscribed there, in what seemed to be a flame. He marveled at this, since the flame did not consume what was burning. No one answered when he knocked at the door, and no one came out to greet him. But at the foot of the door there was a sealed envelope on which his name was written. Inside it, Reb Nachman found a message written in letters which flickered in his sight, as if they consisted of fire, the letters blurred until he brought them into focus. And there he found a list of the duties he was to perform on each floor: on the first story he was to scrub the floor; on the second he was to polish the mirrors; on the third he was to read the first page he turned to when he opened the Bible. And it was written that if he completed these tasks in time, he would meet the one he was waiting for at the entrance to the fourth floor.

Reb Nachman wasted no time at all, but moved efficiently through each task. First he carefully scrubbed the floor and polished the four mirrors so well he was tempted to step inside them, for each reflected something else. The first reflected a desert, the second a forest, the third an orchard, and the fourth a garden. Then he climbed the stairs to the third story, and there he found a Bible on a study stand. There was a ribbon marking a place for him to read. He opened the Bible to that place and saw he had turned to the Song of the Sea. And as he read the words of the Song, it seemed to him he could hear the Song itself, sung in perfect harmony, as if he were hearing it from afar.

He still carried the harmony with him when he bounded up

the steps of the final stairway, calling out the name of the Baal Shem. And at the top of the stairs the Baal Shem emerged from the doorway of a dark room and they embraced. The embrace was long and loving, for the Baal Shem had longed to meet with his great-grandson as much as Reb Nachman had longed for a meeting with his great-grandfather, on whose grave he had so often prayed. That is because, if the truth be known, the Baal Shem Tov and Reb Nachman shared the very same soul, one of the Innocent Souls which had fled rather than taste the fruit of the Tree of Knowledge. In this way they were bound together although they were apart, one living in the world of men, the other making his home in Paradise. But now that which had been parted was brought back together, and the union of the soul they shared shook the world to its foundations. And the Baal Shem told Reb Nachman that they must hurry, for the world is a world of fire, and in such a meeting there is the danger that the world of men might be unable to survive the pure flame burning in Paradise. And the Baal Shem took Reb Nachman to the window in that room and asked him to tell him what he saw outside.

When Reb Nachman looked down from the window he saw a dark woman in a white gown that seemed to be woven out of light. She was traveling along a narrow, winding path, her eyes fixed on the stars that crowded the sky. In her right hand she held a torch that gave off an unearthly light, and everywhere she went it seemed as if a path cleared beneath the moon. The sight of her took Reb Nachman's breath away, and although he saw her there for the first time, still he was certain that he must have seen her before. And that instant she looked up at him, and her eyes met his. And in her glance Reb Nachman read volumes, and found he already knew the words by heart. And in this way he recognized in her the very image of his soul. Finally Reb Nachman replied to the Baal Shem's question and said: "I see she who is the sister of my soul."

"That is true," said the Baal Shem, "but know also that she herself is a princess wandering in exile from her father, a great king. You must let her lead you; she is destined to serve as your guide. Follow her, and do whatever is necessary to keep the flame of her torch in your sight. Know too that all the Fathers in Paradise have faith in you, and that much hangs in the balance of the mission you are about to undertake."

Then, before they parted, the Baal Shem gave Reb Nachman an amulet, a jewel on a chain, with a flame burning inside it. And the Baal Shem said to him: "Wear this amulet at all times. It will protect you, and from it you can know how well your mission is progressing. For as long as the flame burns inside the jewel, hope exists that you will succeed. But if the fire goes out, then know that it is too late to continue, and make your way back to the world of men as soon as possible." Reb Nachman took the amulet and hung it around his neck, and marveled at the flame burning inside it, which had three parts: a bottom part burning darkly, a center part burning deep red, and a top part so pure it was almost transparent. Then Reb Nachman and the Baal Shem embraced once more, and Nachman woke up. And that was the dream of the first night.

As he lay awake after the dream, Reb Nachman saw that the room was illumined by a light which seemed to come from within, as if the moon had slipped inside. And he broke into tears and sobbed, for he still felt the warmth of the Baal Shem's embrace. And now he seemed to have discovered a new awareness of his soul, for he felt that the spirit of the Baal Shem was now a part of him that could not be lost. And when Reb Nachman arose and passed in front of a mirror, he saw to his complete amazement that he was still wearing the amulet the Baal Shem had given him in the dream, and inside it the flame in the jewel was still burning. And for a moment he felt the ground give way beneath his feet, as if the earth had opened up. Then he saw he was walking on the edge of an abyss which yawned beneath him, yet even so he was not afraid, not as long as he kept his balance. And he understood that in being chosen to carry out such a quest he had received a great blessing.

All the next day a fragrance of Paradise clung to Reb Nachman, and that night he dreamed the second dream. In this dream he followed the Princess in her wanderings, and let her lead him to the four corners of the earth, through deserts and forests, through orchards and gardens. During the day she disappeared and he was led by a white bird. But at sunset the flame of her torch would always appear, and then he never let it out of his sight. On the third night he dreamed he followed her to the bank of a river hidden in the darkness. There by the shore was a boat, its hull fashioned from jewels. The Princess stepped into the boat and cast off downstream. When Reb Nachman reached the shore he found another boat hidden in the reeds. This one had been carved from an aromatic wood, and the letter *Bet* was inscribed on its side in a fire that burned but did not consume. There Reb Nachman cast off into the currents. In this way he was led down that river of dreams by the flame of the torch of the lost Princess, who wandered in exile from her father, the King.

In the dream of the fourth night the jeweled boat of the Princess reached a cove at the end of the river, where she disembarked and entered a cave by a secret entrance. Reb Nachman also beached his boat and followed her into the same entrance. Much to his surprise, the walls of the cave shone as if they were lined with pearl, and he saw that the passages spiraled around him as if it were in a seashell. Reb Nachman searched for the Princess in that place, and at every turning of the spiral he encountered a treasure, each more precious than the last. There was a glowing pearl that shone like a full moon; a lamp that gave off an unearthly aura; three golden keys that looked as if they could unlock a palace; a staff with the Name of God inscribed on it in flames that did not consume; a torch that never burned out; a harp that played by itself; a perfect vessel, which glowed from within with a light unlike any other; stone tablets on which fiery letters fluttered; and a *Shofar*, a ram's horn, which Reb Nachman had an overwhelming desire to blow once or twice. But when he picked up the *Shofar* the flame in the jewel he wore flickered and seemed as if it might die out, so he put it down, and proceeded to the final cave, in which he still did not find the Princess. Instead he saw there a Book, whose binding was very beautiful, inlaid with ten glowing jewels. And when he opened the Book he saw its pages consisted of fire, and its letters were inscribed in black fire on white. When he first looked at the letters they appeared blurred in his vision, but as he looked longer they began to come into focus, and in this way Reb Nachman read one page in that Book. And there he read the tale of the lost Princess who had led him to that place, from its beginning to its end, and he learned how she had come to be the sister of his soul.

On the second page Reb Nachman read a story about a prince made entirely of precious gems; on the eighth page he read a story about a rabbi's son; and on the twelfth page he read about a Master of Prayer. All in all he read thirteen pages, and each of them seemed like a lifetime in itself, for in those tales Reb Nachman read the history of his own soul. The last tale he read in that Book was about seven beggars. And when the story ended the seventh beggar still had not appeared. Reb Nachman understood that when the seventh beggar arrived, the Messiah would come. And then he realized that his dream question was about to be answered.

After he had read the thirteen tales, each one a golden branch on a golden tree, Reb Nachman turned to the fourteenth page, and what he read there changed his life for all time. What he read there cannot be fully translated into words, for it cannot be fully understood unless it is read in that same Book, in those same flaming letters. For there Reb Nachman came to understand the silence of the Messiah. He learned that the soul of the Messiah was being held captive by the Prince of Darkness in the Kingdom of Roots on the far side of the River Sambatyon. And there he read that only if two of those among the Children of Israel went in search of the Cave of the Elders in that kingdom and brought back two of the treasures from the cave—the *Shofar* hidden there and the very Book he was reading from—only then would the soul of the Messiah be set free, and the Messiah be able to bring about the End of Days. For that *Shofar* is the horn of the ram which Father Abraham sacrificed on Mount Moriah in place of his son Isaac; and that Book is the treasure of treasures, the Hidden Torah itself, in which every man may read the truth, and in which all truth is to be found.

And the last words Reb Nachman read in that Book told him it was incumbent on whoever read that page to set out at once in search of the Cave of the Elders in the Kingdom of Roots, where the treasure was hidden, and to take with him one other who could be trusted.

No sooner did Reb Nachman finish reading these words than he woke up, resting on his bed, in his room, and it was day. And when he held up the flaming jewel of the amulet he wore, which the Baal Shem had given him, and peered into the flame, the whole dream unwound like a long scroll, and every detail was perfect in his memory. And he drew in a long breath, and felt as if he had just come back from a very long journey.

All day Reb Nachman bathed in the aura of that dream, and by nightfall he had decided to set out on the quest the very next day. He was not worried about how to reach the Kingdom of Roots, for he sensed he was destined to go there. Instead he was puzzled because he could not decide which of his disciples to take with him—Reb Shimon of Medvedevka, his first disciple, or Reb Nussan of Nemerov, his scribe. He was still puzzled when he lay down to sleep, and that night, in his dream, he woke up in a forest. The forest was boundless; he wanted to return. A man approached him whose features he could not discern, for each time he looked at him his sight became blurred. And he spoke to Reb Nachman, and said, "I am one of the Captive Souls who has been kept from being born. This is the forest you have forgotten. It is so long, it is infinite. Nothing could be named until you found your way back to this forest."

Then a second man approached him whose features also were hidden, as if surrounded by some kind of fog. And this one showed him the way to a garden. The distance was endless; he wanted to turn back. And then this man spoke to Reb Nachman and said, "I am one of the Wandering Souls who is unable to find any rest in this world. I wander restlessly from one realm to the next, for the work of my soul is unfinished, and I have been waiting for you to complete the task."

Then a third man approached him, and this one he recognized—it was Reb Nussan, his scribe. And Nussan took him aside and said, "Without you, the letters inscribed in every scroll inside every Ark would be separated from the spirit that animates them like the spirit that inhabits a body, and the words on the scroll would have no more meaning to us than the languages of the builders of the Tower of Babel, after they had lost the ability to comprehend the Holy Tongue."

After this another man approached him, whom Reb Nachman also recognized—Reb Shimon, his first disciple. And Shimon brought with him a torch which he handed to Reb Nachman, and said, "This torch has been handed down from father to son; its light alone has saved us from total darkness; its flame has never gone out." And Reb Nachman took the torch, and its flame rose up into heaven. And then he awoke.

For a long time after he had awakened, Reb Nachman felt his spirit hover between heaven and earth, as if it still had not completed the descent back to his body. And when he contemplated this dream he decided it was Shimon that he would take with him on his journey—for he had been the last to speak, and his gift had taken him from the garden into Paradise itself.

As it happened, Shimon was the first disciple to see Reb Nachman that day, and the Rebbe took this as a sign for his decision. Then he told Shimon the whole story of the dream that had lasted for four nights, and of the captive soul of the Messiah, and of the dream in which Shimon had handed him the torch. And he also told him of the quest he planned to undertake, and he said to Shimon, "Do you want to go with me or not?"

Shimon said, "Of course I will go with you, Reb Nachman! But you must know that I came here in the first place to report a dream that I dreamed last night. In this dream you and I were traveling together in a foreign land. During the day we were led by a white bird, and at night we followed the flame of a torch. Then the dream shifted and you were standing beside a dark woman in the shadow of a cave. She was peering into the bonfire that was burning within. Sometimes she accompanied you with her instrument, and sometimes you prayed with her voice or shared the sound of her breathing, or even her song. Once she showed you how to read your lifeline as if the words were already written. 'If only you would kneel by the fire,' she whispered, 'you would understand why no water can extinguish this flame—why all the logs burst into buds, and all the kinds of wood put forth fruit.' Then I too looked into the fire, and what she said was true—the logs were not consumed by the flames—they were bursting into blossom. I came here to ask you what this dream might portend, and you have answered my question without my having to ask it, for now that you have told me your dream, I know."

When Reb Nachman heard this, he was thrilled, and he decided they must set out on their journey at once, since every moment saved could bring the coming of the Messiah that much closer. Then he hurried to take down a bottle of ink from the shelf, poured a small amount into the hollow of his hand, enough to form a small mirror, and he asked Shimon to look into that mirror and tell him what he saw.

Shimon looked into the mirror of ink and at that moment every shadow and every echo disappeared, and everything became bright as if he were in a sunlit cloud. Then an image came into focus on the surface of the mirror, and he said, "I see worlds that come into being and pass away."

Then Reb Nachman said, "Look again."

This time Shimon looked into the mirror and said, "I see ten vessels of light emerging from a single, unseen point. Now one of those vessels has shattered . . . now the others are breaking one by one. Now there is only one vessel left unbroken, the first one to emerge, and sparks are scattered everywhere like stars."

Then Reb Nachman said, "Look again."

This time when Shimon looked he said: "Now I see the sparks that had been scattered are somehow being gathered together. But the vessels have not yet been restored."

Then Reb Nachman said, "If the sparks are gathered, even if the vessels are not restored, that is enough. Listen carefully, Shimon, for I am going to reveal to you one of the mysteries of creation, as it was once revealed by the Ari.

"Long before the sun cast a shadow, before the Word was spoken that brought the heavens and the earth into being, a flame emerged, as you have seen, from a single, unseen point. And from the center of that flame sparks of light sprang forth, concealed in shells which set sail everywhere, above and below, like a fleet of ships, each carrying its cargo of light.

"Somehow, no one knows why, the frail vessels broke open, split asunder, and all the sparks were scattered, like sand, like seeds, like stars.

"That is why we were created—to search for the sparks no matter where they have been hidden, and as each one is revealed, to be consumed in our own fire, and reborn out of our own ashes.

"Someday, when the sparks have been gathered, the vessels will be restored. Then the fleet will set sail across another ocean of space, and the Word will be spoken again."

At the very moment Reb Nachman said "again," Shimon's gaze was brought back to the mirror of ink, as if by an invisible hand. And there he saw himself traveling through a desert. That is when he realized he had entered that desert and was traveling there at Reb Nachman's side. During the day they were led by a white bird, and at night they followed the flame of a torch. And, strange to say, even though the journey had just started, it felt to Shimon as if it had already lasted forty years. Yet for Reb Nachman there had hardly been time to complete one breath, so caught up was he. But Reb Nachman knew what Shimon did not—that they were no longer traveling in time, and what seemed like years to one was like a single breath to the other.

After the two Hasidim had traveled very far in the wilderness, Shimon said, "Reb Nachman, we have traveled this far and we have not reached a single landmark. Perhaps we should turn back, while there is still time."

And Reb Nachman said, "Let me answer you with a parable. Once there was a man and his son. They decided to set out on a journey around the world. So one day they left home, and set out on the path that led from their own door. But when they had only crossed the field beyond their gate, the man decided to turn back. His son argued with him about it, and asked him how he could turn back when they had just started on their journey. But the man did not reply; instead he took a shovel and covered his footprints with dirt."

When Reb Shimon heard this parable, he looked behind him, and he saw their footprints stretching back as far as he could see. And then he grew ashamed.

Then Reb Nachman said, "You should know, Shimon, that with every step I take in this world, my soul ascends one more rung of Jacob's ladder, climbing towards Paradise. And your soul, Shimon, is holding the ladder steady while my soul ascends, for it is known that my soul will reach down and pull yours up after it."

When Shimon heard this he became firm in his faith once more. And Reb Nachman saw that the *Yetzer Hara*, the evil impulse, had released its hold on him, and that they were free to continue their quest.

Not long afterwards they came to a pillar of stone that stood by itself in the desert, and there was an old man perched on top of it. Shimon asked the old man if he could tell them where they were, and the old man said, "This desert you are passing through is known as the desert Shur. It is a desert full of snakes, lizards, and scorpions. So deadly are the snakes that dwell in this desert that if one of them merely glides over the shadow of a flying bird, the bird falls dead in that place."

While the two Hasidim were standing there, talking to the old man, a wind arose and blew around them something that looked like Hebrew letters. Several of these letters landed at their feet. Reb Nachman and Shimon were confused by this sight, and also worried, for it was not a good sign. And Shimon said, "Tell me, old man, what is the meaning of these letters that blow through the desert like sand?"

The old man said, "For years after the separation from their brothers, the tenth lost tribe tried to find its way out of this desert. Every day the members of the tribe paused at dusk, raised up their tents, and assembled for the holy services. But in the thirty-ninth year of their wanderings they could not agree on where to seek the Promised Land, and one day when they had assembled for prayer no words sang out, for somehow they had lost the word *open*, and from that day on the scroll remained tightly closed.

"Divining the fate that this sign foretold, the prophets so

frightened the people that no man dared lie with his wife. Instead all stretched out alone and discovered the silence of their empty hands, and by morning they had lost the word *hold*.

"Soon afterwards their wanderings were cut short. Day after day they stayed in their tents and refused to continue their journey. At last they agreed among themselves that this place was their home, and that day they lost the word *search*.

"Before long not only the people, but the animals, the birds, and even the winds had become silent. And within a year no one could speak the ancient tongue; its words were scattered through the desert like clouds of dust. Now even the words have broken apart, and these letters are all that remain."

When Shimon heard this story, he despaired, for he was afraid that he and Reb Nachman would also lose their way in that terrible desert. But for Reb Nachman it reaffirmed his determination not to give up being vigilant for even an instant. Then Shimon said to the man, "Tell us, old man, what is your name, and how is it that you have come to spend your life on top of a pillar in such a desert?"

The old man replied, "As for me, I do not have a name—I have been sitting on this pillar for so long I have forgotten it. All I remember is why this pillar was put up. It is to signify the spot where Moses was swallowed by a snake from his head to that place, and spit out and swallowed again, from his feet to that place. And when Zipporah, his wife, saw this, she understood that the Holy One was angry because their son had not been circumcised. And in this place she took a stone and struck off his foreskin, and said to Moses: '*Surely a bridegroom of blood are you to me.*' You should know that to enter this desert is to bring danger on yourself. Still, there is one way you can protect yourself here—if you are willing to reconfirm the covenant of the circumcision. That is the only way you will ever succeed in getting out of this desert alive."

Shimon shivered when he heard these words, but Reb Nachman noticed that the eyes of the old man were not illumined, and that his body did not cast a shadow. And he understood this old man must be a demon trying to deceive them, by discouraging them and by causing them to weaken themselves so much from the circumcision it would be impossible for them to continue their quest. And Reb Nachman said to the old man: "Old man, if what you have said to us is true, you have warned us against a grave danger, and we will do as you say. But first, please show us your *shadow*!"

No sooner had Reb Nachman shouted out the word *shadow*, than the old man vanished from their sight, the pillar vanished with him, and the desert disappeared. Reb Nachman and Shimon found themselves in a forest. And Reb Nachman said, "Now we know that there is resistance to us in this world. No doubt he who has captured the soul of the Messiah must be trying to stop us. But now that we have passed through the desert and reached this forest, I feel that we have passed an important test, though surely it will not be the last."

But in that boundless forest Shimon was afraid. He said, "Reb Nachman, here we are in a strange forest with no guide. How can we find our way? How can we keep from becoming lost?"

And Reb Nachman replied, "Fear not, Shimon. For though I have never been here before, yet somehow it is familiar, as if I recall it from a dream. Although there are no paths here, still I am certain I can find my way."

And so, with Reb Nachman leading and Shimon following close behind, they made their way through the forest. With every step he took it seemed to Reb Nachman that he could make out a path taking form before him, as if the foliage were parting to make way. Nor was the path he took a straight one, but it wandered every which way and sometimes circled back to the same place. Yet Reb Nachman knew that every step he took was necessary, and that it was his destiny to follow precisely that path.

In this way the two Hasidim reached a place in the forest where faint sounds, like distant music, came to their ears. Reb Nachman was perplexed by this strange music and he decided to see if they could locate its source. He and Shimon proceeded in the direction of the music as best they could, and along the way they came to the edge of a stream. And when they started across that stream Shimon felt something brush against his leg. Looking down he saw a snake, perhaps thirty feet long, at his feet, and he let out a great cry. Reb Nachman hurried to him, and at the same time he saw that the stream was crowded with snakes—sleeping snakes. Then he understood that the snakes were hibernating, and that there was no danger unless they woke them up. So he said to Shimon, "As long as that snake is sleeping, Shimon, you need not fear it, and the same holds true for all the snakes hibernating in this stream. But take care not to step on them or brush against them lest they wake up, for then we would truly be in danger."

After this Reb Nachman and Shimon continued to cross the stream by carefully studying the bottom before they took any steps. In this way they arrived safely at the other side, without waking any of the sleeping snakes. And not far from the stream they reached a great-rooted blossomer which seemed to be the source of the solemn music. Shimon was puzzled when he saw that tree, for he could not imagine how a tree could create any kind of music. But Reb Nachman studied the tree very carefully, and just at twilight discovered that as the wind blew through the forest it passed through its roots, which were hollow, and thus created that strange music. And Reb Nachman said, "Although I am not certain of the meaning of this music, Shimon, it is possible it is a sign to tell us that we have finally reached the Kingdom of Roots."

And at that very moment Reb Nachman looked up and saw a clearing in the forest, not far from where they stood. And on the far side of the clearing a river wound through the forest. And just as they reached the shore, they saw a boat casting off that looked as if it had been fashioned from jewels. On the side of the jeweled boat the letter *Aleph* was inscribed in jewels which glowed in the moonlight like distant stars. And although they could not see who was in the boat, they recognized the flame of the torch, and knew that they must follow.

Close by the place where the jeweled boat had cast off they saw the dim outline of another boat, hidden in the reeds. And when they reached this boat they saw that it was wooden, and that the wood had an aromatic scent. And like the boat in Reb Nachman's dream, the letter *Bet* was inscribed on its side in a flame that burned but did not consume. And Reb Nachman said: "Now we know that we have come to the right place, and that we can find what we seek in this kingdom."

Then Shimon said: "But look, Reb Nachman, there are no oars in this boat. How can we guide ourselves on the water?"

Reb Nachman replied: "That the boat is here with the flaming letter on its side—is that not miracle enough for you? Come, help me put it in the water. And have faith, Shimon, for surely the currents will carry us."

So it was that no sooner did the boat ride on the waters, with the two Hasidim sitting inside it, than a current caught hold of the boat and carried it out into the middle of the river, and led it downstream, always at the same distance from the flame of the torch which traveled before them. And as they drifted down that river it seemed to Reb Nachman that a cloud began to envelop them, so that it felt as if they were being carried by the currents of a river of dreams. But he did not know if he were the dreamer, or the one being dreamed. And at the place where the river joined the sea they came to a cove, and the current gently beached the boat as they entered there. And when they had pulled the boat completely onto the shore, they continued to follow the flame of the torch, which seemed to linger, as if to give them time to catch up.

Then Shimon said, "Look, the torch that has led us this far has come to a halt. Let us hurry to find out who it is that has brought us here, for surely this is someone we can trust."

And the two of them hurried toward the flame of the torch, and as they approached it they saw it was burning next to the entrance to a cave. And rooted beside that cave there was a golden tree with branches of gold. And from the branches hung all kinds of vessels, in the shapes of the letters of the Hebrew alphabet. And next to the golden tree there was an ancient carob tree of great beauty, filled with fruit. Both Hasidim marveled at these two trees, and then they entered the cave, where Reb Nachman expected to come face to face with the lost Princess at last. But the Princess was nowhere to be seen. Instead there was an old woman with long, white hair, who smiled when they greeted her, and told them that her name was Iscah. Around her neck she wore a jewel on a chain, which was identical to Reb Nachman's amulet, with a flame burning inside the jewel. In her hands she held a garment she was weaving, that gave off a wonderful glow. And the cloth of the garment had the quality of a mirror, and when Reb Nachman looked into that mirror he saw the lost Princess reflected there. She was standing in a forest beneath a tree with the moon framed in its branches, and it seemed as if she were calling the moon closer. Then she turned and faced Reb Nachman in the mirror, so that he was certain they saw each other face to face. But just then Iscah wove another stitch, and the image disappeared. And it seemed to Reb Nachman that each stitch she took turned in a circle that brought the heavens and the earth a little closer. And when Reb Nachman had seen the amulet she wore and the garment she was weaving, he knew that Iscah had been sent to guide them further on their quest. But he marveled at her name. And Reb Nachman said to her, "But was Iscah not the sister of Sarah, as it is written?"

And Iscah said, "Yes, I am Iscah, sister of Sarah. It was I who was the first disciple of Abraham. And it was I who introduced Abraham to my sister Sarah. Therefore God gave me eternal life, and named me one of the Elders whose role it is to guard the treasure in the Cave of the Elders and to see that the teachings are transmitted and received. I have read in the Hidden Torah that is concealed among the treasures in the cave, and from reading there I have become a seer and a prophet. Thus I have known for a long time that you would be coming here, but still, my waiting for you was like waiting for the Messiah—for, in truth, I do not know what will be the outcome of your quest. That is because it has not yet been decided. It depends on you. So closely matched are the powers that it hangs in the balance."

Then Reb Nachman said, "You have indeed been blessed, Iscah, and we are blessed to have found our way to you. But tell me, for I am very curious, what is the wonderful garment you are weaving?"

Iscah said: "This garment I am repairing is the robe of the *Shekhinah*, which she was wearing at the time the Temple was destroyed. The Sabbath Queen was reluctant to abandon the Sanctuary in the Temple that was her earthly dwelling, and she did not depart until the flames had entered the Holy of Holies. Even then she hovered over the flames so long that, as she rose up, a spark of the flames caught the hem of her robe and it began to burn. By the time she had returned to her heavenly home nothing remained of the robe but a single thread. But this was enough to reconstruct the robe—for if even a single thread remains from the old garment it suffices to transfer to the new one the essence of the old. Since then it is necessary to repair the robe when the moon is waning, so that the *Shekhinah* can wear it when the moon waxes. For once the moon begins to wane the garment goes up in flames, and burns until nothing remains of it but a single thread. Repairing this robe is one of my duties. Guiding you further on your journey is another. Tomorrow morning I will tell you how to continue your quest, for you have already entered the Kingdom of Roots, and you are very close to the cave you are seeking. But tonight let me tell you about what brought you here—let me tell you how the soul of the Messiah came to be held captive."

And Iscah pointed the way for them to take their ease on a fur rug which was spread out inside the cave. And without a word Reb Nachman and Shimon took their places on the rug and listened. And this is the tale that Iscah told:

"The Messiah, who is the Prince of Light, and his brother, the Prince of Darkness, were twins who gave birth to each other at the command of the Holy One, blessed be He. The Holy One had originally intended for the Messiah to bring the End of Days together with his twin, the Prince of Darkness. For each one was meant to complement and to complete the other. What the Prince of Darkness would prepare, the Prince of Light would make manifest; what the Prince of Darkness would receive, the Prince of Light would transmit. This way they would both be vessels of God's word.

"The Messiah accepted his role in creation from the first, but the Prince of Darkness grew defiant and wanted to rule over everything. He said to himself: 'Why should I share the universe with my brother? The world is a world of fire, and he who does not burn will be burned!' That is why the Holy One cast the Prince of Darkness and all of his angels from heaven, into a prison beneath the sea, where they languish to this day. But from his cell the Prince of Darkness is still able to bring harm on heaven and on earth. This is because the *nekevah*, or the feminine soul of the Messiah and the Prince of Darkness, is really one. Because it is shared by them, they are bound together, and the fate of each affects the fate of the other. They are attached like Siamese twins. Just as it is possible for two people to share the same *nekevah* and for their lives to intersect, as the soul they share seeks itself out, so the cosmic soul of the Messiah and the cosmic soul of the Prince of Darkness are linked to each other, and that is the way it has been ever since they came into being.

"The Prince of Darkness is well aware of the power he can exert over his twin, the Prince of Light. Because when the Prince of Darkness closes his soul to the Holy One, the soul of the Messiah is kept captive. And since the day of his Fall, the Prince of Darkness has brooded over his failure and has kept his soul closed, tight. In this way he keeps the soul of the Messiah helpless as if the Messiah himself were imprisoned in the cell beside that of his twin brother. And while his soul is imprisoned the End of Days cannot be reached, for the Messiah cannot come.

"Nor is the soul of the Messiah the only soul affected. There are those known as the Captive Souls. These souls are denied their destiny to be born. For they take their very existence from the soul of the Messiah, and while the soul of the Messiah is held captive, these souls are held captive as well. Each of them is guarded by one of the Watchers, the angels who were cast from heaven along with the Prince of Darkness.

"Also, all those whose souls take strength from the soul of the Messiah—the Hasidim, the *Tzaddikim*, and the *Lamed-Vov*, the Thirty-six Just Men who are the very pillars on which the world stands—all these are denied the radiant strength of his soul. And without this vital support the foundation of the world is weakened, and the hearts of people in the world grow weary.

"Then the Messiah, the Prince of Light, brought his case before the Holy One, blessed be He, and he said, 'Master of the Universe, while my soul is held captive the burdens of the people grow greater. As things stand, it will never be possible for my soul to be set free as long as it is bound to that of my brother, the Prince of Darkness. Please set my soul free, so that I can be born among men and can bring the End of Days, as was promised.'

"And when the Holy One saw that the heart of the Prince of Darkness had grown hard, and that he no longer knew how to nourish, only to poison, He decreed that it be made possible for the soul of the Messiah to be set free from the bondage of his brother. And he gave the decree to the angel Raziel, who announced it in heaven and then delivered it to the Prince of Darkness in his cell. And this is what the angel said:

> The Holy One has decreed that if two of the righteous souls among the Children of Israel shall go in search of the Ten Treasures hidden in the Cave of the Elders in the Kingdom of Roots, on the far side of the River Sambatyon, and if they should succeed in locating this cave and in bringing back the *Shofar* concealed there, let there be a single blast blown on that *Shofar*, and at that time the soul of the Messiah shall be set free. And if it happens that two of the Treasures hidden in that cave should be brought back, the *Shofar* and the Book of the Hidden Torah, then let there be two long blasts blown on the *Shofar*, and at the time of the first blast the soul of the Messiah shall be set free, and at the time of the second the Messiah shall be born among men and usher in the End of Days."

And Iscah continued her tale: "When the Prince of Darkness heard this decree he did not dispute it, for he knew that would be futile. But he laughed and said bitterly that he was certain no one even knew that the soul of the Messiah was being held captive, much less where to begin to search for the Kingdom of Roots. And even if they did reach the Kingdom, they would never find the Cave of the Elders. And even if they did they would never escape the wild currents of the River Sambatyon, which cannot be crossed."

Then Shimon said, "But Iscah, tell us, where is this River Sambatyon, and why did we not encounter it on our way here? For the river which brought us here was placid, and its currents gentle and calm, and they carried us at a leisurely pace."

And Iscah said, "That is because you came here on the eve of the Sabbath, for that is the only time when the River Sambatyon is as calm as any other river."

And Nachman said: "But Iscah, the eve of the Sabbath is not until tomorrow night."

And Iscah said, "No, tonight is the eve of the Sabbath, for in this kingdom we live one day ahead of the rest of the world. That is why there were no oars in the boat, since it can only travel on the waters on the eve of the Sabbath. And then no oars are needed, for those who ride on the waters could not labor, in any case."

And Reb Nachman said, "Please, Iscah, tell us more about this river."

And Iscah said, "As you now know, the River Sambatyon can only be crossed when its wild current stops flowing, and the rocks and sand it constantly throws up come to a halt. True, there are other rivers that dry up from time to time—during the rainy season they swell and overflow, while at other times, they are as dry as a bone. But the Sambatyon is not like any other river. For six days its current is strong and it has plenty of water, so strong it is impossible to cross. But on the eve of the Sabbath a cloud envelops the river, and the waters come slowly to a halt. Then on the day of the Sabbath the waters subside and disappear, and it resembles a lake of snow-white sand, and at the close of the Sabbath it resumes its torrent of rushing water, stones, and sand."

Then Shimon said, "What happens to those who try to travel on the river on the eve of the Sabbath by using oars?"

And Iscah said, "That can never happen, Shimon, since the River Sambatyon is invisible to all but those who have faith that it

exists as a miracle of the Holy One, and to desecrate the Sabbath is
to deny that the river exists. In fact, the whole Kingdom of Roots
exists only for those who have faith in the possibility of its existence. To all others it is invisible, and cannot be found no matter
how hard they try to seek it out."

Then Iscah said, "The strategy of the Prince of Darkness is to
encourage the belief that the Kingdom of Roots does not exist. He
believes that men are foolish and can easily be deceived. So far you
have proven him wrong, yet there are many trials still remaining.
In the morning I will tell you how you are to continue your quest.
For tonight I give you my blessing, and I hope that Duma, the
Prince of Dreams, will remind you of all that you have forgotten,
and all that you have to remember."

Then Iscah finished speaking and left to tend the fire in the
cave. And Reb Nachman and Shimon shivered in the silence at the
thought of all they had been through, and of all that still lay ahead.
And that night both of them dreamed they were sleeping in a
fragrant garden.

When Reb Nachman opened his eyes in the dream, he caught
a glimpse of a tree with a fruit that somehow reflected the sun and
was unlike any he had ever seen. When he sat up he saw one of
these fruits lying at his feet, and when he picked it up and broke it
open he saw it had as many seeds as there are stars, and when he
tasted it he drank of a spring that flowed within, and the taste was
more refreshing than water or wine. Then Reb Nachman knew he
must be somewhere inside the Garden of Eden, for a tree such as
that could not be planted anywhere else. Then he looked around
him and he saw that the ripe fruit of this tree soon melted, and out
of these waters there formed a river, which Reb Nachman knew
must be one of the rivers of Paradise, from which the pious drink
in the World to Come.

Meanwhile, Shimon's dream also found him in a garden.
There he was sleeping beneath a tree that branched above him.
The fruits of this tree were transparent, and in each a fire was
burning so that they resembled jewels with small suns inside. From
where he lay Shimon looked up at the branches above him, and

saw the flames inside each fruit burning against the night sky as if they were stars.

Then it happened that both Reb Nachman and Shimon woke up at the same time, and it was already morning, and the fragrance of the Garden was still on their clothes. And they told each other their dreams, and Iscah also heard them, and she said, "You dreamed of a garden because last night your souls entered the Garden of Eden. For the fur skin you slept on was one of the garments God provided for Adam and Eve at the time of their exodus from Eden, and it still bears the fragrance of Paradise, which will never disappear. The soul of anyone who sleeps on these garments is transported directly to the Garden of Eden. That is how Adam and Eve were able to be restored to their lost splendor, for they used these fur skins to sleep on, and in this way they were able to return to the Garden every night in their dreams. And when they handed down the garments to Seth, they passed on this secret, and after that the garments reached Nimrod, who used the power they gave him to build the Tower of Babel. Later they came to Noah, who took them with him on the ark, and in time they were passed on from Abraham to Isaac. One of these fur skins was worn by Jacob when he disguised himself and tricked his father Isaac into believing that his arm was hairy and that he was Esau. And in that way he received the blessing of the firstborn.

"When the Temple was destroyed, these garments were among the treasures that Jeremiah saved, and he hid them in this very cave. I had you sleep on that fur skin so that your souls could taste the sweetness of the World to Come. And in this way you will know better what it is that you are seeking, for if you succeed in freeing the soul of the Messiah and in bringing the End of Days, this will be the portion for all mankind."

Then Iscah brought Reb Nachman and Shimon a basket filled with carobs, and offered it to them. When she did the two Hasidim realized that they had not eaten anything since they had begun their quest, and yet they had not felt any hunger at all. Reb Nachman remarked about this to Iscah, and she said, "In this kingdom, Reb Nachman, it is the spirit that requires sustenance, not the body. In fact, the only food eaten here is the fruit of the carob, for in no other food is such a pure essence of the spirit contained.

"You might like to know that the carob tree you saw planted outside this cave was the one that Honi tended for seventy years while he was serving as one of the Elders of this kingdom, although when he woke up he remembered his stay here as if it had been only a dream. So too did Simeon bar Yohai and his son sustain themselves on the fruit of this same carob tree during the thirteen years they lived in this cave, hiding from the Romans. For in his wisdom Simeon bar Yohai understood that the carob is a holy fruit, and was in fact the manna that sustained the Children of Israel in their wanderings. Simeon bar Yohai also chose to live here in order to be near the Cave of the Elders, where the Book of the Hidden Torah is concealed. And during that time he transcribed from the Hidden Torah the volumes of the *Zohar*, the Book of Splendor, which contain great secrets, and brought them back to the world of men.

"Among the others who have served here was your great-grandfather, Reb Nachman, the Baal Shem Tov. He found his way here as a young man, and it was here that he came when he disappeared during his long walks in the woods."

After they had heard this tale of the carob tree, each of the Hasidim took one of the fruits of the carob and tasted it. To his amazement, Reb Nachman found it had the taste of the fruit of Paradise he had tasted in his dream that night, while Shimon found that the fruit had a taste so pure that the memory of it haunted him all the days of his life.

Then Iscah said, "Now you shall learn what you have come to know—the Cave of the Elders lies before you, under the waters of the Red Sea. For know that the Kingdom of Roots, where you are, is hidden within the boundaries of the Holy Land itself, and that you have traveled along the route of the Israelites in their wanderings and have reached the very shore where the Children of Israel crossed the Red Sea."

Reb Nachman and Shimon were astounded to hear this, because they had no idea they had reached the Holy Land, much less the shore of the Red Sea. At the same time they were dismayed to learn that the Cave of the Elders was underwater, for there it was beyond their reach. After a long silence Reb Nachman finally spoke: "This news, Iscah, has shaken me to the roots, for I have always longed to walk on the sacred soil of the Holy Land. But tell me, how, then, is it possible for us to reach the cave and its treasures? For surely the waters of the Red Sea have parted only once in the history of creation, when Moses and the Children of Israel stood before it. Then the waters drew back on the command of the Holy One so that the Israelites could cross the sea. But surely such a miracle can never be repeated."

"Yes it can," said Iscah, "for among the souls of the Children of Israel who were gathered by the sea there were present all the souls of all the future generations. And once a soul has experienced the miracle of the parting waters, then it can always be repeated, provided the soul is willing to risk the waters. For the waters can recognize every soul among those who stood there and sang the Song of the Sea. You, Reb Nachman, and you, Shimon, you have souls which stood beside Moses on the shore. I will take you to the very place where the waters parted, and there you must enter the waters and sing the Song. And if the faith of your souls is perfect, then the waters will part for you."

Then Iscah turned and walked out of the cave, and the Hasidim followed her. She led them to a place along the shore which looked like any other. But when Reb Nachman drew near, he saw an almost invisible fog hovering in one site along the shore. And he knew that this must be the place. He asked Iscah if this was true, and she said, "Yes, this is the sacred place where the Children of Israel stood and sang the Song of the Sea. Even the children in the wombs joined in the harmony. Now you too must step into the waters and sing the Song, and if your faith is perfect, the waters will recognize the voice of your soul and part. But remember—the waters cannot stay parted for very long, no longer than it took the Israelites to cross to the other side. Remember, too, that when the waters that have parted come together, they will meet with great force, and the currents will carry you past the cove where the

River Sambatyon meets the Red Sea. You will then be at the mercy of the waters of the River Sambatyon, and this time it will not be the eve of the Sabbath. Then all that can save you from the waves is your faith. For if your faith is perfect when you enter the Red Sea, then the Spirit of the Sea will protect you until you are safely back on the shore. But if your faith is imperfect, then the Spirit of the Sea will not intervene to protect you from the waters.

"Since your time is precious, you must use every second to find your way to the Cave of the Elders. Once you have found it, you must search in the labyrinth for the last of its three secret passages, each of which has a door of fire. Do not even go near the first two doors of fire—you are forbidden to enter there. And I cannot tell you how to find your way through the labyrinth; that is a riddle you must solve for yourself. But this much I can tell you: once you have entered the cave, you can only go forward—there is no turning back. If you turn back for even an instant, your mission will be lost. Reb Nachman, the amulet you are wearing around your neck, identical to mine, is the key which fits the door of fire. Hold its flaming jewel in your hand and raise it towards the door, and it will open.

"Inside the Cave of the Elders you will find the Ten Treasures. Look at them briefly, but remember—if you do not turn your glance away in time, the treasures will draw you to them, and will tell you their tales. But if this happens even once, you will lose too much time. For when the time of the crossing has elapsed, the waters will rush back together, and the cave will be flooded again, and you will be cast into the sea. So search for the two treasures you have come so far to find—the *Shofar* and the Book of the Hidden Torah. And when you find them, be certain to hold them firmly in your grasp, and keep your faith firm. If you do this you will be delivered, and the world will be delivered with you."

And Shimon asked Iscah, "What is behind the first two doors of the cave which we are forbidden to enter?"

And Iscah answered, "The Prince of Darkness and all his angels are imprisoned behind the first door of fire, and behind the second door—there the soul of the Messiah is being held captive. If you were to open the first door, the Prince of Darkness would be set free, and if you try to free the soul of the Messiah before the quest has been completed—then the Redemption of the Messiah will never take place. Therefore you must take great care when you enter that cave, for it is one of the Gates of Heaven!"

When Iscah said this, Shimon realized for the first time the awesome implications of their mission, which Reb Nachman had long understood. He saw that his life hung in the balance above *Gehenna* by a thread, and that one single misstep would be fatal to their hopes. As for Reb Nachman, he was as one who is in a trance—he heard every word that Iscah spoke as if it had already been written, and he so concentrated on their undertaking that he did not even consider the possibility of failure.

Then Iscah continued to tell them what to do: "If you are able to find the treasures, and if you are able to survive the waters when they rush together, and if you are able to cross to the other side of the River Sambatyon with the treasures intact, you, Reb Nachman, are entrusted with the *Shofar*, and you must blow a long blast on it. But listen carefully to what I am now going to say: if you have reached the far shore with the *Shofar*, and there is no sign of Shimon and the Book, then you are permitted to blow on it only once; but if Shimon has reached the shore as well, and brings the Book with him, then you must give two blasts on the ram's horn. As you know, the first blast will free the soul of the Messiah. And after the soul of the Messiah has been set free, the second blast will usher in the End of Days. But remember—only one blast if Shimon does not bring back the Book. For should you blow a second blast which is not deserved, the world will burn up in an instant, and all of creation will come to an end!"

Then Iscah looked into Reb Nachman's eyes for a long time, reading in them as if they were the pages of a book, and she saw he would never be tempted to blow the second blast should Shimon fail. For she saw in his eyes the first day of creation as if it had been imprinted there. And she did not see a wish to end the world. She saw instead a longing for the End of Days, which would bring the world back to the Beginning. Then Iscah gave each of them her

blessing, which carries great power, for she herself had been
blessed by Abraham, and blessed again by the Holy One Himself
when he granted her eternal life. And when Reb Nachman raised
up his eyes during the blessing he saw to his amazement that the
lost Princess was standing before him, where Iscah had just stood.
And when he gazed into her eyes the soul of Reb Nachman was
reunited with she who was the sister of his soul. Then, all at once,
when the blessing had been given, the presence of the lost Princess
vanished, and it was Iscah who stood before them once more, and
she nodded to Reb Nachman and took her leave.

Shimon, who had not looked up during the blessing and thus
had not caught a glimpse of the lost Princess, watched Iscah walk
away. And he marveled that Iscah, who was a very old woman,
still walked like a young girl. But Reb Nachman did not look back,
for he had grown firm in his faith, and he walked forward into the
fog that hovered at the edge of the shore, the Song of the Sea on
his lips and in his heart. Yet at that moment Shimon was seized by
a great fear, and he was unable to move towards the waters and
unable to join in the singing. But Reb Nachman did not know this;
he assumed Shimon was with him in all ways, and even though he
sang alone, it seemed to him that he was joined by the heavenly
hazan and all the angels.

Soon Reb Nachman was deeply immersed in the waters, up to
his mouth, but still his faith remained perfect. He felt certain the
sea would part for him, just as it had for the Israelites. And because he was singing from such a pure depth, the Spirit of the Sea
recognized the voice of Reb Nachman's holy soul, which had in
fact stood among those by the sea. At that instant the waters of the
Red Sea split, and as soon as the path appeared Reb Nachman
hurried down it; thus he did not notice that Shimon joined him
only after the waters had already parted.

Halfway down the path formed by the parting waters, Reb
Nachman and Shimon reached a cavern which lay on the floor of
the sea. The waters which had filled it had also drained away, and
the two Hasidim lowered themselves inside. There they found
themselves in what first appeared to be the inside of a seashell, its

walls lined with a smooth substance like pearl. But unlike a sea-shell, the cavern was immense, and in it there were so many pas-sages it resembled a labyrinth. And there they heard the echo of the original Song of the Sea, which had been reverberating there for all the ages since the Israelites had originally sung it in unison. And Reb Nachman decided to let the Song lead them, and in this way they were guided through the labyrinth, for if they made a wrong turn the Song faded, until they came back on course. Even-tually they reached the first door of fire, where the Prince of Darkness and his angels were imprisoned. And the flames of that door of fire were very dark. And Reb Nachman said, "Hurry, Shimon, past this place where the unholy Prince of Darkness is imprisoned, lest a shadow of his shadow should fall on us and divert us from our quest." So they hurried on, led by the Song of the Sea. And soon they came to the second doorway, where the soul of the Messiah was being held captive. And the flames of that door of fire were a deep red. Here Reb Nachman said, "Let us shut our eyes, Shimon, as we pass by this place where the soul of the Messiah is being held, lest there fall on us a shadow of a shadow of temptation to set the soul free before our quest is complete." And they both shut their eyes, and used their hands to feel their way around the spiral passageway.

Finally the Song of the Sea grew louder, as if they had reached its source, and there they reached the third door of fire, where the Cave of the Elders was concealed. And the flames of this door were pure white, like the top part of the flame which burned in the jewel of Reb Nachman's amulet. Then Reb Nachman raised up his amulet, and saw that the flame in it had never burned so brightly; at that instant the flames parted and Reb Nachman stepped inside the doorway, and Shimon followed him, and the fiery door closed.

From there they saw that the passage spiraled downward. They descended into the first spiral, and there they saw a glowing pearl that shone like a full moon and cast its aura throughout the cavern. And Reb Nachman said, "This must be the pearl that illuminated the ark for Noah, when the skies were dark and overcast for the forty days and nights." And the light of the pearl seemed to curve around the sides of the cavern, for as the two of them turned the corner, spiraling downward, the light never dimmed.

At the turning of the second spiral they found a golden lamp that cast a wonderful glow. And Shimon was curious to know what was the source of that light. And he lingered behind Reb Nachman, and took down the lamp from where it rested, but he was unable to find any source for the light except the lamp itself. And in this way he lost track of time, and stayed in that one place. Nor did Reb Nachman, who was concentrating on the treasures of the cave, notice that Shimon was no longer with him.

At the turning of the third spiral Reb Nachman found three golden keys enclosed within a golden casket. Never had such keys been seen; not even the keys to a king's palace could compare. And Reb Nachman knew that these must be the keys of the Temple in Jerusalem. For when the Temple was about to be destroyed, priests with the keys in their hands had mounted the roof of the Temple and exclaimed: "Master of the Universe, as we did not have the merit to be faithful treasurers, these keys are handed back into Thy keeping!" Then, as they threw the keys skyward, a hand from heaven had reached down and caught up the keys, and now they were hidden in that cave. And Reb Nachman was drawn to those keys, as if in a trance. But as he was about to pick them up he thought he heard Iscah's voice and he remembered her warning, and he stopped himself in time and continued through the next turning.

At the turning of the fourth spiral Reb Nachman saw a wondrously carved wooden staff. And on the sides of the staff there were four letters written in fire which spelled out the secret Name of God. Yet although the fiery letters were burning, the wooden staff was not consumed. And Reb Nachman realized that this staff must be the staff of Moses, which had become a serpent in Pharoah's court, with which he had struck the rock in the wilderness.

At the turning of the fifth spiral Reb Nachman saw a torch burning. And he recognized it as the torch he had taken up in his dream, whose fire had reached into heaven.

At the turning of the sixth spiral Reb Nachman came into the presence of a magnificent harp, with an ornate golden frame. And the breeze that passed through those chambers plucked the strings of that harp, and the music they evoked harmonized with the Song of the Sea. And Reb Nachman realized this must be the harp of King David, which had hung near David's bed, about which it was said that the north wind would come in the middle of the night and pluck the strings of the harp, and the harp would play of itself. And Reb Nachman left that place with difficulty, for the harmony of the harp was so beautiful he longed to remain in its presence.

At the turning of the seventh spiral Reb Nachman saw a vessel filled with light. And although he had never seen it before, he knew that this must be the first of the ten vessels which had sailed forth at the Beginning, sent out by the Holy One like so many ships. Inside that vessel was the light of the first day of creation, the same light which shone before the sun and moon had been placed in the firmament, with which a man could see from one end of the world to the other, and that was the last of that light existing in the world. And because that one vessel was unbroken, it was possible to repent and begin again.

At the turning of the eighth spiral Reb Nachman saw the tablets which Moses had carried down from Mount Sinai. Not the tablets with letters engraved in stone, but the first tablets, whose letters were inscribed in black fire on white. For before the first tablets had shattered, the letters on them had taken flight. Later the Ari found a way to restore the stone fragments to unbroken tablets, and when this had taken place the letters flew back to the stone at once. And those letters appeared blurred in Reb Nachman's vision until he brought them into focus, and when he read them he understood that had those first tablets been received, whole libraries of blank books would now be written by their readers, for whom the lines would first appear blurred on the page. But because those tablets were cast down, the commandments, as we know them, are restrictive. And though the letters are engraved on stone, the curse of that imperfect descent still flows through our blood.

At the turning of the ninth spiral Reb Nachman reached the

Shofar, which lay inside a golden casket. And the shape of that ram's horn was wondrous—it resembled a golden branch of a golden tree. Its luster was so bright it seemed to reflect a hidden sun. And Reb Nachman averted his eyes and reached down and picked up the *Shofar*, and he wrapped it in his prayer shawl, and carried it under his arm.

Only as he left the ninth spiral, with the *Shofar* firmly in his grasp, did Reb Nachman realize that Shimon was not with him. Then he began to tremble, and in his fright that everything might be lost, he cried out Shimon's name. And the echo of that cry spiraled through all the passages of the cave, and crashed against Shimon like a great wave, so that he feared that the waters of the Red Sea had already come back together. And so frightened was he that his hair turned white at that moment, and Reb Nachman almost did not recognize him when he came running breathlessly to catch up. Then Shimon realized that in his rush to reach Reb Nachman he had overlooked the other treasures in the cave, and he wanted to turn back. But Reb Nachman said: "Stop, Shimon. Calm yourself. Remember Iscah's warning—there is no turning back. Yet all is not lost. Although you have deprived yourself of unimaginable treasures, our mission can still be completed." And when Shimon heard these words he was greatly relieved that Reb Nachman had stopped him in time from turning back, and they proceeded together through the turning of the tenth spiral.

When they reached that place it was as if they had entered into a Divine Presence, for it was filled with a pure glow as if the source of the light that illumined those caverns was there, within. Then Reb Nachman understood that they had reached that sacred place where the Book of the Hidden Torah was concealed. And he understood that this sanctuary had existed since the Temple had been destroyed, so that there would be a Tabernacle on earth as well as in heaven. And just as the firmament had been created to divide the upper waters from the lower, so too was there a curtain in the cavern which divided the sacred from the most sacred of all. And there, behind that curtain, hidden behind ten veils, inside the Ark of the Tabernacle, they found the Book of the Hidden Torah, wrapped in a cloth that shone like a mirror in which they each saw something else. Shimon saw the face of his father, exactly as he remembered him best, while Reb Nachman saw a golden mountain from which shone an eternal light, and a waterfall in which was reflected the face of the sun.

When Reb Nachman unwound the mirror of cloth, he held in his hands that most sacred Book, inlaid with ten glowing jewels. And when he opened its pages, he saw they consisted of fire, and that its letters too were inscribed in flames, black fire on white, and that the letters of that Book only took form when they were brought into focus. And those letters, formed out of fire, spelled out the words which were written in the Beginning, to be read over and over until the End of Days. With fear and trembling Reb Nachman handed the Hidden Torah to Shimon, and led him out of that sacred place.

There they found that they had traveled in a circle of spirals to the very place where they had entered the Cave of the Elders, to the same fiery door. And Reb Nachman turned to Shimon and said, "When I raise my amulet this door will open and we will emerge from this cave. Then we must hurry past the other two doors of fire as quickly as possible to the place where we entered from the floor of the sea. Know that at any time the waters which have been parted will come together and carry us apart. Know too that you have been entrusted with this sacred Book of the Hidden Torah. Guard it with your life. God willing, we will meet again on the other side of the sea, with the treasures in our possession." And Reb Nachman and Shimon tied the treasures to their garments, and they took leave of each other. Then Reb Nachman raised the amulet and the flames of the door of fire parted, and at the very moment they stepped outside the waters reached them, and they were swept away through the spiral labyrinth, past the other two doors of fire, and out the place where they had first climbed into the cavern.

In the first rush of the waters Reb Nachman closed his eyes, and when he opened them he found he had risen to the surface of the water, not in the Red Sea, but in the River Sambatyon, and was hovering slightly above the waves in the same fog that he had

stepped into at the shore of the Red Sea. In this way Reb Nachman floated like a cloud down the length of the River Sambatyon,
and before long he arrived at a kingdom which was built on its
shores.

When Reb Nachman reached the shore and stepped on the
sands, the fog which had protected him drifted away. Then he felt
in his garment and saw that he still carried the *Shofar*, and he
looked at the flame in the jewel, and it was still burning. And he
prayed and gave thanks to God for having permitted him to succeeded in traveling so far in his quest, and he prayed to be permitted to complete it.

Meanwhile, because Shimon had hesitated to join in the singing of the Song of the Sea, and did not enter the Red Sea until he
had seen the waters parted, he was not protected by the magical
fog which had hovered there by the shore, and the wild currents
grabbed him as if he were a reed and cast him out into the rushing
waters. And Shimon had to fight off the waters, without rest, just
to stay afloat. Still, he thought only of the Book—that he must
somehow preserve it. And when he had been struggling for hours,
with no sign of the shore, he spied a small rock which rose out of
the waters, and standing on this rock was an old man who held out
a long branch to him. In this way Shimon came to cling to a
branch extended by an old man standing on a rock in the middle of
a great river that flowed through the desert. And no sooner had
Shimon taken hold of the branch, than the old man bent down to
him and he said: "You look like you are weighted down and are
about to sink."

"It is true," said Shimon, "that the Book I am carrying is a
heavy burden."

"I thought so," said the old man. "Tell me, why are you so
foolish as to cling to something that is heavy and causes you to
sink?"

And Shimon said, "Because I promised Reb Nachman that I
would carry it across to the other side, and that I would guard it
with my life."

"That is well and good," said the old man, "but it is very

likely you will lose both the Book and your life. What will you accomplish then?"

"What would you suggest?" asked Shimon, who was afraid that a strong wave would pull him away from the rock at any moment and cast him back into the currents.

"Well," said the old man, "I am also stranded on this rock until the waters subside, and there is not room for anyone else, nor do I have the strength to hold you from the waves much longer. And I am afraid that the waters are going to rise even higher before they recede, and there will be nothing to protect you from the current, which is growing wild. Your only hope is to lighten your load and then try to swim to the other side, before the waters grow worse. If you wish, I am willing to hold the Book for you so that you can cross to the other shore, and once the waters subside you can come back and get it."

It seemed to Shimon that what the old man said to him made sense, and that because of the Book he was in danger of losing his life. So he took the Book from his garment and he gave it to the old man, with great reluctance.

Now, if the truth be known, this old man was actually Asmodeus, the Prince of Demons, who had disguised himself as an old man at the bidding of the Prince of Darkness, in order to take the Book from Shimon, to keep him from completing the quest. The Prince of Darkness had directed Asmodeus to bring him the Book as soon as it was in his possession, and under no circumstances to open it. But this injunction had only whetted the appetite of Asmodeus, and as soon as he had the Book he tore it open, hoping to read in it secrets that would enable him to overthrow the rule of heaven. But at the very instant he opened the Book, Asmodeus was blinded by the perfect mirror of its pages, which seemed to reflect a hidden sun, and the Book slipped from his grasp and was lost in the waters of the river, which soon carried it back to its place in the Cave of the Elders. And when Shimon saw the Book fall from the old man's hands and sink into the depths, he let out a great cry, and at the same instant Asmodeus let go of the branch that held Shimon from the waves, and in a flash the current picked Shimon up and carried him directly to the far shore of the River Sambatyon.

At the same time this was happening, Reb Nachman was walking on the shores of a kingdom he did not recognize, and he wondered where he was, and if this might be the kingdom of one of the ten lost tribes. There he was met by a stern sentry, who asked to know his name and, when Reb Nachman told him, the sentry told Reb Nachman to come with him, for he was under arrest. And when Reb Nachman reached the city that was the capital of this kingdom, the sentry took him to a court of law. There Reb Nachman learned he was on trial, and that the court was in session and was hearing his case. All this was very confusing to Reb Nachman, since no one had told him why he was on trial, nor did he know what he had done wrong. And no sooner did he enter the courtroom than he was ordered to come to the docket, where the sentence would be pronounced.

When Reb Nachman stood in the docket he saw that his judge was the king of that kingdom, and that the king was about to read his sentence. But when he looked up at the king's face, he could not make out his features, for they were concealed as if by a fog. Just then the king pronounced the verdict of the court: "Reb Nachman has been condemned to crawl on his hands and knees for one mile to the gates of the Old City around which the capital of this kingdom has been built." And even though Reb Nachman still did not know why he had been tried, he accepted the sentence. He assumed it was part of his fate. Yet one thing worried him—his hands. His hands were not the hardened hands of a farmer, but the soft, pale hands of a scholar. He was afraid that such labor might harm his hands beyond repair. Still, he was determined to go through with the sentence the court had commanded, and after that to seek aid in crossing the river to the other side.

On the day before the sentence was to be carried out, rain began to fall. The unexpected rain was a shock to Reb Nachman, since it would make his task even more difficult. Now he would have to crawl through both the rain and mud. At dawn on the day of reckoning the rain was still falling and did not stop. Soon nine or ten inches of rainwater washed over his feet. Reb Nachman thought to himself, "This rain must be some kind of curse." Then, before the witnesses who had assembled in the rain, Reb Nachman heaved a great sigh, fell down on his hands and knees and, permitting himself one impatient gesture, pushed away the water in disgust. That is how he found himself afloat. There was exactly enough water for him to cross to the other side like a turtle, swimming through the open gates as the divine rain continued to fall. And there he found a great crowd waiting, and the first one to greet him was the king. And the king embraced Reb Nachman and told him that because of his successful quest the soul of the Messiah would now be set free. And the king told him that everyone in that kingdom had prayed that he would be able to survive the last mile of his journey, for that is what he had just passed. And then Reb Nachman saw that the features of the king were no longer blurred, and that he stood face to face with him, and he knew from the radiance that shone from his face that he must be the Messiah himself, whose soul, because of Reb Nachman, was about to be set free. And in the presence of the Messiah, Reb Nachman was overwhelmed, and he started to sink to his knees, but the Messiah put his arm around him and supported him, and told him that he and all the future generations would be eternally grateful to Reb Nachman when the time came to announce the End of Days.

Then Reb Nachman saw that a great crowd had gathered around them, and that the people were weeping with joy. For the inhabitants of the city were the Captive Souls who would now be free to be born. And Reb Nachman knew the time had come to take out the *Shofar* from his prayer shawl and to blow on it at least one blast, to announce that this part of the quest was complete. But first he asked the Messiah, "Is there any news of Shimon?" And when he asked, the face of the Messiah grew very grave, and he said, "Shimon has been deceived by Asmodeus, Prince of Demons, who disguised himself as an old man and took the Book from his possession." And when he heard this, Reb Nachman was filled with grief, because it meant the End of Days had been delayed once more. Then the Messiah said to him, "Do not mourn in this moment of joy, Reb Nachman." And then Reb Nachman remembered the occasion they were about to celebrate, and with great joy and relief he raised up the *Shofar* and drew a long breath and gave a long blast on that horn, so long that afterwards it was said that all those assembled there witnessed the whole drama of creation, from when the earth was unformed and void, and darkness was upon the face of the deep, until that time. And at the first note of that long blast a great wind began to blow, and a gentle rain of blessings began to fall, and everything flourished.

As for Reb Nachman, he himself had not known that his celestial soul played an instrument in the Celestial Orchestra. And when he put his lips to the *Shofar* his celestial soul entered his body and sounded the ram's horn for him instead, and the soul of Reb Nachman ascended on high on this note. There the heavens opened to receive him, and the gates of all seven heavens were opened. And Reb Nachman was taken into the highest heaven, *Araboth*, where he was greeted by his great-grandfather, the Baal Shem Tov, who embraced him and then introduced him to the Fathers, Abraham, Isaac, and Jacob, and to the saints and martyrs who had all gathered to greet him there. And all of them, including Simeon bar Yohai and the Ari, Rabbi Isaac Luria, welcomed him and clasped him to their breasts, and told him that he had performed a great *mitzvah* and that the world would prosper because the soul of the Messiah had been set free. And they told him not to grieve over Shimon's failure, for since the soul of the Messiah had been freed, the Redemption could come in any generation.

Then Reb Nachman took leave of the Fathers and of the Baal Shem. His soul re-entered his body just as his celestial soul completed sounding the long blast. And at that very moment the kingdom of the Captive Souls disappeared, for it was no longer needed, since the Captive Souls had now been set free to be born. And Reb Nachman found himself on the far shore of the River Sambatyon, with the *Shofar* still in his hand. And there he saw Shimon, and he was not grieved with him, for he understood they had accomplished all that they could in that generation. Just then a golden casket washed up upon the shore and came to rest at Reb Nach-

man's feet. And he knew that it had been sent to take back the
Shofar to the Cave of the Elders. And he took the *Shofar* and placed
it inside the casket and carried it back into the waters. And no
sooner had it entered there than the whole river vanished from
their sight, and Reb Nachman and Shimon found themselves sitting in Reb Nachman's study, both of them staring into the mirror
of ink in Reb Nachman's hand, which had grown dark.

The First Rung

ONE of the primary ways in which Reb Nachman communi-
cated with his Hasidim was through the vessel of the dream. For it
was in dreams that Reb Nachman came face to face with the souls
of his Hasidim, and there were no veils between them.

Once it happened that Reb Nussan, Reb Nachman's scribe,
dreamed he was walking at night with Reb Nachman down a
seemingly endless path. All at once they came to a place where
there was an immense ladder which reached from earth into
heaven. And when they first saw it, they were speechless. They
approached the foot of the ladder and looked up, and even though
it was illumined by the moon, round and full that night, still they
could not see its top, which seemed to reach to the very stars.

At last Reb Nussan asked Reb Nachman what they should do,
and Reb Nachman replied that the answer was obvious—they must
climb the ladder until they reached the top. And without further
hesitation, Reb Nachman stepped upon the first rung and began to
mount the ladder, even though it appeared to be an endless ascent.
But Reb Nussan hesitated to begin such an undertaking, and did
not know if he should follow, and before long Reb Nachman had
climbed so far ahead that Reb Nussan lost sight of him on the
ladder. Then Reb Nussan grew frightened because he was alone in
that place and scrambled up the ladder, hoping to catch up with
Reb Nachman, but no matter how hard he climbed the ground

remained beneath his feet, and after the longest effort he was still standing on the first rung of the ladder.

That was when Reb Nussan awoke, feeling like a leaf about to be torn away by the wind. And because the dream had left him shaken he decided to go to Reb Nachman, in hope that he might be able to shed light on it. So Reb Nussan went to the House of Study where Reb Nachman spent his time in the study of the sacred texts. There Reb Nachman listened with complete attention as Reb Nussan told him the dream. And although its meaning had escaped Reb Nussan, it was readily apparent to Reb Nachman, who said, "Your dream is very wonderful, indeed, Nussan, for it reveals how powerful is the spiritual longing within you. Surely you can recogize that the ladder in your dream was the very same ladder of Jacob's dream, which the rabbis say is one of the paths by which we may reach Paradise. Therefore climbing the ladder represents the ascent of our spirits as we purify ourselves. And how is this purification accomplished? By first immersing ourselves in the sacred waters of the Torah. And because I have spent my life in those waters, I was able to ascend the ladder in your dream. Yet this same path was closed to you. Why was that? Not because you have neglected the Torah, but simply because you were afraid. Remember, Nussan, the whole world is a very narrow bridge, and the main thing is not to be afraid.

"'We came to that bridge together, Nussan, and I did not hesitate in crossing because I knew that to do so is to be tempted to look down, where the abyss yawns below. That is how I was able to cross. For that bridge and the ladder in your dream are one and the same, and he who crosses the one is able to ascend the other."

And when Reb Nachman said this, his words rang true, and it was then that the veil of the dream was torn away, and its meaning became apparent. And suddenly Reb Nussan found himself standing on one side of a bridge. And at that instant he was shaken by a mighty wind and heard it roaring through the abyss, but he did not look down at the depths below. Then he hesitated no longer, but took the first step and then the second and crossed the length of the bridge in one long breath. And before he knew it, he stood next to

Reb Nachman on the other side and the roaring was gone, and in its place he heard the music of the Torah as it is heard when every echo has disappeared and the Word is spoken in the silence as it was in the Beginning.

The Four Who Entered an Orchard

REB Nachman was once walking at night with four of his Hasidim. They asked him to speak to them of the Mysteries of Creation. Reb Nachman agreed to their request, but asked them first to enter the orchard they were passing and to bring back the fruit of the first tree they came across.

Anxious to hear what Reb Nachman would have to say, the four entered the gate of the orchard, and hurried to the first tree they saw in the distance, illumined by the light of the moon. As they approached it, they saw that the tree bore a unique jewel-like fruit, which glittered in the night like precious gems and was illumined by a light from within. The four Hasidim were dumbfounded to see such a tree, and at a loss as to whether they should pick such precious fruit.

One of the four turned to the others and warned them: "Most certainly this tree has been enchanted, and so must be the fruit. If we attempt to pick it we too may become enchanted. Even to touch it is dangerous." The second Hasid nodded his head in agreement: "Yes, it is possible we have stumbled on the tree that bears the forbidden fruit. If we pluck it we may bring a great sin down on ourselves." But the third Hasid protested this conclusion: "Reb Nachman has directed us to bring back the fruit of the first tree we come across. This is the tree, whose fruit is no doubt a great blessing that must not be ignored." For a while after this there was silence, then the fourth Hasid spoke: "I, for one, do not believe this tree and its fruit exist in this world; therefore, it is an illusion, and we must be dreaming."

In this way the four Hasidim fell into a dilemma, and each argued for his own theory, and each was like a ram butting his head against the wall of the others' explanations. At last, with nothing decided, they came back to Reb Nachman empty-handed. They found him waiting outside the orchard, his features lined with grief. He asked them, knowing the answer in advance, "Did any one of you bring back the fruit of the Tree of Life?"

The King's Treasury

ONE day Reb Nachman said in the course of his *D'var Torah* that "Every good deed is made into a lamp." And no sooner had he said this than he saw a look of confusion cross Shimon's face. He asked Shimon if there were something he wished to ask, and Shimon said, "I long to know more about these lamps of which you have spoken, which are created from every good deed. Tell me, if you can, where they shine and for how long, and what they illumine, for such a light would be a great reward indeed for every man's good deeds."

And no sooner had Shimon asked this question than Reb Nachman's face revealed that he was far away, even though he was with them. He was silent for a long time, and when at last he spoke, he spoke as if from a great distance, in another land. And this is what he said:

"Once there was a kingdom hidden in the darkness. The existence of this kingdom was unknown to most inhabitants of the world, although it had long been rumored. But those who had had the good fortune even to glimpse it were aware of its immense value. For that dark kingdom was actually the treasury of a mighty king, filled with the most rare and precious treasures to be found anywhere, whose value far exceeded the total of all other treasuries in the world.

"Now in the darkness of that kingdom there was an occasional light, a beacon cast from a lamp that burned briefly, sometimes lasting only for a few seconds. Occasionally such a lamp lasted as long as a full day, although this was rare. And rarest of all was the lamp that continued to burn and did not go out, but this was so rare that some went through an entire lifetime without even knowing that such a beacon existed. And what were these brief illuminations in that all-pervasive darkness? Somehow these lamps were mysteriously ignited by a deed of one of the inhabitants. What kinds of deeds accomplished this? Good deeds, of every kind. Someone who had taken the wrong path was shown the proper way, or someone crying in the darkness was consoled. The deed itself was not predictable, but the result was—a beam of light began to burn in front of a man's eyes, illuminating the landscape that had been lost in the darkness for so long. And what did he see there? He saw the treasures in the king's treasury, wonders without parallel in the world.

"For the brief moment that the lamp burned, he who was fortunate enough to glimpse the true nature of that landscape feasted his eyes on the wonders surrounding him, or sought to explore, as quickly as possible, the many mysteries of that unparalleled treasury. And even when the light burned for only a short time, whoever caught even a glimpse of the wonders surrounding them attained a new perspective of life in that world, which was far richer than most of the inhabitants imagined. Still, it was hard for any of them to accept the loss of that light, and the return to a life in the darkness was not easy to accept at all. For once they had known what it meant to be a true seeker, there was no greater punishment than not to be able to seek any longer.

"Now there were also those whose light did not burn merely for a brief moment, but for a full day. And they were blessed by gazing upon the treasures that much longer, giving them more time to probe these mysteries. And among the inhabitants of that dark kingdom, those whose light had burned even once for a single day were regarded as the righteous of that kingdom, and were universally admired.

"And then there were those who had the most wonderful

lamps of all. These lamps were never extinguished, but burned and shone forever. And it naturally occurred that these rare individuals soon found many who wished to remain in their presence, where life in that world was illuminated and not left in the darkness. For they knew the hunger of wanting to explore the mystery, once illumined for them in a brief instant, and recognized that the greatest treasure of all was one who possessed such a lamp, for without the light that it cast into the darkness, all truth was obscured. But in their presence the treasures of the king were revealed, and the mysteries which had beckoned so long were at last revealed in all their glory."

Here Reb Nachman stopped speaking and a faint smile played around his lips. Then he looked directly at Shimon and said, "The voices of the angels call out to us all the time, but rarely do we hear them. And when I said that 'Every good deed creates a lamp,' I was echoing the voice of an angel, although I did not realize it at the time. And only because Shimon heard the other words of the angel, even though he did not know it, and asked his question, did I listen hard enough to hear all that the angel said, and thus learned about the realm of which I have spoken, and of how it is that the light of a great *Tzaddik* is never extinguished, so that his exploration of the king's treasuries can go on forever. And so it is that I have learned that the lamp of Shimon's deeds burns far brighter than any of us may have imagined, for only such a one could be attuned to the faint words of the angels."

And after that the Hasidim all treated Reb Shimon with a new respect, and heeded his words far more than they had before; for they never knew which words he spoke were his own and which ones he had heard from the angels.

The Order of the Torah

ONE day, while Reb Nachman gave a *D'var Torah* to his Hasidim and Reb Nussan wrote down every word he spoke, Reb Nachman said, "If the Torah were written in order, we would know the precise reward and punishment for each commandment."

Now as Reb Nussan wrote down these words he began to puzzle over them, and he found that he could not pass beyond the first phrase, no matter how many times he read it. Was the Rebbe saying that the Torah was not written in order? What could he possibly mean? After all, the Torah began with the description of the creation of the world, and proceeded to the creation of the first man. And while Reb Nussan was so musing to himself, perplexed, his pen stopped writing, for his pen refused to write unless he had listened to what had been said. Now Reb Nussan was normally the best of listeners and had no difficulty in taking down all that he heard. So it was that Reb Nachman noticed Nussan's pen had become still, and he realized something was wrong. He said to him, "Tell me, Nussan, how many fingers-breadths separate the Upper Waters from the Lower?"

Now Reb Nussan, who was concentrating on the order of the Torah, did not expect such a question, and it took him by surprise. In that instant, when he realized what was being asked of him, his spirit suddenly took leave of his body and took flight. Before he knew it he found himself hovering in space, above him the great expanse of the Upper Waters, and below him the great sheet of the Lower Waters. And there, in that place, Reb Nussan was able to examine the crack between them, which he found to be no more than three finger-breadths.

And it was then, just as his spirit was poised to tumble back into his body, that he wondered whether it was the Upper Waters which had separated from the Lower, or the Lower which had been the first to pull away. At that instant he heard a voice speak, which he recognized as his own, and the voice said, "I shall remain suspended here until I know which was the first to separate from the other." And then he heard a voice reply out of nowhere, and he recognized this voice as that of Reb Nachman, which said, "The Holy One Himself is not certain, Nussan, of which was the first to separate. For just as God said, '*Let there be a firmament in the midst of the waters, and let it divide the waters from the waters,*' all of the letters of the Torah, which had existed since before the creation, cried out at the same time, for some were attached to the Upper Waters and some to the Lower, and there was a great pain of separation which took place. And in the confusion that followed all the letters took flight, so that for one terrible instant the scroll of the Torah in Paradise was blank.

"And only when the Holy One commanded the letters to take their places did they return, swarming guiltily to the eternal scroll they had abandoned. In the confusion that followed the order of the Torah was changed, so that it never again resembled exactly what it had been during the time before all the letters had taken flight. This new order was not that far removed from the original, in fact it was quite close. But the fact remains that in some ways it was different, and as a result nothing had stayed the same. So it was that the precise reward and punishment for each commandment is not known, for the Torah is not written in order."

Suddenly Reb Nussan found himself back in his body, seated among the Hasidim as they listened to Reb Nachman's *D'var Torah*. And Reb Nussan's hand wrote down all that he heard, for this time he understood.

The Tale of a Wandering Spirit

WHEN the need to tell a tale came to Reb Nachman, he would begin to speak to his Hasidim at once; and it was as if a spirit were speaking through him for he seemed unaware of anyone else's presence. Therefore his scribe, Reb Nussan, sought to remain with his Rebbe as much as possible, in order to be present whenever he spoke. But sometimes it happened that Reb Nussan was called away, and then he would have to reconstruct from the other Hasidim what Reb Nachman had said in his absence, so that it too could be recorded. But he recognized that much that remained of what had been said on such occasions was fragmented, and it was apparent that much had been lost.

Now it happened that Reb Nussan was once called away from Bratslav for a fortnight. And on the very evening he departed, a wonderful tale revealed itself to Reb Nachman in all its glory, from the first to the last, with every word in its place, as if it had already been written. Reb Nachman recognized that it was a very important tale that had descended from the *Yenne Velt*, the Other World, to be told. Normally Reb Nachman did not hesitate when such a tale revealed itself, but would share it with his Hasidim at once. But as he considered this tale, he recognized it could be of immense importance in transmitting secrets that might hasten the coming of the Messiah. Therefore he hesitated telling that tale while Reb Nussan was not present. And why did he simply not retell it when Reb Nussan returned? Because Reb Nachman never told the same tale twice. It was as if he were forbidden to repeat more than once the truths revealed to him from on high. And Reb Nachman knew that while his other Hasidim would listen carefully to the tale, still much of it would be lost. And he could not bear for that to happen. No, every word of that tale had to be preserved. Therefore Reb Nachman undertook to remain silent. From that moment on he said nothing to anyone, for he feared that if he spoke at all the longing to set the tale free would overcome him, and he might let it slip from his grasp and be lost.

Neither did Reb Nachman inform his Hasidim of his decision to remain silent until Reb Nussan's return; but they recognized at once that their Rebbe had chosen not to speak, and so great was their respect that they did not press him to reveal the reason. So it was that Reb Nachman wrestled with this tale for thirteen days and nights, concentrating all his attention on recalling every aspect of it.

Then, on the day that Reb Nussan was scheduled to come back, a terrible thing happened. Reb Nachman awoke in the morning and discovered that he no longer knew the tale—not a single detail, not even the general outline remained. It had flown from his memory like a lost dream that no effort could restore. This unexpected event cast Reb Nachman into despair, so that he was not unlike the minister in his tale of the lost Princess, the one who grieved so after he lost the right to set her free, by falling asleep on the last day of a year-long vigil. His soul was afflicted as if he had broken the Yom Kippur fast at the last minute and lost his right to all the blessings he had earned.

That morning Reb Nachman began to speak again, since the tale had been lost, and he began his *D'var Torah* with this passage from the Psalms: *Thou shalt search and be lost.* And it happened that Reb Nussan arrived just as Reb Nachman began to speak. In fact, as Reb Nussan entered the *Beit Midrash* the first words he heard Reb Nachman say were "Even a *Tzaddik* who searches after lost things is himself sometimes lost." And Nussan noticed at once that Reb Nachman was teaching with a broken heart. And Reb Nachman saw that Reb Nussan seemed to glow, as if he had been fulfilled. And after Reb Nachman embraced his scribe, and blessed his safe return, he finished his teaching and was about to reveal the tragedy of the tale that had been lost, when he recognized that Reb Nussan had something he longed to say and motioned for him to speak. And Reb Nussan said, "From the very first day that I left Bratslav, a dream haunted me every night. In this dream, Rebbe, you called me into your study, and told me you had a tale to tell me, which you wanted me to record. But when I tried to find a pen with which to write, and paper on which to record it, I could not. In some of the dreams I succeeded in locating a pen, but then the paper would still be missing, while in other cases the paper was present, but no pen was to be found. And in every case I awoke before you began to tell the tale. At last I dreamed I was sitting in your chamber, and this time both pen and paper were present. In fact, I held the notebook which I use to write down the gems of wisdom that pass your lips. But just as you were about to begin the tale, there was a knock at the door, and when I answered it there was an old woman with white hair standing there, who insisted on speaking to you."

"What was it that this old woman wanted, Nussan? I must know!" Reb Nachman exclaimed, certain that the mystery was about to be revealed.

"She said she had been given a story to tell," said Nussan, "but to her dismay she found she was unable to write it down. She had carried this tale with her for many years, and it had become like a stone child to her. She said that she had come to tell you the tale, that she might bequeath it to you, for she knew she was shortly to leave this world and could not bear to think it would be lost."

"Tell me, Nussan, without delay," said Reb Nachman, "did I accept the tale or not?"

"Of course you accepted it, Rebbe," said Reb Nussan. "You welcomed her and bid her to speak, and swore to guard everything she said and see that not a single word was lost. And as she began to speak you signaled for me to take the tale down, which I did, word for word. Then the old woman proceeded to tell a wonderful tale, with many twists and turns and tales within tales, that was not unlike a labyrinth. But you and I followed her through every turn, for our concentration was complete. And when the old woman had finished telling the tale, and I had written down the last word, I awoke. That was this morning, and I wasted no time, but took out the notebook in which I record your teachings, which I had used in the dream, and opened it, intending to write down the tale, which was still vivid in my memory. But imagine my surprise when I discovered the tale had already been set down in my handwriting, exactly as the old woman had told it!"

And when Reb Nachman and the other Hasidim heard this, they all recognized that a miracle had truly taken place, and that one of the tales hovering on high had at last taken root in this world, where it would serve as a guide and consolation to all those who searched in this life, even those who searched and became lost.

Then Reb Nachman held out his hand, and Reb Nussan handed him the notebook, that he might read the tale written there. And as Reb Nachman's eyes flew across the letters, a wonderful smile grew on his face. For the tale he read there and the tale he had carried with him for thirteen days and nights were one and the same; he had lost it only that morning, after it had finally been set down. And he turned to Reb Nussan and said, "Now I see that the effort I made to preserve this tale was not wasted. For had I not held it close to my heart, it would have been gone when the time came for you to record it. And if we had failed to hold it, it would have been lost, who knows for how long?"

Then Reb Nussan said, "But tell me, Rebbe, who was this woman, and why did she seek you out?"

Reb Nachman replied, "Surely she was a spirit who was condemned to wander until this tale had been told to someone in this world who would preserve it, so that it could exist in the world below as well as in the world above. Who knows how many times she circled the long labyrinths of *gilgul* without ever finding the way out, and who knows how many others she offered to entrust with the tale, who failed to accept it? But you and I, Nussan, were brought into this world to be vessels through which the holy spirit can be received and transmitted. And I did my best to hold the tale until you were ready to receive it, for that was what was required of me. For know, Nussan, that I am rooted in the Oral Law, and you in the Written. But just as these are the two Torahs which were given, as Rabbi Nehemiah said, so you and I serve to renew their truths in this world, that they may last for all time.

"But next time, Nussan," added Reb Nachman, "please be certain to keep a pen and paper with you at all times, day and night, whether asleep or awake. For remembering that tale was far more difficult than trying to hold a cloud to a single shape, or

trying to weave a *tallis* out of the wind. Rather, it was like trying to
ascend to Paradise on a ladder of prayers, where a single weak link
could cause it to collapse. That this did not happen is truly a
miracle, for which we must celebrate!"

The Lost Tzaddik

ONE day Reb Nachman led Reb Shimon on a walk in the
forest. When Shimon asked him where they were going, Reb
Nachman replied that he wanted to reach the river. And although
Shimon wondered what Reb Nachman wanted to do there, he said
no more about it. So too did he wonder at the path he took, for it
was not the usual route to the river, and seemed much longer. And
secretly Shimon wondered if the Rebbe might be lost. But he
dared not say such a thing, and followed wherever Reb Nachman
led.

When they had been walking all day and had still not reached
the river, Shimon at last spoke up and said, "Rebbe, are you certain that this is the path to the river we want to take?" But no
sooner had Shimon said this than they first glimpsed the river in
the distance. Shimon was ashamed that his patience had run out at
the last moment. They hurried to the edge of the hill overlooking
the bank of the river below and the river itself, with its quickly
moving currents. And there at the bottom of the hill they saw a
small wooden hut and beside it a boat, tied up next to the river-
bank. Going down the hill, they came to the hut, just as dusk
began to fall.

Shimon thought to himself that Reb Nachman must have been
leading them to that place, since they had arrived there just before
sunset. Shimon asked him if this were the case, and Reb Nachman
replied, "No, I have never been here before in my life." Then
Shimon became afraid and said, "But was it here that you were
leading us?" Reb Nachman replied: "I don't know where I have led

you. For I myself was lost. Therefore I simply continued walking, for to stop would be to accept defeat. And like Lot's wife I somehow knew that I must not look back."

Shimon was frightened to hear this, for he had completely entrusted his soul to the Rebbe, and now the Rebbe had confessed that he was lost. And yet at least they were not alone in the forest as night fell—they had reached a place where they might be able to find shelter. And Reb Nachman said, "Let us go to the door, Shimon, and see if we might spend the night." Then Shimon knocked on the door, wondering who might dwell there. And when the door opened they were greeted by an old man, whose clothes were old and tattered. And when he saw them, he welcomed them at once, without hesitation. For very few were the guests who came to his door, and his life there was very lonely.

The old man motioned for them to enter, and the Hasidim stepped inside. There they saw at once that the old man was a fisherman, for his net was hung inside the hut. Without even waiting for the Hasidim to introduce themselves and request shelter, the old man told them they were welcome to remain there for the night. The Hasidim accepted this offer with gratitude. Then the old man said, "It is remarkable that you have arrived here today, for only this afternoon I captured a large and beautiful fish with silver scales. Never have I seen such a fish in my life. I have just been preparing the fish and was about to cook it. You have come just in time. Please join me."

In a short time the old man began to cook the fish, and when its aroma reached the Hasidim for the first time, they marveled at it, for it bore the scent of Paradise. And when the old man served the fish they were astonished, for never had they seen such a beautiful fish in their lives. Then the old man cut the fish open, and as soon as he did a bright light shone forth from inside it. All of them saw it and wondered what it was. The old man reached inside and pulled out a key—a golden key. Shimon could not believe his eyes. How was such a thing possible? And even Reb Nachman seemed awestruck, as if this were the last thing he had expected to find.

The old man held up the golden key before his eyes and studied it. Then he handed it to Reb Nachman, who observed it intently. At last Shimon held it in his hand, and saw that it was a key like any other, except that it was made of gold. For a long time no one spoke, as they contemplated that key. At last the old man said, "This key cannot be for me. I do not need the money the gold could bring; I have everything I need in this place, and the river never withholds food from me. Nor am I young enough to find whatever it is that this key opens. No, it seems clear that this key was not meant for me, but for one of you, although I do not know which one. For you arrived on the same day as did this fish, and surely such a key could not be found by mistake." And when the Hasidim heard these words, they knew that the old man was filled with wisdom, and had learned how to recognize signs.

Then Shimon was the next to speak, and he said without hesitation, "If, as you suggest, the key was intended for one of us, then there can be no doubt that it was intended for Reb Nachman. For it is he who has found the key to every mystery we have encountered."

The old man considered these words, and handed the key to Reb Nachman and said, "Here—both of us are certain that it was intended for you. Take it, and may you discover the purpose for which it was intended." And all Reb Nachman said was "I will do my best."

That night, as they slept on the fishing net, since the old man was so poor he did not have a fur rug to offer them, Reb Nachman dreamed about that golden key. In his dreams he traveled to many lands and searched for many places in which to insert the key, for he knew that he could not rest until he had found the lock for which it was intended. In one dream he found himself ascending into the heavens, but even though he tried to open all of the Gates of Heaven, the key fit none of them. And in another dream he traveled through a vast desert until he reached a golden mountain, thinking the golden key might fit there, but it did not. Before waking he even dived to the bottom of the sea, since the key may have been found there by the fish and perhaps unlocked a palace beneath the sea. But the key did not open anything he found there either, and when he awoke and recalled these dreams, Reb Nachman began to wonder if there were any lock in the world for which the key was intended.

Then Reb Nachman took out the key, which he had placed beneath his pillow. He held it up to his eyes and for the first time peered through the round opening in the head of the key. And he was astonished to find that he was looking into another world, which passed before him, slightly out of reach. That world was surrounded by a hazy aura, as if everything consisted solely of images like those existing in a mirror. And all of a sudden Reb Nachman understood that he had discovered the purpose of the key—to open the way into that shimmering world, which appeared to be so near and so far away at the same time. Thus, remarkably, the key unlocked itself.

While Shimon slept, Reb Nachman stared with rapt amazement into the mirror of the key, which he now saw was illumined by its own light, as if by its own galaxy of stars. He understood at once that it would take very long to probe that abundant mystery, for the secrets of that world were not simple. And so Reb Nachman had found the key to unlock the Other World, a key that makes its way to only one man in every generation.

And there, in the mirror of that key, Reb Nachman also saw the old man who had welcomed them to that hut. But when he saw him there, his true appearance was revealed, so that Reb Nachman recognized him at once even though he had never seen him before. And when Shimon at last awoke from a deep, dreamless sleep and saw that the old man had gone, he looked questioningly at Reb Nachman, who replied, "Elijah always departs when he has completed his task."

The Upside-down World

RɛB Nachman and Reb Shimon were sitting together on the bank of a lake, discussing the Mysteries of the Chariot. Shimon said, "Reb Nachman, how is it possible to travel from one world to the next?"

Reb Nachman said, "Shimon, look at that tree on the other side of the lake."

Shimon did this.

Then Reb Nachman said, "Now look at the shadow of that tree in the water."

Shimon looked at the shadow of the tree and he saw that he was peering into another kingdom, an upside-down world, where all the forests were inverted. Then he noticed that the shadow of the tree also resembled an immense leaf. And he noticed that the leaf resembled the wings of a bird. And then Shimon realized he was flying on the back of that bird, and cities were whirling by, when he looked down and saw a jewel glowing in the darkness. And that jewel was Jerusalem, which he saw from a great distance. Ahead was the Garden of Eden. The bird came down into the Garden, and he saw three angels standing around a well, and one by one they came and drew water and poured it out into three vessels, one of wood, one of clay, and one of stone. And from the wood grew a tree that gave birth to a woman who grew ripe; and from the clay the angels formed the features of the first man to see her face; and from the stone they carved a seat, and sat back for centuries, waiting for the wind. After he had watched for what seemed ages, Shimon walked over to the well and leaned over the side and looked down. There in the well he saw a shadow that resembled the wings of a bird. Then he noticed that the shadow also resembled the shape of a leaf. And then he saw that the leaf also resembled the shadow of a tree. He looked up and found himself sitting on the bank of the lake, beside Reb Nachman. And Reb Nachman said, "Does that answer your question?"

Reversing the Order

ONE night Reb Shimon dreamed that time was moving backwards. Everything reversed its order, pulling him inexorably
along. Soon the sun that had just set rose up in the West, and the
light that had been banished was restored. And Shimon felt that he
was being drawn upwards toward that sun like a moth into a flame.
Just as he was about to be swept into the red eye of the sun, he
awoke.

Still disoriented, as if he were lost in a wilderness, Shimon
hurried to the *Beit Knesset* to share his dream with Reb Nachman.
As soon as Reb Nachman saw his face, he knew that something
momentous was about to take place. When Shimon related his
dream, in which everything had moved backwards, the mystery
suddenly became clear to Reb Nachman, and he embraced Shimon
and then hurried to the *bimah* to begin the morning prayers. But
instead of starting with the first prayer, Reb Nachman began with
the mourner's *Kaddish*. The Hasidim were startled and mystified by
this, for Reb Nachman had said nothing about it, and none of them
had ever heard of such a thing being done.

When the mourner's *Kaddish* had been said, Reb Nachman
began to chant *Alenu*, the final prayer of the service. Again the
Hasidim joined him with disbelief, and in this way he led them
backwards through the morning service from the last prayer to the
first. Even though they were greatly mystified, all of the Hasidim
joined in this strange service, for above all they were loyal and true
to Reb Nachman and knew he would not lead them astray.

As for Shimon, the order of the service did not seem as
strange to him, for the dream in which time had moved backward
still cast its spell on him, and he found the order strangely natural.
At the same time, however, the sense of being inexorably pulled
towards the unknown became even stronger. Suddenly the sensation was overwhelming, and Shimon felt like a leaf being pulled

into the depths of a whirlpool, and at that moment he had a vision in which he saw himself swept into the eye of the sun, merging for a moment of death into the memory of an infant sun, tail of a comet, breath drawn back and forth through countless stars. And from a very high place Shimon looked down at the husk of his body, and came to know with certainty which part of him would pass away and which part was eternal.

An instant later Reb Shimon's soul was restored to his body, and he found himself standing in the *Beit Knesset*, where Reb Nachman was still leading the prayers. And although he had his soul back, still it seemed to be drawn upward, as if it were hovering slightly above the ground. It was at that moment that Reb Nachman reached the beginning of the backwards service, and without hesitating proceeded to repeat it, this time in the proper order. Still mystified, the Hasidim joined in the prayers until the service reached its natural conclusion.

When the final *Kaddish* had again been said, and the service had truly come full circle, Reb Nachman hurried to Reb Shimon, and put his arm around him. Shimon felt light and dizzy, but his soul no longer seemed to tug upward, and his feet were firmly planted on the ground. And from out of the fog that surrounded him, he heard Reb Nachman say: "While you told me your dream, Shimon, I saw the *Shekhinah* hovering in your presence, waiting to kiss you. Now the kiss of the *Shekhinah* is the greatest possible blessing, but it is so powerful and all-consuming that Moses and other sages departed from this world in that way." By then all of the other Hasidim had gathered around Reb Nachman, listening intently to all that he said, for at last the mystery was beginning to unravel. And Reb Nachman said to Shimon, knowing that all of the others heard him as well: "That is why I first led the service backwards, in order to guide you into that divine embrace. And that is why I immediately repeated it in the proper order once we had reached the beginning, in order to lead you back to this world, and assist you in completing the transition from the world above to the world below. Yet the kiss of the *Skekhinah* still clings to you." And when Reb Nachman said this, all of the Hasidim looked closely at Reb Shimon and saw that his face was surrounded with a ghostly aura. And then they understood for the first time how blessed is one who is sheltered in the embrace of the Divine Presence.

Before the Pargod

Now it was a practice of long standing that Reb Nussan wrote down everything Reb Nachman said. None of the Bratslaver Hasidim could remember a time when Reb Nussan did not record Reb Nachman's words the moment they were spoken, except on the Sabbath. And then all the Hasidim would retell among themselves the tales Reb Nachman had told them on the eve of the Sabbath, until the time when they could be written down.

But one day, not a Sabbath, it was seen that Reb Nussan had folded his hands while Reb Nachman spoke, and did not stir from that position. Afterward Reb Shimon came to Reb Nussan and said: "But tell me, Nussan, why did you not write down the Rebbe's words?"

Reb Nussan said, "On the contrary, I wrote down every single word." With that Reb Nussan went to his studystand and brought back several pages. These he handed to Shimon. First he, and then the rest of the Hasidim, read the pages with amazement, for every word that Reb Nachman had spoken was to be found there.

Then Reb Nachman said, "What Reb Nussan has said is true. This morning I merely repeated what I had said to him in a dream last night, when we both stood before the Pargod in Paradise. I repeated those words today only to be certain they took root here below. Thus Reb Nussan did not need to write the words down, for he had already done so when we returned to this world, and as you have seen, every word is there, and nothing is missing."

Then there was a long silence, and at last Reb Nachman

added: "As you know, the words I speak to you in Yiddish Reb Nussan translates into Hebrew. Yet when we stood together before the Pargod, and saw face to face the Eternal Forms that flicker on that Curtain, I could only think and speak in the Holy Tongue. And as I spoke I saw that every word had been inscribed in Reb Nussan's memory as if it had been graven in stone."

The Vision of the Burning Branch

for Dennis Crowe

ONE day Reb Nachman spoke to his Hasidim on the Mysteries of the Pargod: "All souls are woven into that Curtain, which hangs before the Throne of Glory, and the entire past history and the future destiny of every soul is recorded there. Together all the souls form the flaming letter *Bet*, which burns on that Curtain in black fire on white. But it is impossible to look directly on that flaming letter and live; it must be glimpsed in a mirror. Nor is there one mirror which suffices for all men, but each man must seek out his own mirror. For some the waters of the streams of Paradise serve, while others seek out a mirror in the eyes of an angel. Then he who peers into the black fire will see the whole past history of his soul unfold before him, and he who peers into the white fire will see the whole future history of his soul unwind before his eyes."

After Reb Nachman had said this he paused and was silent for a long time. Finally Reb Shimon spoke, "Tell me, Reb Nachman, why are we not permitted behind the Pargod?"

A flash of anger and dismay passed through Reb Nachman's eyes when he heard this question, and he swayed on his feet as if he had grown faint. Then he turned and left his study and walked off alone. Later that day he approached Shimon and said, "In order to answer your question it will be necessary for you to perform an exercise. I want you to sit before the curtain in my study and pretend that it does not exist; just let your eyes blur when you look at it, and imagine it empty."

For the next three days Shimon performed this exercise for several hours every day. He let his eyes blur as he stared at the curtain, telling himself that it had no more knowledge than a plate of glass, perhaps less. And he succeeded in wishing it away. But soon he discovered that this was an error. A curtain may be pulled apart, but only by the cords which control it. It is not about to relinquish its propriety, much less its existence. On the fourth day Shimon took up a pen and wrote down one word, his name. But even before he finished, the letters dissolved into a black powder and disappeared. After that he regarded the curtain with awe and respect; he no longer attempted to transcend it. But the curtain, once denied, was not about to reaffirm its trust. Often he feared he had only seen a glimpse of its wrath, the first of its brooding.

That day Shimon described the effects of his vigil to Reb Nachman, and asked to know why he had given him this exercise. Reb Nachman said, "When you asked your question, Shimon, about not being able to go behind the Pargod, I was already there, and your question brought me back to the other side. I knew at that moment that I had left you far behind, and that you were afraid. As I told you once before, Shimon, it is your duty to hold the ladder steady while I ascend it, so that afterwards I may pull you up after me. This time I had reached the top rung of that ladder when you became distracted and loosened your grip. And for me it was like clinging to a branch at the top of a tree tossed and shaken by a great wind. And I knew that if I fell from that height I might not survive. Then I became afraid that I had brought this on myself, and that I was trying to climb too high, before my time. And when I looked down from that place I saw how wide are the jaws of the Abyss."

"No!" cried Shimon, like a man who had been hanging above *Gehenna* by a thread that had just broken. And he started to sob. And between sobs he said: "Tell me, Rebbe, how is it that you survived?"

"That . . ." said Reb Nachman, "is because I did not fall. When the ladder gave way I remained suspended where I was." "Where was that, Rebbe? Tell me!" Shimon almost shouted.

"I found myself balanced in the Tree of Life like a bird in its nest," said Reb Nachman. "And I was held there ever so firmly because I have always clung to the Torah, as it is written, '*The Torah is a Tree of Life to those who cling to it.*' "

Then it happened that at the very moment Reb Nachman said this, the blue bowl used for washing before meals, which was empty, broke into two parts with a loud crack. And at that same instant Reb Shimon also broke open and had a vision which later sustained him all the days of his life. In that vision he saw the very branch of the Tree to which Reb Nachman had clung; that branch was wrapped in flames, but the flames did not consume what they were burning. Shimon saw this from a great distance, as one whose soul has ascended. And when he looked down from that high place and saw the branch revealed inside that flame, Shimon knew for certain that the fire was the fire of his soul, and that the fire was eternal, and that his soul burned with an eternal flame.

When the vision of the burning branch came to an end, Shimon found he had fallen to the floor. At first he was overwhelmed, and then he was convulsed with weeping. For many moments he wept, but when he stopped and started to describe to Reb Nachman what he had seen, Reb Nachman smiled and said, "I already know, Shimon, for I was with you in that place. Until now you have been a hard vessel to break open, but this time your eyes opened enough to glimpse a branch of the Burning Tree. And that Tree, Shimon, burns in Paradise, behind the Pargod. Now do you know why I asked you to perform that exercise?"

Reb Nachman's Mirror of Ink

ONE night, in a dream, Reb Nachman of Bratslav entered his study and took down the leather-bound Bible, which had belonged to his great-grandfather the Baal Shem Tov, and he opened it to the first page, and read the first letter of the first word. And in the dream he tried to comprehend this letter, *Bet*, but he found he knew nothing about it except its name. And he knew he could not continue to read in that book until he understood the first letter of the first word. And when he woke up he was still puzzling over what the letter meant.

When Reb Nachman was fully awake and considered this dream, he put on his prayer shawl and poured a small amount of ink into the palm of his hand, forming a mirror. Then he unfolded from a prayer book a paper on which he had written the Name. At that moment every shadow and every echo disappeared, and everything became bright, as if he wore a garment of light. And when he looked into that mirror of ink he saw the letter *Bet* inscribed in white fire on the dark surface, and the letter was like a map of constellations. He studied the letter, and in this way he saw the *Aleph* concealed in the dot at the flaming center of the *Bet*. The *Aleph* was illumined by a light from within, and he saw inside it as if it were transparent.

Inside the *Aleph*, he saw the earth from a distance as if it were a glowing coal, as if it were a black pearl, glowing like a dark sun at the bottom of a deep well. And he saw the dark sun recede into the distance, like a sunstain growing faint. Then he saw the face of the moon take form out of the dark, and the face that took form spoke of the future as if it were the past. From those whispered words he learned how to read the letters written in the stars circling his soul. And as he read in the stars, he glimpsed the future lashed to the mast of an ark, rolling over the waters of a dark sea. There he saw a black swan rise up from its cradle beneath the waves, unfold its

wings, and prepare to fly, in its beak a black pearl, a silence of two sides, a dream song, a seed from which grew a silver tree, its branches only an arm's reach away. And he reached into the ark and took out the silver tree. And he wrapped himself once more in his prayer shawl, and in his garment of light. And he unwound the scroll and the letters fluttered and a sacred presence rose up from the page. And he became lost in a single letter, *Bet*, and he read it over and over until he heard its voice rise up from the silent page; until he held it like a half moon in his arms, the center itself, turning its dark side down.

A Message from the Yenne Velt

It happened one year that Reb Nachman of Bratslav received an invitation from a devout couple in a neighboring village with whom he had been acquainted for many years. Even though Reb Nachman seemed pleased with this invitation, he replied with a message saying that he would be unable to come at that time, and asked that they invite him at a later date. Then, a few weeks later, the couple sent another invitation, and Reb Nachman replied in the same fashion, asking that the evening be delayed. So it was that for several months Reb Nachman continued to refuse the invitations of this couple, but always in the most polite fashion, and always requesting that they invite him again in the near future.

Then late one afternoon a messenger arrived from this same couple with an invitation that Reb Nachman be their guest that same evening. And this time, without hesitation, Reb Nachman replied that he would be happy to comply and began at once to make preparations for the journey. However, when everything was ready for the departure and the horses stood saddled, Reb Nachman sat down and began his studies as if he had no intention of going anywhere. This behavior mystified and frustrated his Hasidim, who had been invited to accompany him, but they dared not ask for an explanation. Finally, after they had all been waiting almost an hour, a visitor arrived at the door, a bookseller who made it his practice periodically to bring the books he had collected to Reb Nachman, to let him examine them and keep any that he chose for himself. Reb Nachman welcomed this bookseller with great warmth, as if he had been expecting him, and without waiting for him to carry his books inside, he searched through the new acquisitions on the bookseller's wagon. In a short time he examined and turned away many dozens of *siddurs*, *mahzors*, and commentaries, among them some very rare books. And although the bookseller tried to bring the more valuable books to Reb Nachman's attention, he dismissed them all, and persisted even in ignoring the titles of the books, glancing only at the page on which was written the name of the previous owner. At last, near the bottom of the pile, Reb Nachman seemed to find what he was looking for, and that was the only book he selected. This choice mystified the bookseller, since the book was a plain and rather worn Lurianic *siddur* such as was commonly used by all the Hasidim, and seemed to have nothing at all to distinguish it. Yet from the expression on Reb Nachman's face it seemed as if he had located a veritable treasure, so pleased with it was he. And with this book in hand Reb Nachman ordered the horses to depart at once for the neighboring town, since they were already late.

When Reb Nachman and his Hasidim arrived at the home of the couple they were greeted warmly and invited at once to the table, where a fine dinner was served. The primary dish was an exceptionally large and tasty fish, which satisfied in full the hunger of everyone. After dinner the host expressed thanks to Reb Nachman and his Hasidim for coming on such short notice, and did not mention the many occasions their invitation had been declined. He explained that he had caught the remarkable fish that day and had felt that such a fish should be shared by no less than Reb Nachman himself.

After the dinner and the blessing after meals, Reb Nachman took out the *siddur* he had received from the bookseller and gave it to the wife of the host. After such a splendid dinner the other

Hasidim were embarrassed by this modest gift, since the book appeared to be ordinary in every respect. But when the wife had opened it no further than the page on which the name of the previous owner was inscribed, and read what was written, she was overcome with emotion, and began to weep. At last she found words and said, "But how is it possible that you have come into possession of this book, which has been lost for so many years?" And Reb Nachman replied: "I received it today from a Hasid who is a bookseller, for I found it among the books on his wagon."

By then the curiosity of the host and the other Hasidim was keen, and the woman offered this explanation: "This *siddur* once belonged to my brother, who has been dead for six years. But it was lost long before that; for my brother, I am sorry to say, who was once a promising artist and one of the finest students in the *yeshivah*, later lost his way and abandoned his art and heritage, and in the end the grief he brought upon himself led him to suicide. Now I am amazed that his *siddur*, which has been lost at least twelve years, has turned up this very day—for tonight is the sixth *yahrzeit* of my brother's death!" And then the Hasidim looked up, and noticed for the first time the *yahrzeit* candle burning on the mantle, and a shiver passed through every one of them.

Then the woman continued to speak: "It is because of several incidents related to my brother that we invited you to join us in the first place, Reb Nachman. And now I see that it was not an accident that it was tonight, of all nights, that you agreed to accept our invitation. Perhaps, then, it is *beshert* that you assist us in comprehending these signs, which so far have escaped our understanding."

Reb Nachman nodded, and motioned for the woman to continue. And she said: "Some months ago, at the time of our first invitation to you, I discovered in a closet three woodcuts carved by my brother, may his soul rest in peace, that I had never known about. They were a great surprise, for, as you can see from the dates inscribed on them, they come from the period after he had renounced both his art and his religion." And the woman took out the woodcuts from a drawer and handed them to Reb Nachman, who examined them carefully.

The first showed a young man with a stern, bitter demeanor, sitting in a chair. On his shoulder was perched a parrot, whose expression was identical to his own. In fact, it did not seem possible to determine whether the parrot was imitating the man or the man the parrot, but in any case the expressions were one and the same. The second woodcut, dated after the first, was also a self-portrait, which revealed to the world the young man's great torment. The waves of lines that crossed his face were lines of grief, and it was apparent to all who saw it that his decision to abandon his faith had cast him into a sea of sorrow. But it was the third woodcut, the last of the three, which was the most mysterious of all. For it showed an exceptionally peaceful scene of a river running through a garden, and there were no people in that place at all.

Then, after Reb Nachman had examined the woodcuts and passed them to the other Hasidim, the woman continued her tale: "Some weeks after finding these woodcuts, a second discovery was made. In order to add a room to our house, since I had recently given birth to a son, whom we named after my brother, we tore down a wall, and after doing so we discovered concealed within the wall a bag containing my brother's *tallis* and *tefillin*, which had long been lost. For when he had cut himself off he had hidden these, even from himself. After his death we searched for them everywhere, but they were not to be found until the wall was torn down, while his *siddur* remained lost until you recovered it this very evening.

"Finally, you should know that I had a dream this morning that is surely relevant to this mystery. In the dream I was standing once more in my brother's room, which was exactly as it used to be, and while I knew that he was no longer among the living, I still felt his presence there. And as I looked around the room, I noticed a journal, which I realized must be his own. I opened it, and the page I turned to seemed blurred, but as I focused on it line by line I brought the words into being. And there I read a poem my brother had written, and because I knew it was of great importance, and because I sensed even in the dream that I could not take the journal with me from that place, I read the lines over and over, until they were engraved in my heart. And upon waking I wrote down the lines at once, and in this way preserved that poem." And then she handed Reb Nachman the page on which she had written down the poem, and this is what he read:

> Along thy streets of dust and stone,
> Only one night left to stay,
> An ancient zither plays its tone
> From nearby passage place and way.
> O not thy will shall beckon me
> To walk among dark faces all,
> And of these eyes which only see
> Lives that spring and those that fall.
> Is what said the prophet true,
> Of all things just ye shall obey?
> Or shall I turn my back on you,
> Or shall I turn my eyes and stay?
> Lest the night should change and slow reveal
> The pathos that your walls bemoan
> In blindness I should grope and feel
> Along thy streets of dust and stone.

After he had read this poem and heard all that the woman had to say, Reb Nachman was at first silent. But when he began to speak the words flowed from his lips, and all who heard him were caught up in the clarity of his thought. "There can be no doubt," he said, "that all these occurrences, coming as they did during the sixth year after your brother's death, are not coincidences, but, rather, constitute a message from him, whose soul resides in the *Yenne Velt*, the Other World. Even the fish caught today, which brought us together this evening, was not an accident but another sign. Now it is for us to decipher the meaning of all that has taken place, so that the efforts of your brother's spirit to reach us will not be wasted, and so we can understand the truth as it exists.

"Therefore, let us consider these discoveries. The first, that of the woodcuts, reveals the stages through which the soul of your brother was condemned to pass. Now it is known that those who die a natural death are usually required to purify their souls for at least a short period, which lasts as long as eleven months. That is why we pray the *Kaddish* each day for eleven months, to assist in this process of purification, and to console the *neshamah* of the departed one while it is still within our reach. After eleven months the souls of those who have died a natural death are, with few exceptions, purified, and able to ascend into the upper realms. What, however, is the fate of those who die by their own hands? For this is not only a sin against man, but also against God, who created man in His image. And just as we are slow to forgive one who takes his own life, so too does the soul of such a one receive a terrible stain, which takes much longer to be purified.

"If we examine the first of these woodcuts we can see that the soul of your brother was dominated by a force which entered his life from without. In this way the pure soul of your brother was tainted and overshadowed, so that the purest part found itself in exile. This is what the parrot represents. For this parrot tells us that a *dybbuk*, a dangerous wandering spirit, entered the body of your brother and dominated his soul. And from that time on his words and actions were not his own, but those of the *dybbuk*, who repeated his bitterness and hatred of this life so often that your brother came to believe it was his own. The second woodcut shows us how tormented his soul became, and how deep ran the waters of his grief. But it is the third woodcut that must give you comfort, for the serene landscape it portrays shows he sensed that one day his soul would free itself of these torments and find its true home in Paradise. For this last woodcut represents the ascent of his purified soul into Paradise, freed of the stain of the sin which had tainted it so long.

"Now the discovery of the bag containing his *tallis* and *tefillin*, which had been lost, reveals it was then that his true soul had at last freed itself of the alien spirit which drove him from his family and made him an exile in this world and the next. So too is the cause of this discovery of great importance. For the son you have recently brought into the world bears the name of your brother, and because you saw fit not to banish his memory from this world, but to renew it in the presence of your son, you lifted a great burden from his soul, and brought it that much closer to release. In this way the discovery in the wall you tore down to make room for your son is more than one miracle, but two at the same time, just as the *tallis* and *tefillin* each represent a separate *mitzvah*. The recovery of the *siddur* also tells us that the final stage of the *tikkun*, the restoration, has at last taken place; for with the recovery of the *tallis* and *tefillin* and *siddur*, what was lost has been found, and the process has become complete.

"Then there is the poem itself, which is the most direct message of all, sent to you by the very soul of your brother to announce that after six years of exile his soul has at last become purified, that as it enters the sabbatical year after his departure from this world it is prepared to ascend into the upper realms. He has sent this message to inform you that on the day of his *yahrzeit*, at this time of transition, his thoughts are with you, as your thoughts are with him. So too does he have one last request to make—that you should cease to mourn over him, and in this way release the hold you have on his soul and let him freely enter that place where at last he can receive the reward of the long process of purification he has endured."

And when Reb Nachman had spoken these words every one in that room sensed the powerful presence of the *neshamah* of that woman's brother among them, taking in all that transpired. And these were the final words that Reb Nachman spoke, directed to the soul itself: "Fortunate soul, your message has been received from the *Yenne Velt*. And just as you have reached out to us, so have we reached out to you. Know that you are now released from all that bound you to this world of men, and your purified soul may now ascend into the upper realms in peace. Your family bids you farewell and sends you love, and in the future will cherish your memory and cease to mourn over the sufferings of your soul, from which you have now been set free for all time."

The Miller's Dream

for Rabbi Zalman Stein

In the town of Berditchev there was a Jewish miller who made his home in a windmill. This miller had been a widower for ten years. He and his wife had been childless, and he had lived alone for a long time. One night this miller had a vivid dream. In the dream he was walking along the shore of a great sea. All at once a boat appeared on the horizon and came closer. Before long he perceived a woman in the boat, alone, without oars, carried by the will of the current. Suddenly a wave arose and delivered the boat into the cove where he was standing. As the boat approached, he glimpsed the woman's face, then awoke.

When the miller arose he found himself in the grip of a vague but powerful emotion. The dream was completely vivid to him, as if he had lived through it. He thought about it all that day, and at last he decided to go to Reb Levi Yitzhak of Berditchev to seek an interpretation of that dream.

When the miller arrived at the home of Reb Levi Yitzhak, he found a long line of petitioners waiting to see him, and his heart sank, for he doubted if he would be received that day. But when the door to the rabbi's study opened, and the rabbi appeared there, he looked straight at the miller across the crowded room, and beckoned to him to come in at once. Much amazed, the miller entered the study and told the Rebbe the dream. And when he finished speaking, Reb Levi Yitzhak said, "You were right to seek assistance, for a dream not interpreted is like a letter left unread. Therefore you should depart for Bratslav at once, for the spirit of Joseph in our day is found in Reb Nachman, and he will surely comprehend its meaning." Then Reb Levi Yitzhak wrote out a letter of introduction and gave it to the miller, and the miller took his leave and set out for Bratslav. For although it was a three-day journey to Bratslav, and it was almost time for

124

the harvest, that dream called out to him like a melody he recognized but could not identify. And he longed to know what it meant.

The miller arrived in Bratslav on the third day and went straight to the *Beit Midrash*, where Reb Levi Yitzhak had told him Reb Nachman could be found. He entered and found Reb Nachman sitting alone, studying the pages of an ancient manuscript. The miller wondered what book it was that so absorbed the Rebbe's attention. At last Reb Nachman looked up and asked how he could help him. The miller gave him the letter of introduction Reb Levi Yitzhak had written, and when Reb Nachman had read it, he said, "Tell me the dream."

Reb Nachman listened with complete concentration as the miller spoke, and afterward he said, "I will tell you its meaning in three days." Then he turned back to the ancient manuscript and did not look up again. The miller did not know what to do—he had to return in time for the harvest. But he dared not disturb the Rebbe, nor question him. Therefore he tried to keep his heart steady while he waited.

On the morning of the third day, the miller approached Reb Nachman, who said, "I will tell you before sunset." So it was that the miller waited in great anxiety, as the hours passed. Then, just before sunset, a carriage pulled up before Reb Nachman's house, and a woman descended and sought an audience with the Rebbe. And when the woman entered the house, the miller was astonished to see the same woman of his dream, the one who had been alone in the boat. He stared at her, while her eyes looked only at the ground. Then Reb Nachman appeared and told the woman to be seated, and told the miller that he too should remain to hear what she had to say.

So it was that the woman revealed that she was the widow of a merchant who had died at sea. And since there were no survivors, there were no witnesses to confirm his death, and she had been left an *agunah*. Therefore she had set out three years before, in order to gather the signatures of two hundred rabbis to free her from that terrible status, in which she was forbidden to remarry. She had gathered one hundred and ninety-nine signatures, and Reb Nachman's signature would free her, so that it would be possible for her to remarry. Reb Nachman did not hesitate after she had spoken, nor question her further, but nodded and put his signature to the document. The woman sighed with great relief and smiled, and when the miller saw that smile he lost his heart to her, and knew he would seek to make her his wife.

Then Reb Nachman arose for the afternoon prayers, and when the miller saw the smile on his face, he understood that Reb Nachman had kept him there so that he would not miss the arrival of his future wife. In this way Reb Nachman had not only brought them together, but had interpreted the meaning of the miller's dream as well.

The Destroyer of Books

REB Shimon said, "Reb Nachman, last night I entered your study in my dream and I was led like one in a trance to a book on the shelf. And when I took down this book and opened it, I found that the pages were blurred. But then I discovered that if I focused on the words line by line, I could bring them into being. In this way I read that page. And on that page I read a very beautiful poem. The poem was fragile and balanced, and I read it over and over until the words were written in my heart.

"Then there was a knock at the door, and when I answered a woman was standing there, who said that you had sent her. She asked me what I was reading, and then took the book from my hands as if to examine it. Then she told me you had sent for me and led me to the door, and only when it was too late to turn back and I was almost awake did I realize that because of her I had lost the precious poem. Can you tell me, Rebbe, who is this woman, and why did she deprive me of my poem?"

Reb Nachman replied, "Yes, I know her, Shimon. She is a

jealous slave to Silence known as the Destroyer of Books. Believe me, I did not send her to you; rather, all day I have been trying to send her away. Even now, while Nussan is writing down our words, she is the dark woman standing behind him who is tearing these pages to pieces."

And Shimon looked up at Reb Nussan and behind him he saw the same woman of his dream, and even as Reb Nussan wrote down their words she was tearing up those pages. The sound of tearing rose around them; the torn pages fluttered to the floor. Soon even the silence between syllables had been broken, so that Shimon almost could not hear the last words Reb Nachman spoke: "Nothing, not all the forests that scatter their seeds in circles, can restore those pages fallen at her feet."

A Tale of Two Sisters

JUST after the start of the Sabbath Reb Shimon began the discourse, and said to Reb Nachman, "Why is it that Lilith, whom the legends tell us is the sister of the *Shekhinah*, the Sabbath Queen, turned her face so far toward the darkness and away from the divine light?" "It is true," Reb Nachman replied, "that when the Temple was destroyed the *Shekhinah* accompanied us into Exile. And it was then that Lilith raised her voice to heaven and demanded that the Holy One make her his consort in place of her sister. But the Holy One, Blessed be He, never considered this brazen proposal for even an instant of an instant, nor did he stop mourning for the Queen from whom He had separated Himself, and Lilith, made ashamed, slipped off into the night to haunt the cradles of the newborn and to become the mother of demons. Her fate is exactly the opposite of that of the Sabbath Queen now present among us, who is like the light that everywhere surrounds the flames of the candles. How is it possible that the fate of two sisters could be so far apart? Let me explain it to you as a tale."

And this is the tale Reb Nachman told:

Once there were two sisters who were the daughters of very poor parents, although it was rumored that they had descended from a family of kings. Almost from birth the elder sister had taken it upon herself to serve her family in any way she could, but the younger, infatuated by the rumor of their former glory, liked to imagine she was a princess who should always be served.

One day, as the elder sister lowered the bucket into the well, the rope broke, and the bucket filled with water and sank to the bottom. But since this sister was reluctant to return without the bucket, which was the only one her family owned, she climbed into the well and clasped the rocks on the inside and slowly lowered herself to the level of the water. There she took a deep breath and dived after the bucket, but once she was under water she became aware of a bright light shining from a place that seemed close at hand, a light so beautiful she could not resist abandoning the bucket and swimming in that direction, and when she came up for air the next thing she knew was that she had come to a land she had never seen before. There ice-covered mountains in the distance radiated the light of the sun she had seen reflected in the well, and large, ancient oaks were everywhere to be found. Then she heard a gentle voice, and when she turned around she saw an old man who was wearing a garment which seemed to be woven of light. The old man greeted her from his place on the ground under the most magnificent of the ancient oaks, and when the elder sister returned his greeting she looked into his eyes for only an instant and saw that a light shone from them that was almost blinding. Then she turned her gaze to the ground, for she knew she was in the presence of a holy man.

When the old man spoke again he asked her if she would be willing to bathe him, for it had been a long time since he had taken a bath. She nodded her head to say yes, and then the old man pointed out the iron vessel which would serve as his bath and told her to listen carefully to his instructions and to obey them exactly as he told them to her. First she must fill the vessel with stagnant water; second, she must gather dung and light a fire under it; and finally she must take a pumice stone and use it as a sponge with which to wash him. The old man closed his eyes and said he would sleep until the bath was ready for him.

Now although this young woman had great respect for the old man, she had prepared many baths in the past, and she had no intention of using stagnant water when there was a freshwater stream nearby. So she carried the vessel down to the stream and filled it with the fresh, clear water. Then she walked into the nearby woods and found a large quantity of the best kindling wood, and since that would serve to make a fire far better than dung, she built the fire from that instead. Finally, she plucked three large leaves from one of the ancient oaks, for she knew that although a pumice stone closely resembled a sponge, it was far too hard to absorb water and far too rough to rub against the old man's skin. And when the bath was ready she saw that the old man had opened his eyes, and she led him to the vessel and proceeded to bathe him with gentleness and care.

When she had finished bathing him, the old man told her that she had done precisely the right thing in ignoring his orders. As a reward he gave her a bag filled with diamonds and told her that if she went back into the water at the same place she had emerged from, that she would arrive back in the well. The elder sister thanked the old man many times for his gift, took the bag of diamonds, and returned in the way he had told her. When she emerged from the water she was back in the well, and she noticed that there was now a ladder on the inside of the well which had never been there before, and on the bottom rung of the ladder was the bucket that had fallen into the well. Then she climbed out of the well, filled the bucket with water, and brought it and the bag of diamonds back into the house and told her poor parents and her sister of her good luck that day.

Now when the younger sister saw the bag of diamonds the elder sister had received she gasped at their beauty, and she became very jealous. That night, while everyone else was preparing the evening's meal, the younger sister took out the bag, thinking perhaps to steal the diamonds. But when she reached in and grasped a handful, she found that the diamonds turned to water in her hands. Then she knew the diamonds were enchanted, and that she must do whatever it was her sister had done in order to receive a bag of diamonds of her own. So early the next morning she went to the well, climbed down the ladder, and when she reached the water she saw the same light her sister had seen and took a deep breath and dived after it, emerging in the same land her sister had come to the day before.

Now the younger sister cared for nothing but her own image in the mirror, so she did not look up to see the sun reflecting on the ice-covered mountains, nor did she look into the eyes of the old man when he greeted her and asked if she might be willing to give him a bath. She was repelled at the idea of bathing an old man, but when she asked him if another girl had visited that land the day before, he replied that it was possible. And when she asked if that girl had given him a bath, he replied that it was possible. And when she asked if she had been given a bag of diamonds as a reward, he replied that it was possible. And so she agreed to give him a bath. Then the old man gave her exactly the same instructions he had given to her sister: to fill the vessel with stagnant water, to build the fire with dung, and to wash him with a pumice stone. The young sister was disgusted by these demands, but in her greed she did exactly as she was told, and at the very moment she touched the pumice stone to the skin of the old man she was changed into a frog that hopped back into the water and emerged in the well where she lives to this day, croaking day and night for someone to save her from the fate she has earned for herself.

A Single Flame

REB Nachman and his Hasidim were gathered at the Sabbath table. After the meal had been finished and the blessings had been said, Reb Nachman began to speak. He said, "The soul of every man is like a flame. Like a flame it has three parts: a dark part at the bottom, where the soul is submerged in darkness; a part in the middle that is dark red, where the soul starts to emerge from the darkness; and a third part at the top that is pure white. Thus it is that the soul of every man must pass through these three gates. For it is only when a soul has been purified that it is permitted to pass through the fourth gate, which is the Gate of Mystery."

Reb Shimon wondered greatly at this, and he asked, "For how long is the soul condemned to the Gates of Darkness before it is permitted to enter the realm of light?"

Reb Nachman replied, "If only you understood what it means to be a flame, Shimon, you would understand very well how long a man's soul is condemned to suffer trying to travel from the realms of darkness into the realms of light!"

And no sooner had Reb Nachman said this than Reb Shimon happened to glance up at the Sabbath candles that burned on the table before them. At the very instant he glimpsed the flame of the candle burning in the center, he suddenly realized that his own life was like the flame of that very candle, burning only because it consumed the wax of the candle beneath it, and at the mercy of any wind. And then Shimon became one with that flame, and saw the world as would a flame burning atop a candle. And that flame had three parts, which blended into one another, and it was impossible to determine where one part ended and the next began. And the bottom part of that flame was dark. It was the darkness before the creation of the world, where the soul of man returns to when his life is ended. And in that darkness Reb Shimon felt as if he were pinned down to an iceberg in a world in which there was nothing but a voice repeating the same words over and over, while hills rose up and collapsed around him. That is when he looked down at his hands, and saw to his horror only bones. And in his shock he looked away, and that is when he saw the first glimmer of the light that flickered above him. And when his eyes fell back to his hands, he saw that they were wings, and that he was already flying upward, towards the source of the light.

And when Shimon reached that place, where the darkness was divided from the light, he saw an opening no more than three finger-breadths, and he knew at once that it was a gate meant to be passed through. And that is when he found himself rising toward a Kingdom of Light, where he was rocked in a cradle of light, which emerged from a hidden point, eternal and unmoving. And that hidden point was a flame consisting of three parts, the Spirit, the Voice, and the Word. Yet at the same time it was only a single flame which would never burn out.

It was then that Reb Shimon emerged from his vision, and found himself seated with Reb Nachman and his disciples, with the Sabbath candles still burning brightly on the table, and the room filled with light. And the source of that light came not from the candles, but from Reb Nachman, and that is when Shimon recognized that for him Reb Nachman was the trunk of a tree of light, and that he, Shimon, was one of the branches of that tree. And he also understood that the other Hasidim made up the other branches of that tree, and that none was complete without the others or without the light of the Holy One, which illumined Reb Nachman's words like the white flames burning atop the Sabbath candles that swayed before his eyes.

The Boy Who Blew the Shofar

IN the month of Elul, three days before Rosh Hashanah, a young boy whose name was Eliyahu had a strange and vivid dream. In it he found himself walking at night on the path that led to the synagogue in Bratslav. And when he arrived there, he entered the *Beit Knesset* and found it empty. But he saw that a *shofar* and a large *tallis* had been left on the *bimah*. For throughout that month of repentence, the *shofar* was sounded after the morning service. Just then a man entered the synagogue who was wearing a shroud, and although this was very strange indeed, Eliyahu found that he did not feel afraid. The man approached him, and the boy saw at once that he had the appearance of one tormented. When he reached the boy, the man said, "Please, you must help us. There are forty-eight imprisoned souls, and only you can set us free." "But how can I help?" asked Eliyahu in the dream. "I am only twelve years old and I am too young to put on a *tallis*." The shrouded man repeated himself, "Only you can save us. For if our souls are not freed before Rosh Hashanah, we will be condemned to wander in the *Yenne Velt* until the Messiah sets us free at the End of Days." "What is it that I must do?" the boy asked. "You must take the *tallis* and *shofar* from the *bimah* and go to the cemetery outside town, where all the imprisoned souls have gathered. And you must sound the *shofar* exactly as is done on Rosh Hashanah." "But I cannot steal from the synagogue!" said the boy, "Nor can I blow the *shofar*." "Only you can set us free, Eliyahu," said the shrouded man. And he turned from the synagogue and departed. And just as he passed through the door, the boy awoke.

When Eliyahu realized this encounter had taken place in a dream, he was at first relieved. But then the plea of the shrouded man began to haunt him, and he wondered if he were truly expected to perform this strange and forbidden act. Eliyahu had the greatest respect for all that was sacred, and he could not imagine

stealing a *shofar* and *tallis* from the *Beit Knesset*. Nor could he imagine blowing the *shofar* in a cemetery, for such a thing is never done. Furthermore, he had never even held a *shofar* in his hands. He did not know the first thing about how to sound it. And even the rabbis had to practice during the month of Elul in order to recover the skill required to sound the *shofar* on Rosh Hashanah. Eliyahu did not doubt that to perform these acts would be a desecration. And who would believe him if he said he had been told to do so in a dream? Therefore he did nothing, and a day passed, although the dream weighed heavily upon him.

The next night Eliyahu again dreamed that he followed the path at night to the synagogue. This time he found the door open when he arrived, and wondered about this, since the door was always closed. Inside he saw a shrouded figure standing at the *bimah*, facing the Ark. As he entered this figure turned around, and Eliyahu saw it was a woman. He could barely believe his eyes—a woman standing at the *bimah*, and a shrouded woman at that! Yet when this eerie figure stepped down from the *bimah* and approached him, the boy did not take fright, but instead felt compassion for her, for he saw the look of suffering in her eyes. Then the woman began to speak. She said, "Eliyahu, only two days remain before Rosh Hashanah. I am speaking for forty-eight souls, whose fate is in your hands. You must take up the *tallis* and *shofar* and blow great blasts on it before dawn in the cemetery where we are clustered together in bondage. Hesitate no longer, for without you we are lost." Then the shrouded woman departed, and no sooner had she passed through the doorway than Eliyahu awoke.

This time the boy found himself paralyzed with fear. He began to be afraid he was losing his mind. Why would such a heavy burden fall upon him? He was no Rebbe! For performing such an act he could become an outcast for the rest of his life. Who would forgive him such a desecration? Who would believe his reason for doing so? With these terrible thoughts tormenting him, another night passed, and when dawn arrived Eliyahu knew it was too late to go to the cemetery, and then he suddenly felt a great wave of remorse.

Haunted by guilt and dread, the day dragged by for the ex-

hausted boy. He wondered if he should undertake the bizarre task
that night, but he was unable to decide. Then, just as it grew dark,
he fell into a deep sleep, and slept until an hour before dawn. Then
he dreamed again, and once again stood before the open door. This
time, however, the synagogue was not empty when he entered it.
Everywhere he looked he saw shrouded worshipers chanting
prayers with great intensity, and among them he recognized the
shrouded man who had approached him in the first dream, and the
shrouded woman who had spoken to him in the second. The boy
was amazed to see such a strange congregation, yet he did not feel
terror at the sight of them, but compassion mixed with grief. For
he saw that all of them were suffering terribly. He counted quickly
and saw that there were twenty-four men on one side of the aisle,
and twenty-four women on the other, and he was able to count the
women because the *mehitzah* was missing, and the shrouded men
and women stood in full view of each other. And as strange as that
would have been when he was awake, it did not surprise him at all
in his dream, but seemed perfectly natural.

Just then Eliyahu noticed there was no one standing at the
bimah, although the *tallis* and *shofar* were still lying there. And he
turned to the nearest man and said: "How is it that you are praying
without a prayer leader?" "Because we are waiting for him to put
on the *tallis* and take up the *shofar*," said the man. "And when do
you expect him to come here?" asked the boy. "He has already
arrived," said the man. "And where is he?" the boy asked, for he
was very curious to know who he was. "It is you we have been
waiting for," said the man. And Eliyahu looked around, and saw
that every eye in that congregation was fixed upon him. Then the
man said: "Only an hour remains. Then it will be too late."

Just then Eliyahu woke up in a cold sweat. Then he leaped
from bed like one impelled and ran in the darkness to the *Beit
Knesset*. And when he reached it, the first thing he noticed was that
the door was open, and his heart almost stopped beating. He
stepped inside and saw, to his great relief, that the synagogue was
empty. But then his eyes were drawn to the *bimah*, and he saw the
tallis and *shofar* lying there. And he recognized the *tallis gadol* as

that of Reb Nachman. This discovery staggered him, for he dared
not put on the Rebbe's *tallis*. Yet time was swiftly passing, and
soon it would be too late. There was no other choice. He hurried
to the *bimah* and took the *tallis* in his hands and put it on, and it
covered him like a long robe. But, strange to say, when the *tallis*
was on his shoulders he felt suddenly strengthened. Then he
picked up the *shofar* and ran out of the synagogue, hoping that no
one would see him.

In a short time he reached the cemetery. Normally he would
never have entered there at night, when spirits and demons are said
to freely roam. But now he gave no thought to this fear, for
another fear, that of being too late, gnawed at his soul. And when
he stood amidst those tombstones, in the presence of all those
departed souls, he had the same sensation he did in the dream that
all eyes were fixed upon him. Then, hesitating no longer, Eliyahu
took up the *shofar* and blew on it for the first time in his life. He
sounded the first long, unbroken note, *tekiah*, and when it came
forth from the *shofar* with perfect clarity he was completely
amazed, for the sound had a resonance fuller than any he had ever
heard. Then, in succession, he sounded the broken notes, *shevarim*
and *teruah*, which resemble sobbing and wailing. And as he blew
those notes he thought he heard a great sobbing and wailing surrounding him on all sides. Then he repeated the long, unbroken
blast and held it for what seemed ages to him. And as he did,
Eliyahu suddenly felt a wind emerge and surround him. The instant he finished blowing that long note, the sound of rushing
winds encircled him for several seconds, as if caressing and em-
bracing him, and then he heard a distant clanging, as if a great gate
had opened far away. Soon afterward the winds grew calm, and
the first light of dawn appeared. For a few moments Eliyahu stood
in the cemetery, wearing the large *tallis*, with the *shofar* in his hand.
He felt a sense of calm and relief more complete than he had ever
imagined. But all at once he remembered that the Hasidim would
arrive at any moment to pray, and in a panic he ran back to the
synagogue as fast as his legs could carry him.

When he arrived, Eliyahu saw at once that the door he had left

open in his haste to reach the cemetery had been closed, and a
great fear descended on him. For a moment he wanted to run
away, but he managed to force himself to open the door and step
inside. When he did, Eliyahu saw that there was only one person
there, a man who was praying at the *bimah* with *tefillin* but without
a *tallis*. This man turned around as he entered, and Eliyahu saw
that it was none other than Reb Nachman himself. The boy was
overcome with terror, for he was certain that the Rebbe would
never forgive him. And so he was much amazed when he saw that
Reb Nachman did not seem angry at all, but smiled broadly as he
approached him and embraced Eliyahu while the boy was still
wearing his *tallis*. And when the boy looked up in confusion, Reb
Nachman said: "They were right you know, Eliyahu, only you
with your pure soul could set them free, acting on your own. And
now those forty-eight souls have been freed from their wanderings
and have reached their final destination. But they would never
have reached that Sanctuary had you not opened the Gates of
Holiness, which had been closed to them for so long."

A Message from the Messiah

ONE day Reb Nachman spoke to his Hasidim of the Shattering of the Vessels and the Gathering of the Sparks. Of how the
vessels had emanated from the *Ein Sof*, the Beginning before which
there was no beginning, filled with primordial light. How these
vessels had somehow shattered, scattering sparks of light everywhere in the world. And how it was the purpose of every Jew to
search for those sparks no matter where they were hidden, so that
the vessels might someday be restored. For since waking that day,
Reb Nachman had felt as if he had come close to an understanding
of this divine mystery, but it was still concealed from him, although he felt its presence as if it were palpable. So he spoke to his

Hasidim in the hope that one of them might be the vessel through which this secret would be revealed.

Therefore Reb Nachman encouraged each of his Hasidim to question him that day, and because Reb Shimon had been Reb Nachman's first disciple it was his honor to ask the first question. Reb Shimon asked, "Tell me, Rebbe, where shall I search for the sparks that must be gathered?"

And Reb Nachman said, "Look first, Shimon, in your own soul. For a man's soul consists of many sparks. From where do these sparks come? From the light given off by great men after their death. For you must know that no longer does a man inherit a single *neshamah*. Remember: there were only six hundred thousand *neshamahs* created at the beginning of time, and the same number were present at Mount Sinai to receive the Torah. But today there are more Jewish bodies than there are Jewish souls. Therefore the souls of men have become fragmented, and it is a rare soul indeed that is inherited from a single source. Even in my own soul I have recognized the sparks of many souls—of the souls of Moses, of Simeon bar Yohai, of the Ari, and, of course, of the Baal Shem Tov. In addition I have recognized sparks of the souls of both Messiah ben Joseph and Messiah ben David. And the seventh soul is one that had not been reborn since the days of the Wandering in the Wilderness. So long had it searched for a resting place."

After Reb Nachman had spoken his Hasidim were silent, for they too sensed the mystery hovering above them. Finally Reb Nussan, Reb Nachman's scribe, spoke up and said, "But tell me, Rebbe, why did the vessels split apart in the first place?"

And Reb Nachman replied without hesitation: "It is little understood, Nussan, that it was the destiny of the vessels to shatter, just as seed-pods break open when they are ripe and cast their seeds into the wind."

With these words the current quickened and carried all of them a little closer to the edge of a waterfall, and all of them became afraid, and none of the others dared to speak. But at last one other spoke up. It was Reb Naftali, the musician; he played many instruments, but when he played the violin, the music

evoked in all who heard it long lost memories of the Garden of
Eden, and left a taste as sweet as manna. And Reb Naftali said,
"All of us, Rebbe, seek to gather the sparks. But who will restore
the vessels so that they can contain the divine light?" And to this
question not even Reb Nachman dared to reply, for the restoration
of the vessels could not be accomplished by any man.

But that night Reb Nachman had a dream that was a crystal
vision, in which the veil was at last torn away from the mystery
that had hovered among them like a dove above its nest. In that
dream Reb Nachman found himself in the Holy Land, in the
sacred city of Safed, where the Ari, Rabbi Isaac Luria, had made
his home. And the path Reb Nachman followed led him directly to
a *Beit Knesset* in that city. The walls of that House of Prayer were
made of stone, and the shape of the building was round, so that it
resembled a dome. And when Reb Nachman entered there he
found that the Ark of the Covenant had been placed in the center
of that synagogue. And the curtains of the Ark had been pulled
back so that the scrolls of the Torah were revealed, and there were
seven scrolls inside that Ark.

It was at that moment that the door of the *Beit Knesset* opened
and a man entered there whose face was glowing. And when this
man saw that Reb Nachman was already there, he said: "I hope I
have not kept you waiting." And Reb Nachman said, "There is
only one for whom I am waiting, and that is for the Redeemer who
shall restore the shattered vessels." And the man replied: "It is he
who has sent me here with a message to deliver to you." And he
took out a sealed letter from beneath his white robe and gave it to
Reb Nachman. When Reb Nachman had broken open the seven
seals he saw that the words were written in large Hebrew letters
and the script of the letters was similar to that of the Torah.

Reb Nachman was staggered to receive such a message. He
asked the man, "Where have you come from?" And the man replied, "I have come from a kingdom quite distant from here, and
from a place more than two years journey from where the ten lost
tribes live, on the other side of the River Sambatyon." And Reb
Nachman asked, "Then how have you come to this place?" And

the messenger replied, "I traveled in the underground caverns that cross the earth, through which all souls will travel to reach Jerusalem at the End of Days, when the Messiah takes his place among men."

And when he heard this Reb Nachman grew afraid. And he asked, "What is your name?" And the man said: "I am the spirit of Hayim Vital. In the afterlife I have been made the messenger of the Messiah, just as I was the messenger of the Ari."

In the presence of Hayim Vital, Reb Nachman was in awe, for it was through the pure vessels of Hayim Vital's writings that the sacred teachings of the Ari had been preserved and transmitted. He opened the letter and this time the letters of the words burned in his vision, black flames illumined by white. And at that very moment Reb Nachman stepped outside his body and his soul broke into blossom. And when he looked up he saw the twenty-two letters of the alphabet flying everywhere around him like dark birds. And then he saw that every letter was actually a vessel filled with light, and that every one of them understood what it meant to receive. And he saw that when the vessels became so full that they overflowed, they spilled sparks of light into the world, and each spark was a primal seed taking root wherever it touched down.

Then Reb Nachman woke up, and as he lay back on his bed and remembered this dream he felt as if he had swallowed one of those sparks, for inside him a sun seemed to be growing ripe. And every word Reb Nachman spoke to his Hasidim that day was inscribed in their memories and took root in their souls. And those were the very same words that the Messiah had written in the message that he had sent.

The Sea of Ink

In his dreams Shimon was always traveling with Reb Nachman, consumed by a quest, although he was not exactly certain what it was. Especially in the three-year period he spent apart from Reb Nachman, the Rebbe haunted his dreams. Once Shimon dreamed they sailed together on a *tallis* and were sustained from manna which dropped from the sky upon that very prayer shawl. Once he dreamed that he and the Rebbe ascended into the heavens in a chariot of fire, surrounded by stars on all sides, the world illumined as never before. And once he dreamed that they were sailing together across the Black Sea. And to his amazement, when Shimon looked down at the water, it was indeed black. Shimon wondered if Reb Nachman knew the reason for this, and one day he asked him. Reb Nachman replied, "Lower a bucket, Shimon, and fill it with water. And bring that water back to our cabin and examine it. Then, I am certain, you will know the reason."

So Shimon did as Reb Nachman had said, and lowered a bucket from the deck until it reached the water. When the bucket was full he raised it up and carried it back into the cabin he shared with Reb Nachman. And he filled a glass with that water, and saw that the water was in fact pitch black. Then he smelled the water and detected an odor that reminded him of ink. Shimon laughed and turned to Reb Nachman, "This water not only looks like ink, it smells like it too!" Reb Nachman also laughed, saying, "Let us try an experiment, Shimon. Why don't you dip your pen into this 'ink' and let us see how well it can write."

Carried away by their jest, Shimon took out his pen and dipped it into the black water. Then he took out a page and attempted to see if it would write. But the instant he set his pen down on the page, his hand began to write of itself. Shimon was astonished when this happened, and pulled the pen back, but Reb Nachman said, "No, Shimon, don't stop. Keep your pen fixed to the page!" And when Shimon saw the look in Reb Nachman's eyes, he turned back to the page at once and continued to write. And there unraveled before him a tale, although he did not know whence it came. And this is the tale that was written by the hand of Reb Shimon: "At the dark bridge, the black border, I paused between two breaths." These were the words Shimon's pen wrote before he raised his hand. After Reb Nachman told him to continue to write without stopping, these were the words that followed: "Ten men were mourning for me. They spoke a lost language, planting something in the sand. All edges called me closer; only a sea breeze held me back. Too soon I surrendered myself to sleep, searching for an entrance, an angle of repose, a lock in which to exchange a key for a crown. It is your hand that charts the seasons, the circle I can no longer comprehend, for where I have lain down in the darkness I can only measure a minute of death. Yet when I have taught you my one word, I will put my dark cloak behind me, let new waters form nightly, and await the blessing of a rainbow to carry me across."

Suddenly Shimon's hand came to a halt, and no other words were written. And when it became apparent that there was no more to write, Shimon read the words he had written out loud to Reb Nachman, who listened ever so carefully. After this he considered their meaning, but the words seemed to be a riddle, which he could not decipher, although Reb Nachman did not seem to question their meaning in the least. And Shimon said, "Please, Rebbe, cast light on these words if you can, for their meaning eludes me, although I do not doubt that what is being said is of great importance."

And Reb Nachman said, "In this you are correct, Shimon. For know that it is a spirit who has spoken through you, a wandering soul of whose presence I have been aware ever since we stepped upon this ship. And when you asked your question about the Black Sea, and said the water resembled ink, I saw how it might be possible for this wandering spirit to communicate with us at last. When you filled your pen with that 'ink' you made it possible for the spirit to speak through you and reveal the tale your hand has written." Shimon was amazed at this explanation, and realized that for once he had served as a perfect vessel. And already he longed for the spirit to speak through him once more.

"What is it that this spirit wants of us?" asked Shimon, for he suddenly realized that he did not understand the meaning of the words his own hand had written down. Reb Nachman replied, "Know, Shimon, that he who approached us is the spirit of a young man from our very own town who is entreating us to bring redemption to his soul." "And how can this be done?" asked Shimon, who felt that he had a stake in bringing salvation to that tortured soul. Reb Nachman grew very serious and said, "He who has approached us is only the first of many souls who have accompanied us, Shimon. There are flocks of them on every side. If you could only see them, you would be astonished. For they are waiting for us to take the key in our hand and open the gate so that they can flock through, to the destiny they have desired so long. Yes, Shimon, there is far more at stake than our own souls, for there is a multitude of souls surrounding us, each of them bearing prayers that have been exiled for many ages. And until we accomplish our task, those prayers will be forced to remain in exile; but once our quest is complete the prayers will be woven into a garland of prayers by the angel Sandalphon, and worn by the Holy One, blessed be He, as a crown of prayers, as He sits on His Throne of Glory."

And as Reb Nachman said these words, Shimon had a glimpse of that multitude of prayers languishing in exile, and just before waking he glimpsed as well the crown they would make when they had been woven into a garland that shone even brighter than the sun.

The Tale of the Palace

"To understand *Maaseh Bereshith*," said Reb Nachman to his Hasidim, "it is necessary to understand the meaning of the word *Bereshith*, which in itself contains all the Mysteries of Creation." To this Reb Shimon replied, "But how is it possible for a word to contain all of creation?" Reb Nachman replied, "That is because the world was created through it. But let me explain by a parable, for in this case the most direct route is not the shortest." And this is the tale he told:

Once there was a king who ruled a great kingdom. And one night this king had a dream about a magnificent palace. And when he awoke he remembered every detail of its dimensions: that the palace had four sides, and that each side had ten gates. And there were also nine openings heavenward, and there was reputed to be another opening of which nothing definite was known, and that was called the Mysterious Gate. And the king also remembered that this palace had contained within it the form of everything in the world: every kind of treasure, every kind of flower, and every kind of ocean. In fact, nothing was missing from that remarkable palace.

When he awoke, the king called in his seers and told them the dream. And when he called them forward to tell him its meaning, they said, "It seems, your majesty, that you were destined to have this palace built. That is why the dream came to you, for you are a king. If the dream had come to a poet, he would have written a poem about a palace. If the dream had come to a musician, he would have set music to it. But since the dream has come to you, it can only mean that the palace is intended to be brought into this world as an actual building."

When the king heard this he was pleased, for that is how he had interpreted the dream. But one matter disturbed him greatly. And he said, "By and large your reading of this dream is the same

145

as mine. But how can we solve the most difficult problem? For in the dream the palace contained everything in the world."

For a long time the seers were quiet, but at last one of them replied, "The truth is, sire, that we do not know how to reply to this question. For surely any palace that the king could have built could not fulfill that one condition. It is said that every dream loses something in its translation to reality. Perhaps you would be best to abandon such a desire, since it can surely never be fulfilled."

But the king was not at all happy with this reply. And he said to the seers, "Either I will build a palace that contains everything, or I will build no palace at all. For I know that it is incumbent on me to be true to my dream. That above all." And the king dismissed his seers, and told his servants to call in the king's architect. And so they did.

When the architect arrived the king told him his dream, in every detail. And after the architect had listened, he said: "Your wish is my command, O king, for those things that it is in my power to do. But how can I build a palace which will contain all things? After all, it is possible to contain a garden in the world, but how can the world be contained in a garden?"

And the king replied, "Go hence, architect, and wander across the land. Do not return until you are ready to announce that it is time for the palace to be built." With that the king turned away, and the audience came to an end.

Soon afterward the architect packed a few of his belongings and set out into the world, for he knew that he must discover the secret of the palace the king wanted built or else be condemned to a life of wandering. Therefore he sought everywhere to decipher the mystery. But as he journeyed through one kingdom after another, no one could tell him the solution to the riddle. Like a man obsessed, he traveled to every corner of the earth, where he sought out every experience, even those that are counted by some as sins. For there was no aspect of this world that he wanted to ignore in his search. And even though he did not succeed in solving the central mystery, he became a man of great wisdom, who was recognized and honored by all who crossed his path.

Then one day the architect heard it said that in another country there lived a wise man known as a *Tzaddik* who was said to know how to contain a kingdom in a nutshell. Therefore the architect decided to seek out this *Tzaddik*, for he had searched on every other path. For if the *Tzaddik* could contain a kingdom in a nutshell, then surely he would know how to contain everything in a single palace.

So it was that the architect journeyed to that far-off kingdom, which could be reached only by ship. It was a very dangerous journey and took many months, but at last he arrived. In a short time he succeeded in finding his way to the *Tzaddik*, for his fame had spread to every corner of that land. And when the architect spoke to the *Tzaddik*, he came directly to the point: "I have heard it said that you know the secret of how to contain a kingdom in a nutshell. Tell me, is it also possible to contain everything in the world inside a single palace?"

The *Tzaddik* replied, "Such a palace already exists."

The architect was very surprised to hear this, and he said, "But where can such a palace be found?"

And the *Tzaddik* said, "It is said that the Torah received at Mount Sinai by the Children of Israel contains within it everything in the world. And this has been proven to be true over the generations, for in the Torah my people have found the answer to every question that we have asked. So too is the Torah a palace, as it is written: *to enter into the king's palace.*

"Now it is also said that the first word of the Torah, *Bereshith*, which means 'In the Beginning,' contains within itself the entire Torah. It is also known that once the first letter of the first word, which is *Bet*, contained the entire Torah in itself. And there are those who believe that the whole Torah once fit in the dot in the center of the letter *Bet*. Those who believe this also believe that the outside of the letter is actually a map whose purpose is to lead the seeker to the center, where the secret of how to contain everything can still be found.

"In order to fulfill the command of your king, you should build the palace as he has specified, but in the shape of the letter

Bet, with his own chamber located in the place of the dot, for that place serves as the center. Then the palace will be complete in every respect. For that letter contains the Torah, and the Torah contains everything that exists. Know too, architect, that since you set out on your wanderings as a young man you have shared every experience. So it is that you too bring with you everything in the world. With the wisdom you have obtained, the king should be able to accomplish anything."

When the architect had heard what the *Tzaddik* had to say, he did not understand at first how the world could be contained in one place. But it was a long journey home from that far-off kingdom, and the architect had many months in which to consider the meaning of the *Tzaddik*'s words. When he finally reached his own country he was at once given an audience with the king, and it was then that he announced he was ready to start building the palace.

The Scribe

THE teachings and tales of Reb Nachman of Bratslav have come down to us only because one of his disciples also became his scribe. Reb Nussan of Nemerov recorded everything his *Tzaddik* said, including his long fairy tales. When Reb Nachman told these tales on the eve of the Sabbath, his Hasidim would retell the stories among themselves, until the Sabbath ended and it was permissible to write again. Then Reb Nussan would write the stories down, word for word, as close to the original as he could recall.

In all accounts it is said that Reb Nussan became a disciple of Reb Nachman's after having met him in a dream. In one version, Reb Nussan dreamed of a ladder which rose up from earth into heaven. Reb Nussan began to ascend that ladder, in order to reach the heavenly realm. But after climbing only a few rungs, he fell backward to the ground. Many times Reb Nussan attempted to ascend the ladder, and each time he climbed closer to heaven, but each time he fell backward before he reached the top. Then, at last, Reb Nussan succeeded in climbing close to the top rung of the ladder. Suddenly the figure of a man whose face was radiant appeared at the top. And this man said to Reb Nussan: "If you never allow yourself to give up hope, Nussan, you will surely reach the top." Just then Reb Nussan lost his balance and fell backward to the earth once more. At first he was dejected, but when he remembered the words of the man, he decided to try again. But then he woke up.

A year later, while on business in Bratslav, Reb Nussan decided to spend *Shabbat* at the house of Reb Nachman, in order to hear his discourse on the Torah. As Reb Nussan entered the house he found the Hasidim had already begun to pray. Slowly Reb Nussan made his way through the maze of Hasidim, and found a place just behind the Rebbe. When Reb Nachman began to distribute the wine of the *Kiddush*, and turned in the direction of Reb Nussan, their eyes met, and Reb Nachman said, "Welcome. We have already known each other a long time." Then Reb Nussan remembered the dream of the year before, and recalled the radiant face of the man who had spoken to him out of the heavens. And in this way began the lifelong bond in which Reb Nussan came to serve as Reb Nachman's scribe.

Yet, there is still another version of this meeting that has come down to us. In this rendering, Reb Nussan dreamed he was traveling in the Holy Land. There it happened that he encountered Reb Nachman by chance in Jerusalem, and Reb Nussan, who knew that Reb Nachman was the great-grandson of the Baal Shem Tov, requested a meeting. Reb Nachman agreed that they should meet, and showed Nussan the way to his house. Then he wrote the address down inside the book he was carrying with him, and gave the book to Nussan. Reb Nussan watched him disappear into the house, turned to go, and then woke up. At first he was angry because the meeting had not taken place. But it was then he decided that he must depart from Nemerov and travel to Bratslav, where Reb Nachman held his court.

The next day Reb Nussan announced his plans to his family, but it was almost a month before he could resolve his business and placate his father-in-law, who had no use for Hasidim, to take leave for Bratslav. Then on the night before his departure, one month to the day after his earlier dream, Reb Nussan dreamed again of Reb Nachman, and in this dream he was already a disciple in his court. Reb Nachman spoke to the gathering of his Hasidim, and the subject was a book. He held the book open and read from the pages one by one. The story took place in the past and in the present at the same time. The subject of the book was a dreamer, and the author of the book was his companion, who took down his every word. They traveled together to many lands, and everywhere they went the dreamer reported his dreams and the author recorded them so that nothing was lost. In this way that book had come to be written, and brought back truths to this world that had long been lost.

But once, during their travels, the dreamer disappeared inside a cave, and when he did not emerge his companion was forced to leave the land without him. From then on his life lost its purpose; he slept during the day without dreaming, and lay awake all night. Needless to say, his writing stopped. And only many years later, when he crossed a black border, did the author return to the mouth of the cave into which the dreamer had disappeared. This time he called into the cave and the voice of the dreamer answered back. The author begged the dreamer to come out so that they could resume their collaboration, but the dreamer said he could not emerge until the spirit of the author had been sought out by a living man. And it was only then that the author realized that he had left his body behind him when he had crossed over that border, and now his being consisted solely of the kernel of the spirit that had once animated his body. So too did he realize that he had been called upon by the dreamer to undertake a new task— to seek out a living man, one he could transmit the dreamer's tales to, one who could write the tales down.

It was at this point that Reb Nachman stopped reading. His court was quiet. All of his Hasidim understood that one of them was about to be chosen to write the dreamer's tales down. And like all of the others, Reb Nussan was certain he would be the chosen one.

Secrets of the Holy Tongue

REB Nachman discoursed to his Hasidim in Yiddish, his native tongue. His scribe, Reb Nussan, wrote down everything he said in Hebrew, the Holy Tongue. Thus it happened that every word that passed between them had to be translated.

One day, while Reb Nachman was speaking to his Hasidim, and Reb Nussan was writing his words down, Reb Nachman saw a look of bewilderment pass over Reb Nussan's face.

"What is it, Nussan?" asked Reb Nachman.

"Rebbe," Reb Nachman stuttered in Yiddish, "God forbid, I am afraid I have completely forgotten the Holy Tongue. It has vanished from my lips. How could this happen?"

Reb Nachman looked very grave, and was silent for a long time. Then he dismissed the other Hasidim and brought Reb Nussan into his study.

"It is said of scribes, Nussan," Reb Nachman began, "that Hebrew is inborn to them, and that they know the secrets of the Holy Tongue from the day they are born. And for four generations their descendents are also born with this blessing. And if any one in those four generations becomes a scribe, the gift is perpetuated another four generations. But if no descendent becomes a scribe within that time, the gift is lost.

"This loss you have suffered is a sign, I am afraid, Nussan, that there will be no other scribes in your family for four generations. But in the fifth generation a scribe shall be born, and because the gift has been lost to him, he will not speak the Holy Tongue."

"But Rebbe," Reb Nussan interjected, "how can there be a scribe who does not speak the Holy Tongue?"

Reb Nachman said, "It is to spare him this tragic deprivation that you have lost your language, Nussan. For in giving up the Holy Tongue you have bequeathed to your descendent what you yourself hold most precious. It will come to pass that at first the scribe who will arise from your seed will not recognize his destiny as a scribe, and will not even know that something precious has been lost. Later, when he becomes aware of his loss, he will mourn over it. And then he will rejoice when he wakes up one morning and discovers that the language has been restored to him, and has not been lost after all. So too will your soul rejoice that day, Nussan.

"By tomorrow morning, I assure you, Nussan, the Holy Tongue will be restored to you as well, for the flight of the Spirit is swift."

And so it was that when Reb Nussan arose the next morning and said the first blessing of the day, he found that he spoke the Holy Tongue once more, and it was hard for him to imagine that it had ever been lost.

Translation

ONE day a visiting Rebbe happened to sit next to Reb Nussan while he was writing down a *drash* of Reb Nachman's, and he noticed that while Reb Nachman spoke in Yiddish, Reb Nussan wrote down what he said in Hebrew. He said to Reb Nussan, "Tell me, Reb, why is it that you translate what your Rebbe says? Can you not understand it directly, without translation?"

Now Reb Nachman overheard this question, and he made the reply: "If there is one secret at the core of my teachings, it is that every sacred act is an act of transformation, in which we take what we are given, and remake it into something new. If not for the very act of translation between one realm and the next, from the heavens to the earth, how would we transform what we receive, and therefore make use of it?

"Perhaps you will understand if I put it this way: Once there was a man who wrote a *drash* which, unknown to him, turned out to be the word-for-word translation of a rare manuscript that had never been published. And this fact was not known until the manuscript was finally published fifty years after the translation. How is this possible? Because both translated, in the first place, from the same source; both learned how to read the letters written in the stars that circled their souls. And because they were born beneath the same constellation, they both read in the same dreambook, and thus translated from the same inexhaustible source.

"Now one part of my soul is rooted in the soil of Poland, one part is striving to reach the Holy Land, and one part has already arrived in that sacred place. But because of that one part rooted in *Galut*, my language is Yiddish. Yet for my words to be understood in the celestial realms and to perform the *tikkun*, the act of restoration, they must be translated. In this way it should be apparent to you that Reb Nussan is vital to my work, for if it were not for him my words would be like eyeless needles, sworn to silence. But with his help it is possible to thread the needle and for the *tikkun* to begin."

After Reb Nachman finished speaking, Reb Nussan added these words: "The truth is that what Reb Nachman speaks was originally spoken to him in Hebrew by the angels that ascend and descend Jacob's Ladder and bring him words from on high. But so that we can share these secrets, he translates what he hears into Yiddish, for that is how we best understand. My work is simply to restore his teachings to their original state, for that is what happens when I translate Reb Nachman's words into the Holy Tongue."

The Soul of Reb Nussan Journeys to the Holy Land

ONE morning, when Reb Nussan woke up, the first thought that entered his mind was that it was the Sabbath. While his wife slept late, since it was the Sabbath, he washed and prayed as he did on every Sabbath. But that day he felt at ease and at peace with the world in a way he had not felt in a very long time. Nor did he know why, but a man does not question a blessing of peace. And it seemed to him as if the garment of the Sabbath Queen, the robe of the *Shekhinah* that is woven out of light, had descended around him like an invisible cloud.

So it was that Reb Nussan was completely taken aback when his wife reminded him at midday to go to the market to buy a fish for the Sabbath—for then he realized that it was Friday, and not the Sabbath at all. And when this truth sank into him Nussan became dejected.

The next morning, when it was truly the Sabbath, Reb Nussan told Reb Nachman what had happened. Reb Nachman said: "For that half a day, Nussan, your soul celebrated the Sabbath in the Holy Land, where everything takes place one day before it does here. When your wife spoke to you your soul was called back here.

"Now it is known, Nussan, that on the day before the Sabbath, all the souls in *Galut*, in the Exile we share, strive to make their way to the Promised Land, to the Holy City of Jerusalem. But on each Sabbath there is only one soul in *Galut* that succeeds. And this Sabbath you were the guest in the Holy Land. What a shame, though, Nussan, that you could not stay for *Havdalah*!"

The Lost Menorah

THE silver menorah had been in Reb Nussan's family for four hundred years, and family tradition held that it was even older than that. Needless to say, this menorah was precious in the eyes of Reb Nussan, and so he was clutched with fear when he discovered, the morning of Erev Hanukkah, that it was missing. How could such a thing happen? Reb Nussan and his wife looked everywhere, but it was not to be found. Then Reb Nussan's wife recalled that a man who had been collecting trash to leave at the dump had come to their house with a covered wagon a few days before. Reb Nussan's wife had filled several sacks with things for him to take away—sacks of the same kind in which the menorah had been stored. Somehow he must have taken the sack with the menorah as well, and carried it off to the dump!

When Reb Nussan realized that this was the only explanation, he was devastated, for the menorah must now lie at the bottom of the deep valley that served Bratslav as the town dump. There, he was certain, it would never be found. And when this likely truth sank in, Reb Nussan became dejected. He left the house and sat under a bare tree, sinking into gloom and melancholy.

When Reb Nussan's wife saw how this loss had harmed him, she could not bear it, and she blamed herself. So she came to Reb Nachman in tears and told him all that had taken place. When Reb Nachman heard what she had to say, he left his home at once and came to Reb Nussan, who sat blankly at the foot of the tree. So lost was he in his grief that he did not even notice Reb Nachman standing above him, and he was greatly startled when the Rebbe spoke and said, "Why are you sitting here, Nussan, when it is almost Hanukkah and you do not even have a menorah with which to light the candles?"

When Reb Nussan heard these words he was so startled he leaped to his feet in anger, and then he realized it was Reb Nachman

who had spoken. But he could not understand why the Rebbe would rub salt in his wound, and he said, "Why must you remind me of this, Rebbe, at such a moment, when I have just sustained such a great loss?" And Reb Nachman said: "Because, Nussan, the menorah cannot be considered lost until someone has searched for it."

"What do you mean, Rebbe?" said Nussan. "Surely you do not think it is possible for it to be found?" "And why not, Nussan," said Reb Nachman. "If it was possible for the coffin of Joseph to be recovered even though it had sunk to the bottom of the Nile, surely it is possible for this precious menorah to be found. Waste no more time brooding, Nussan, for if you do not find it by Hanukkah, then it will surely be lost for good."

Now Hanukkah began that very evening, and in that valley was piled fifty years of trash. Still, Reb Nussan was suddenly filled with hope and determination, and he took leave of Reb Nachman and hurried off to borrow a horse, so that he could complete the task in time. He made the old horse trot as swiftly as it could, but it was noon by the time he reached the valley where the trash was dumped. He tied the horse to a tree and slowly climbed down the sides of the valley until he reached the bottom. There he was overwhelmed by the vast piles of trash which were spread out as far as his eyes could see. Still, Reb Nussan refused to be discouraged, and he waded into the trash, digging with his bare hands. Before long, however, his hands were raw and sore, and he wished he had remembered a shovel, for in his haste he had not brought one. All of a sudden Reb Nussan saw a shovel sticking up from the trash. He rushed to it and pulled it out and was completely astonished to discover that it was not only a shovel, but his own shovel as well, a rusty one that he had once thrown away. Then he knew that the shovel was a sign from heaven that there was still hope, and he continued to dig with confidence and determination.

For three hours he dug and dug, and suddenly he came upon a sack which resembled one of his own. And when he tore it open he was blinded for an instant by the reflection of silver in the sun—for he had found the lost menorah at last. Then, with tears rolling down his face and his clothes filthy from the trash, he held up the undamaged menorah and raised his voice in prayer: "*Shema Yisrael, Adonai Elohanu, Adonai Ehad*—Here O Israel, the Lord our God, the Lord is one.*"

The Tale of the Mirror

ON Simhat Torah, when the cycle of the reading of the Torah begins anew, Reb Nachman spoke to his Hasidim about the passage *And God created man in His own image, in the image of God He created him.* Reb Nachman said: "What is meant by this passage? That man was created with the attributes of the higher beings? That man was created in the likeness of the *Shekhinah?* That it is the soul of man referred to, and not the body? Perhaps all these interpretations are true. But more important is the great mystery hinted at in this passage concerning the image of God Himself. But since this mystery can be revealed only to those worthy of understanding, I shall present it in the form of a tale." And this is the tale Reb Nachman told:

When the Holy One, blessed be He, decided to create man, He wondered what he should look like. Therefore He first created a mirror and looked into it, and the image of Himself that He saw when He looked there was the image after which He formed man. After Adam and Eve had been created, God gave that mirror to them as a wedding gift, so that they would have at their disposal any truth they needed to know. All they had to do was to look into that mirror, and the answer to their question would take form in front of their eyes; and the image would remain fixed and clear until they had fully understood its meaning. Then it would disappear.

Adam and Eve greatly treasured this mirror, for from it they came to know a great many mysteries, among them that they had been created in the image of God. And so precious was the mirror to them that when they were expelled from Eden they took it with them, for they could not bear to leave it behind. But when Adam

approached the mirror for the first time after taking it out of the
Garden, he discovered to his dismay that it had grown dark; not a
single image took form within it, not even his own. But when he
began to repent of his sin by standing in the River Gihon, the
mirror gradually began to grow lighter, little by little, until a time
came when he was able to make use of it again.

Then it happened that when Eve learned the news of the
death of Abel, she took a stone and smashed the mirror, shattering
it into a thousand pieces. For she never again wanted to see the
image of one who had lived to bury her own child. From then on
nothing remained of the mirror except for those fragments, which
were divided among the children of Adam, beginning with Seth,
each of whom took the largest remaining piece. During the Flood,
however, all of these fragments were lost but one, which Noah
carried with him on the ark. This fragment that Noah preserved
still remains among men, hidden in some dark place, where light
does not illumine the secrets it reflects within. And among these
mysteries is that of the image of God, which was the first to be
reflected there. This secret is within our reach, could we but penetrate to the corner in which that mirror is hidden and permit the
light to shine on it once more.

The Mystery of the Unripe Fruit

ONE day Reb Nachman spoke to his Hasidim about the origin of souls. He said, "All souls, except for those of the *Lamed-Vov*, the Thirty-six Just Men in each generation, are suspended like sleeping infants from the Tree of Souls, where they are rocked in so many cradles. They alone hear the long note rising up from the roots, and the song echoing in the branches of the tree. They alone see the aura that surrounds the tree like the faint flame of a burning bush."

This vision of a Tree of Souls caught the fancy of all of the Hasidim, who envisioned it in their mind's eyes and were silent. But Reb Naftali, the musician, perceived in the Rebbe's words an even greater mystery, which had not been revealed. And at last he said: "Tell me, Rebbe, from whence do the souls of the *Lamed-Vov Tzaddikim* come?"

And Reb Nachman said, "Those souls are carried like seeds in the living waters which spring forth from beneath that Tree of Souls. When the waters carry them to fertile ground, they take root in that place. And that is how the souls of the *Tzaddikim* who sustain every generation come into being."

Now because he was a great musician, Reb Naftali knew that sometimes the waters of inspiration flow and all goes well, and sometimes the stream runs dry. And he wondered if this were also the case with the waters that carried the souls of the Just Men. And he said: "But tell me, Rebbe, for I am very curious to know, do such waters ever run dry? For it is well known that if not for the presence of the *Lamed-Vov Tzaddikim*, the Holy One might well bring the world to an end."

And Reb Nachman smiled because Reb Naftali was so perceptive, and he said: "Let me reply to you with a tale. It is the mystery of the unripe fruit."

Once there was a king who was famous in all the world be-

cause of the marvelous fruit of his enchanted orchard. For the
fragrance of that fruit was like the perfume of Paradise, and it had
the taste of the Garden of Eden. So prized were these fruits that
they were worth their weight in gold.

And why were these fruits so treasured? Only because of their
fragrance and taste? No; also because of the remarkable effect these
fruits had on those who ate of them. For these fortunate ones were
permitted to see the world washed free of all taints and sins. They
saw the world as it was before the Fall, even as it was before the
Shattering of the Vessels. So moved were all those who shared this
vision of purity and perfection that they carried its glow with them
all the days of their lives. And the memory of this vision sustained
them through every trial.

Now did everyone who tasted of this miraculous fruit share
the same vision? The answer is no. Many said they had seen a
beach without boundaries, surrounded by a golden glow, while
others had seen the Holy Land in all its glory and some were
certain they had reached the Garden of Eden. There were also a
few who swore to having had a vision of a pure woman dressed in
white, while others saw a body of light that was an angel, and still
others saw a star taking root in the branches of a tree. And each of
these visions was crystal clear and unforgettable. No wonder all the
world wept the year the fruit of the trees in the king's orchard did
not grow ripe.

How could such a thing happen? It was not due to an early
frost, for the winters in this kingdom were very mild. Nor was it
due to any disease. It simply happened that one day the fruit on all
the trees in the king's orchard stopped growing. When this happened, the fruit had not yet grown ripe. Nor did it wither and die
on the branch, but remained as if frozen in time, never rotting,
never growing ripe. And that fruit had none of its powers until it
grew ripe, just as it had not yet acquired a fragrance or taste.

Now it had been the custom of that king to let each inhabitant
of that kingdom taste this precious fruit when they had reached a
certain age. And all who grew up in that kingdom looked forward
to that moment and its pure vision. But now a new generation was

deprived of this blessing, and it was as if they had lost their own language, so much a part of their lives had these pure visions become.

The king was greatly distressed by this turn of events. Above all, he wished to know what spell had caused the enchanted orchard to be robbed of its powers. Therefore he called in all of his wise men and asked for their advice. They consulted among themselves, and finally told the king that his enemies had caused this blight. They advised him to declare war, in order to release the frozen fruit. But the king did not heed this advice, and instead he called in all of his astrologers. And they gazed at the stars, and consulted among themselves, and finally declared that the trouble had been caused by a constellation of stars, which in time would set itself aright. But the king could not wait. And he called in all of his soothsayers, and they sought the mystery in every kind of divination—in fire and in water, in coffee grounds and in tortoise shells. And there they read signs and symbols that explained many a mystery. But this did not include the mystery of the unripe fruit.

Then the king became dejected, and lost the desire to rule his kingdom. And for a time his memory of the pure vision began to fade and to be forgotten. He had reached the point where he was about to abdicate his throne and go into exile when a wandering beggar arrived in that kingdom. Like all strangers who crossed the border into that country, he was brought before the king. Once more the king repeated the tale of the unripe fruit; the beggar listened to the tale and then asked, "How is the orchard watered?" The king replied, "There are four rivers that water the orchard." And the beggar said, "What is the source of these waters?" The king replied, "All stem from the same source—from a fountain in the center of the orchard." And the beggar said, "Let us examine this fountain." The king agreed to this, and together with all his court he accompanied the beggar there. And when they reached the fountain they found that it no longer flowed out of the rock. And when they examined it, they found that the fountain was blocked by a small stone, no larger than the seed of a peach. Yet that small stone had held back the fresh waters, and therefore the waters that remained had grown stagnant, and had caused the fruit to remain unripe.

That is when the king realized that the source of his kingdom's blessing lay in the water, not in the fruit. For it was the water which nourished the fruit. And what was it that gave this water its great potency? But it is impossible to answer that question without revealing an even greater mystery. If this mystery should be revealed, everyone would be nourished merely by comprehending it. No one would any longer eat or drink. Everything in the world would stop. Therefore this mystery cannot be revealed.

And how did that small stone come to rest in that place? The wise men said that they were right to accuse the king's enemies, for surely it was no accident. And the astrologers said that they were right in saying that the evil would pass. And as for the soothsayers, they foretold a time of abundance. And the wandering beggar? He has been put in charge of the king's orchard, to see that the fruit grows ripe.

The Book That Was Burned

BETWEEN Purim and Pesach, when Reb Nachman was in Lemberg, he went into a special room and cried a great deal of the time. At last he called Reb Shimon and said: "I have a terrible dilemma, and there is no one I can turn to for advice. In my house in Bratslav there is a book in which I invested my soul. And because that book contains truths taken from on high, it has already caused me a great tragedy. For the existence of that manuscript caused my son, Shlomo Ephraim, to lose his life. And now I have heard a *bat kol*, a heavenly voice, which has announced that if that book is not burned my own life will be lost."

Shimon then spoke up and said, "In that case, Rebbe, how can there be any doubt about what you must do? If your life is at stake, surely the book must be burned!"

Reb Nachman relied, "The decision is not as easy to make as you may think, Shimon. I have already been loyal to that book, and I have paid a great price for having done so. For in that book there are mysteries revealed that I cannot even hint at. The Ari was once in such a predicament. It happened that he was studying the sacred *Zohar* with his disciples, when he said, 'Here lies hidden a great secret, but it is too dangerous to reveal.' Then his disciples begged him to interpret that passage. At last he succumbed to their entreaties, and he revealed the secret to them. But no sooner had he done so, than he heard a *bat kol* decree that his son Moses would die within seven days. And when the Ari returned to his home, he discovered that his young son had suddenly taken ill, and was consumed with fever. And even before the week had passed, the boy died."

When Shimon heard this tale, a shiver passed through his body, for he realized how great was the Rebbe's dilemma. He realized that a decision of this magnitude could only be made by Reb Nachman, and he remained silent. As far as Shimon was concerned, the life of the Rebbe was the most precious thing in the world. But for Reb Nachman the truths revealed in that book were so precious that he seriously considered sacrificing his life to preserve them.

Then Reb Nachman said, "All of the secrets contained in that book were revealed to me in dreams, for in dreams the soul is free to ascend into the highest heavens. And there were great obstacles I had to overcome in order to recall all that I learned there when I awoke, for the angels did everything in their power to make me forget. Thus I paid a great price in order to bring this book into being, and its continued existence in this world will now cost me my life." And Reb Nachman broke out weeping, and Shimon saw that his heart was broken, for never before had he seen the Rebbe weep that way. Then Shimon repeated his belief that Reb Nachman's life was more precious than the book. He said, "If there is even a thought that our Rebbe's life depends on this, it is far better, in my opinion, to burn the book so that the Rebbe will remain alive."

Reb Nachman weighed these words, then he said, "If the book is burned, I will still depart this world at some time, and the holiness of this book is inexpressible. Yet there are many other truths that I am permitted to reveal, which would also be lost if I leave this world prematurely. And it is these truths and not my own life that must be weighed in the balance." Then Reb Nachman was silent for a long time, and Shimon saw that he was weighing this matter in his mind, and he dared not interrupt.

Suddenly Reb Nachman reached into his pocket and took out a key and handed it to Shimon and said, "If the book must be burned, here is the key to the bookcase in which it is kept. A second copy is to be found in the trunk beneath my bed. Go quickly, before I change my mind. Run, don't walk. Take a carriage and go to Bratslav and see to it that the copies of the book are burned. And do not burn only one copy and keep the other, for that would be the same as not burning either one." And when Shimon took the key from the Rebbe's hand, he saw that his hand was shaking. And he did not manage to say anything, but nodded and hurried off to complete the terrible task. For next to taking a life, what is more terrible than burning a book?

Shimon immediately hired a carriage to go to Bratslav. But when he tried to climb into the carriage, he suddenly fell and hurt his leg badly, and it pained him so greatly he feared it might be broken. He recognized at once that there must be forces trying to stop him from fulfilling the mission and he was determined to continue, despite his pain. So Shimon ordered the driver to help him into the carriage and drive to Bratslav at once. Thus the carriage proceeded to Bratslav, where Shimon intended to direct the other Hasidim to burn the books in his presence.

But when the carriage finally reached Bratslav, Shimon discovered that all the pain in his leg had disappeared. He hurried and took the two copies of the book from where they were hidden, and set a fire in the stove and burned the books, and their truths were returned to smoke and rose into the heavens, from whence they had come.

About this book Reb Nussan, Reb Nachman's scribe, adds the

following: "When I was writing down the book for Reb Nachman that was burned according to his order, the Rebbe said to me, 'If only you knew what it is that you write.' And I said to him, 'Surely I do not know.' And he said, 'You don't know how much you don't know.' "

As Above, So Below

In Memory of Nathan Schwartz

ON the ninth *yahrzeit* of his father, Reb Naftali Hertz, which fell on a Sabbath, Reb Nussan of Nemerov came to the *Beit Knesset* for *Maariv*. No sooner had he stepped inside the House of Prayer, however, then he discovered that he had lost his voice and could neither pray nor sing. While he was wondering how this could have happened, the *gabbai*, Reb David, approached Reb Nussan and informed him that Reb Nachman had assigned the honor of the first *aliyah* to him. Reb Nussan whispered that he had lost his voice and would be unable to accept this honor. And when the *gabbai* relayed this information to Reb Nachman, the Rebbe replied: "Tell Nussan he has been chosen instead to take the Torah out of the Ark and to return it there." And when Reb Nussan was told this, he nodded his head in agreement, for this honor required no use of his voice.

The time came to read that week's portion from the Torah. Reb Nussan ascended to the Ark and opened the curtain hanging before it, known as the *parochet*, and reached inside and took out the ancient scroll, which had been passed down for many generations. And as he lifted it up, the bells of the silver ornaments on the handles of the Torah, known as *rimonim*, began to tinkle so that it seemed as if he heard a distant voice calling out to him. And when he picked up the *Sefer Torah* he found it exceptionally light— it seemed as if the Torah had leaped into his arms and was resting like a feather on his right shoulder. Moreover, he felt so light walking with the Torah that he almost had to hold himself down so

as to keep from floating away. And as he held the Torah he felt as if he had stepped into the presence of his father, and into the shelter of his embrace.

Almost reluctantly, Reb Nussan took the Torah down from his shoulder and held it between his hands while the *hazan* lifted off the decorative cover, now quite worn, and uncovered the scroll of the Torah. And as Reb Nussan stood there while the words of the Torah were read, his thoughts insisted on turning to his departed father, who had so often stood before the Ark himself and whose presence he sensed that day more so than at any time since his death.

Before long that week's *sidrah* had been read, and it was time to return the Torah to the Ark. Reb Nussan picked up the wooden handles of the Torah and held it while the *hazan* replaced the cover. Then he rested the Torah against his shoulder once more and carried it back to the Ark, and with considerable emotion he replaced it in the Ark and closed the curtain.

No sooner was the curtain closed, than Reb Nussan's voice was restored, and when he returned to his place he was able to chant the *Alenu*, the closing prayer, with the others, and to join in the *Kaddish*.

After this Reb Nachman began his *D'var Torah*, and it seemed to Reb Nussan that he spoke directly to him, and kept his eyes fixed on Nussan's own. The subject of Reb Nachman's *D'var Torah* was the Kabbalistic concept of "as above, so below." First Reb Nachman said: "What is meant by 'as above, so below'? It is said that the *Merkavah*, the heavenly Chariot, is carried by the angels. But it is also said that the angels are carried by the *Merkavah*. What is above supports what is below, and what is below, what is above." Then he related this mystical premise to that week's *sidrah*, *Va-ayra*, which concerns the Egyptian plagues. Reb Nachman said: "After the ninth plague Moses began to despair, for despite all his efforts, Pharoah had remained unmoved, and still refused to set his people free. Moses offered up a prayer to the Holy One, blessed be He, and in reply he was told that although no change was discernable in this world, it was clear in the invisible realm that each of those plagues was a necessary step that could not be avoided.

"So too is it with prayer," Reb Nachman continued. "Often it seems as though our prayers have remained unanswered, when in fact the necessary changes are being made ready, for heaven has to be prepared before anything can be manifested on earth." And to Reb Nussan these words had a strange relevance which he could not quite explain to himself. For Reb Nachman's words formed a window in which an ocean of mysteries could be seen taking form, its waves rushing towards him and then retreating beyond his grasp.

After the service, Reb Nussan approached Reb Nachman and told him of his strange experience with the *Sefer Torah* that day, and of how his voice, which had been lost, was restored the moment he had returned the Ark to the Tabernacle. Reb Nachman was very moved by this, and he said, "Know, Nussan, that every departed soul clings to the scroll of the Torah on its *yahrzeit*, when that *yahrzeit* falls on the Sabbath. So it was that your father's soul was clinging to the Torah today. And so that you might be reunited for this brief moment, his soul saw to it that your voice was lost, so that you would receive that honor instead. Thus you were able to embrace your father's soul when you held the Torah in your arms. And at the same time the two of you were able to embrace the scroll of the Torah together. This is what is meant when we say 'as above, so below.' "

A Crown of Prayers

AFTER a long and difficult journey to the Holy Land, Reb Nussan finally reached the Holy City of Jerusalem. The first place he sought out was the *Kotel*, the Western Wall that is all that remains of the Temple built by King Solomon. No sooner did he enter into the presence of the Wall than Reb Nussan realized its level of *kedushah*, of holiness, was even far greater than he had expected. And when he finally stood before the Wall, he was amazed to find every crack in it stuffed with the prayers of the ages. He himself, as was the custom, wrote down a prayer on a slip of paper, folded it carefully, and found a place for it in one of the crevices between the stones of the Wall. At last he prayed before the Wall, and said *Kaddish* in memory of his departed father, and at the moment he finished praying a single raindrop fell from the sky and ran down his cheek, as if it were a tear.

On his return to Bratslav, Reb Nussan described to Reb Nachman his travels in the Holy Land, and he especially emphasized the wonders of the Wall. Then he said to Reb Nachman, "But tell me, Rebbe, how is it possible for the Holy One to take into account so many prayers?"

And Reb Nachman replied, "To understand how, you must first know the history of the Western Wall. For when the building of the Temple in Jerusalem had been completed, and the Temple stood perfect in its beauty, the *Shekhinah*, the Divine Presence, descended from the celestial realms and rested upon it; and the Lord chose the Western Wall, and He said: 'The Divine Presence shall never be removed from the Western Wall.' Since then the Divine Presence has rested eternally upon the Wall, hovering in hidden and mysterious waves.

"But when the allies of the forces of darkness tore down our House of Glory—may it be rebuilt in our days—the angels on high descended and spread their wings over the Western Wall, and a

Voice went forth, and proclaimed: 'Never shall the Western Wall be destroyed.' And the commander entrusted with tearing down that Wall backed away, and retreated from that place. Later he told Caesar he let it stand so that succeeding generations would be able to gaze upon it and see what a glorious thing Caesar had conquered and destroyed.

"After the destruction of the Temple a dove was seen to appear at the Wall on the eve of *Tisha B'Av*, a dove among doves. And that dove would appear during the night and join Israel in mourning. Among the people it was understood that the dove was the Divine Presence, still in mourning over the loss of her Sanctuary on earth. But very few have been found worthy of seeing the Divine Presence hovering over the Wailing Wall, as it is now known. For sometimes—very rarely—it has happened that an image of a woman, clad in black, has appeared on the face of the Wall, and she has been overheard to say: 'Console yourself, my son; there is yet hope that the Children of Israel will be restored to their inheritance, for surely I shall have mercy on them.'

"The northern corner of the Wall is where the Divine Presence is believed to have revealed herself. And anyone who stands in that place, before those stones, and prays—that prayer flows from the very heart of the worshiper to the *Shekhinah* herself, who then conveys it to the Holy One, blessed be He. And there are those who say that the Holy One receives those prayers directly, for He stands behind the Wall, and from there peers through the crevices and keeps vigil over the sons of men, seeing but not seen.

"You should know too, Nussan, that the prayers in the cracks of the Wall are but one portion of the prayers that ascend, which the angel Sandalphon daily weaves into garlands of prayer, which he adjures to ascend as crowns for the supreme King of Kings. For each of these garlands requires six hundred thousand prayers to form a single crown of prayer for the Holy One, blessed be He, to wear while He sits on His Throne of Mercy."

Reb Nussan asked, "But Reb Nachman, how long does it take for so many prayers to accumulate?"

Reb Nachman said, "In the time it has just taken you to

breathe in and out one time, Sandalphon has completed a new crown and given it to the Holy One to wear."

Reb Nussan asked, "But how is that possible? Surely it would take a day or two to accumulate enough of the prayers of Israel to form a single crown?"

Reb Nachman said, "That may be true enough, Nussan. But you must realize that there are many kinds of prayers. In fact, everything in existence has its own prayer, which it repeats at least three times every day. There is the prayer of the rain, and the prayer of the golden coin buried in a black box, as well as all the prayers in the cracks in the Wall. Then there are the prayers of all the sunsets never seen—prayers closed like sleeping flowers, prayers whose fire is forgotten, whose darkness is not enough. Listen . . . ," said Reb Nachman, gesturing toward the window, and as he did, Reb Nussan was certain that he could hear a multitude of prayers rising up, where before there had only been silence, " . . . there is also the prayer of the daughter who waits for the seasons like a tree, her wishes silent. And the prayer of the son who waits for the fruit to fall, for the seeds to break open in the earth.

"These are the prayers the angels take up together, that fuse to form the crown of prayers they receive in return. But you should know, Nussan, that there is one prayer which in itself suffices to create a crown of its own, and this is the crown which the Holy One, blessed be He, loves to wear above all. And this is the prayer that the newborn child brings with him into this world from the dark sun of its source."

Three

THE GOLDEN DOVE

The Golden Dove

And he sent forth a dove.
Gen. 8:8

ONE night Reb Nachman of Bratslav was awakened from his sleep by the sound of knocking, which seemed to come from his bedroom window. Startled, he sat up and saw that a bird was beating its wings against the windowpane. Then Reb Nachman did not hesitate, but leaped from bed and opened the window, and the bird flew inside and perched upon his study stand, near where the pages of the Torah lay open. In that instant the room became illumined as if the moon had slipped inside. And Reb Nachman saw that the bird was a golden dove, whose feathers shone as if they were woven of moonlight. And he averted his gaze, for he knew he was in the presence of a powerful spirit.

Before his eyes the dove was transformed into a beautiful woman, pale as moonlight. She wore robes of white, of a substance that seemed to consist of woven light. And Reb Nachman recognized her at once, although he had never stood directly before her. For it was the *Shekhinah*, the Sabbath Queen and Bride of God, who filled the room with her presence.

And the *Shekhinah* said, "Know, Nachman, that you are a blessing unto the generations." When he heard this, words rose up within him, and he said, *"My dove in the hollows of the rock, show me your face, let me hear your voice."* And the *Shekhinah* said, "Let me tell you a tale." And Reb Nachman felt himself to be an empty vessel, and waited for her words, ready to receive them. And at the first word she spoke he was transported to a faraway land, where he experienced all that she described as if it were happening to him. And this is the tale that the *Shekhinah* told:

Once there was a king, the ruler of a great kingdom, who one night had a vivid and unforgettable dream. In this dream he found himself riding in a caravan, which threaded its way through the

desert. The caravan journeyed for what seemed a great distance, through the sweltering heat. At last it came to a modest oasis, where there was a small freshwater pool that bubbled up from under the earth, and in the center of the oasis grew a single palm tree. But in the desert that pool appeared like the very Garden of Eden to those in the caravan, including the king. The travelers stopped there to refresh themselves. And after they had eaten and rested, they reluctantly departed, for they had to resume their journey.

Now in the dream the king was not a king, but merely another member of the caravan. In fact, his only possession was a lead cup, which had been handed down in his family for many generations. That cup was battered and worn, for it had always been in use, and its value was very little except to him. Still, it was his only possession, and reminded him of much that had gone before him; and thus it was quite precious in his eyes.

Then it happened that after they had departed from that oasis and had traveled for a considerable distance, the king realized that he did not have the cup—it was missing. Suddenly he recalled that he had left it by that pond in the oasis and had forgotten to take it with him. And he also realized he could not leave it behind. But he dared not tell the others that this was the reason he was going back there. They would surely argue that the cup was not worth the danger of being stranded alone in the desert. And if he debated with them, he would be left even further from the site where the cup was to be found. So instead he told the others who rode before and after him that he had left a golden dove at the oasis. And when they heard this, they all told him to hurry back to retrieve it, for such a precious object could not be abandoned.

So it was that the king made his way back to that oasis, but when he finally reached it and searched for the cup, he could not find it. It was not where he thought he had left it. The king was greatly distressed when he discovered this, for he had assumed that if he risked the dangers of leaving the caravan to return there, the cup would at least be his reward. He became determined not to give up the search, for in the desert the sand quickly covers over everything. Therefore the king began to dig in the sand. And before long his hands came upon something about the size of a cup. Then he dug faster, until it suddenly became apparent that it was not his cup he had found, but something else. At first this realization disappointed him, but then he began to wonder what was buried there. Perhaps it was only a bone, for those were scattered through the desert, having accumulated over many generations. His hand brushed away the sand, and all at once the object gleamed brightly in the sunlight, and to his complete amazement the king found that it was a golden dove, a remarkable treasure. Not only was it fashioned out of the purest gold, but it was set about with rubies, moonstones, emeralds, turquoise, mother-of-pearl, and diamonds. And in the beak of the dove there was a golden twig, from which hung three golden bells like buds.

The king was awed as he studied the golden dove, for it was lifelike in its perfection. And he understood that a miracle had taken place—his leaden cup had somehow become that golden dove. For a moment he took the golden dove in his two hands and saw that it fit inside his closed palms. But at that instant he felt the dove begin to stir, as if it were alive. The king was so startled he opened his hands, and the dove flapped its wings and flew away. Astounded, he watched it fly off until it became a speck on the horizon. And at that moment he awoke in the royal chamber and realized he was still the king. But this recognition meant little to him at that moment—for he had never valued the whole of his kingdom the way he had treasured that golden dove. And the first thought that crossed his mind was that he would trade his kingdom for the golden dove, so great was his longing to possess it. Then the fact that he could command such a dove to be made crossed his mind. And although it would not be alive, at least it would console him, for the absence of the dove was palpable, so vividly was the dove's image imprinted upon his memory.

Therefore the king had it announced that any goldsmith in the land who could create such a golden dove would be greatly rewarded. And he had it described the way he had seen it in his dream. But even though every goldsmith in that kingdom attempted to create a golden dove to the king's precise specifications, none of their creations resembled the dove of the king's dream, and all were shortly melted down again. When the last of these attempts had failed in the king's eyes, and he was about to give up hope his dream could be brought into being, a wandering beggar arrived at the palace who insisted he had brought a golden dove for the king to examine, although he refused to show it to the guards, saying it was for the king's eyes only. The guards did not really believe that the beggar possessed such a treasure, but they had orders to report such things, and this is what they did.

Now since the king had no hope left for the goldsmiths of the kingdom, he did not dismiss the beggar out of hand, but ordered that he be brought before him. And when the beggar arrived, the king saw that he had a sack slung over his shoulder, and the king was very curious to see what he had brought. He said to the beggar, "Waste no time, old man, but show me what you have in your sack." "I have come a great distance to do just that," said the beggar, "for I am merely a messenger." "And who is it that has sent such a ragged messenger?" asked the king. "He who has sent me is also a king," said the beggar, "whose kingdom is far away." "If that is so," said the king, "why has he sent such an impoverished messenger?" "That was the king's decision," said the beggar. "He knew that I had to travel through many countries in order to reach you, so he decided I would be safer if I appeared to be penniless. If I rode on a noble horse, I might be the target of robbers." This made sense to the king, and he said, "Let me see what you have brought." But the beggar said, "The king who sent me insisted that I was to reveal this gift to you, and to you alone. And he said that once you had seen it, you would understand why." Now the king was suspicious about this, but he was also very curious, so he signaled for his guards to leave. And when the guards had withdrawn, the beggar waited no longer, but opened his sack and took out a golden dove. Not only was it made of gold with precious gems arranged as the king had described, but it was identical in every respect to the golden dove of his dream! The king was speechless, and stared at the dove with disbelief, for it truly existed in the waking world and was not merely a dream. The king held out his hands, and the beggar placed the golden dove there, and no sooner did the king's hands encircle the dove's body than he realized it was throbbing and alive. Although it appeared to the eye to consist entirely of gold, yet it was alive. This was far more than the king had believed could ever be possible, for even when he had imagined finding a golden dove exactly like that of his dream, he did not dare to hope it would be alive.

And the king looked at the beggar and realized he had brought him a great treasure, priceless and beyond words. And he wondered who it was who had sent it to him, and how long ago the messenger had set out, since it had been exactly three months since the king's dream had taken place. He asked the beggar, who said, "I set out on this journey three years ago, sire." And the king could not understand this at all, for how could this distant king know what he would dream even before he himself had dreamed it? He protested to the beggar that such knowledge was impossible, and the beggar replied, "My king, your majesty, has an enchanted mirror in which he can peer into the future, and there he can see anything and everything, even dreams which have yet to be dreamed. And when he saw the dream of the golden dove that was winging its way to you, he recognized how much you would long for it once you had awakened, and therefore he decided to send you the golden dove, for he knew that you were destined to receive it. For he had the golden dove in his possession but he realized that the time had come when it must be transmitted to another. That fortunate one is yourself, my lord."

When the king heard this he could bearly believe his ears. And he began to realize that there was an even greater mystery here than had been revealed so far. Therefore he beckoned the beggar to continue, and he said, "This golden dove is much older than you could ever imagine, O king, for it has been in existence since before the very creation of the world, and in each generation there is one who is destined to receive it. It has belonged to my ruler ever since he began his reign, but that was many years ago, and now the time has come for the dove to be delivered to you."

"And what is it that I am supposed to do with the dove?"

asked the king. "That I do not know," said the beggar. "For the
king did not tell me any more than what I have just told you."
"But tell me please," pleaded the king, "do you at least know
something about the dove itself?" "No, your majesty, I do not,"
said the beggar. "And now I must go. For the king commanded
that I must begin my journey back on the same day you receive
the dove, within the same hour. And thus I must not delay any
longer." And as the king stood there, with the golden dove
perched on his hand, the beggar bowed and took his leave. And
as soon as he had departed, the king realized that he had many
more questions for the beggar about the powers of the golden
dove, and he ordered his guards to find him and bring him back
at once. But even though they continued to search all that day
and the next, the beggar was nowhere to be found and was never
seen again in that kingdom.

So it was that the king came into possession of one of the
wonders of the world while still ignorant of its powers and of its
purpose in his life. Yet he did not regret all that had happened, for
the golden dove had already given his life a new meaning and he
longed to devote himself to probing its mystery.

At first the king thought he would build a magnificent golden
cage in which to keep the golden dove, for he did not doubt that it
was a unique and invaluable treasure. But he realized that such a
treasure would cause great envy among the kings in the surrounding kingdoms, who might judge it worthy of going to war to obtain. Then the king understood why the beggar had insisted on
showing him the golden dove when he was alone, for its existence
was something that had to be kept secret. The king then called
upon his most loyal servant, and when he appeared, the king told
him to take the golden dove to one of the chambers on the top floor
of the palace and to keep it there and attend to its needs. The
servant was filled with awe to see such a wonder, both alive and
inanimate at the same time. But when he took it in his hands they
sank from its weight, for it was as heavy as solid gold. And he
looked at the golden dove and found that it did not seem to be the
least bit alive, although the sculpture was very lifelike. And when

the king saw this he became terrified that the dove had died, and snatched it back from the servant. But the instant it rested in his hands, the dove was as light as any living bird and flapped its wings.

Both king and servant were amazed to see this, and the king understood he had just learned one of the secrets of the golden dove—that it was alive when it was in his hands, but when it left his hands it became nothing more than a golden sculpture. The king made the servant vow to keep silent about all that he had seen, and the king decided to retain possession of the golden dove himself. He brought it to his own chamber and let it make its home there, for he did not doubt that the dove preferred to remain alive, and this appeared to be possible only when it was in his possession.

A week passed, in which the king spent a great deal of time in the presence of the golden dove. But so far he had discovered nothing more about it, except that it seemed to be free of the need to eat and drink. For the dove ignored all food and drink he set out for it, yet it did not seem to suffer from hunger pangs, nor did it change its size. So the king accepted that it was enchanted, and in its enchantment was free of such needs.

Now in that kingdom there lived a sorcerer, who spent his days in the study of the Torah and his nights in the study of the stars. In this way he had discerned the secret link between them, for all the truths which are revealed in the Torah can be discerned in the stars, though the mystery of how to read the stars has been discovered by very few. And the wisdom of this sorcerer was known far and wide in the land.

So it was that while the king was certain the golden dove possessed miraculous powers, he was not able to discern what these powers were, nor how to bring them under his control. The king asked his wise men for advice, and they told him to send for the sorcerer who knew how to read the stars, for surely the mystery of the golden dove could be found there.

The king did as they suggested and sent a messenger in a golden carriage drawn by two of the finest horses in the royal stable, one black and one white. Now when the messenger arrived

the sorcerer was studying the pages of the Torah. He was reading
the passage where Noah sent out first a raven and then a dove to
see if the waters had receded. And when he looked out the window
and saw the two horses pull up, one black and one white, he knew
at once that this must be a sign. Therefore he agreed to accompany
the royal messenger at once, and the horses sped back to the kingdom as if their hooves rode upon the wind.

When the sorcerer arrived, the king took him into his own
chamber at once and showed him the golden dove. The king explained how it was transformed into a golden object when held by
anyone but himself. And the sorcerer looked at the dove with
wonder and said, "Let me take it in my hands." So the king gave it
to him, and as soon as it touched the sorcerer's hands it flapped its
wings and took flight, flying around the chamber seven times before returning to the hands of the king, who regarded all that he
had seen with astonishment. Then the sorcerer said, "What is it
that you wish to know about this dove, sire?" The king replied, "I
would like to know its history and its powers." And no sooner did
he say this than the dove took wing from the king's hands, flew out
the window, and vanished. The king was distraught, for what if
the dove never came back? But all at once they heard the sound of
the beating of wings and the dove flew back inside, in its beak an
olive branch, with three ripe olives on it. It landed in the king's
hands, as before, and he took the olive branch from its beak and
observed the olives with amazement. At last he said: "But there are
no olive trees in this part of the world!" The sorcerer replied,
"That is right. For that olive branch has surely come from the
Holy Land, for in this way the dove has replied to your question."
The king was confused by this, and said, "Please, interpret its
meaning for me." And the sorcerer said, "This dove, which just
flew so far away and returned in the blink of an eye, is surely a
messenger, bearing messages from the Supreme King on high to
this world, as well as from here to on high. I discerned this when
the dove circled the room seven times, hinting that it had descended from the highest heaven. Now, by bringing the olive
branch the dove has demonstrated how it serves as a messenger, for

it bore your question on its wings, and the olive branch is the reply. Let me explain.

"As everyone knows," the sorcerer continued, "Noah sent out a dove to see if the waters had receded from the land. The first time he sent forth the dove it found no place to perch, and returned to the ark, for the waters still covered the face of the earth. The second time the dove returned with a freshly picked olive branch, to signify that the trees had emerged from the sinking waters. And the third time the dove did not return. This golden dove which has come into your possession is likewise a messenger. This I discerned from the presence of the olive branch. And I do not doubt that its value to you shall be a precious as was that dove to Noah. Know too that the dove of Noah was one of the seven things created before the creation of the world. And if that is so, this means that Noah's dove was eternal, making it possible that this enchanted dove, which has fallen to you from heaven, may be the very dove of Noah!"

The king regarded this remarkable turn of events as an enigma which continued to unravel before his eyes. And he said, "How can you discern all these truths?" And the sorcerer said, "I merely serve as the vessel, through which the voice of the golden dove speaks." And the king marveled at the mysteries that had been revealed and the mysteries still concealed. "If you are able to receive the message of the dove so clearly while merely in its presence," said the king, "perhaps you will be able to hear its voice even more clearly if you hold it in your hands."

So the sorcerer took the golden dove into his two hands, and closed his palms lightly around it, so that he could feel the regular beating of its wings against his hands. And before long he heard the voice of the dove rise up in his soul, and when he spoke he translated its words into his own, and he said, "This dove was indeed created even before the heavens and the earth were brought into being. So too was it the dove of Noah, for at that time it was first incarnated as a living creature. For before it became a living being it existed in heaven without shape or form, like all of the other angels and spirits that inhabit the heavens. It lived a long life

as the dove of Noah, and when it died a natural death it returned
to its prior existence as a spirit being. In this way it continued to
serve as a messenger—bearing the prayers of the righteous of each
generation to Paradise in its beak, and bringing back the blessings
that are dispensed from above. Eventually, however, the dove
came into the possession of King Solomon, the wise and great
monarch who built the Temple in Jerusalem."

"How did that happen?" asked the king, who had heard, as
had all the world, of the greatness of King Solomon, and who was
very curious to know everything about the miraculous dove that
had so suddenly illumined his life. And the sorcerer continued to
translate all that he learned, and said, "During his long reign King
Solomon invariably made the right decision, but once it happened
that he greatly erred and became vulnerable to the powers of Asmodeus, the king of demons. He entrusted Asmodeus with his
magic ring, because Asmodeus had promised to reveal a great secret to him if he did. Then Asmodeus picked up Solomon from
where he sat on his throne and hurled him hundreds of miles, so
that he landed in a foreign country, where he became a wandering
beggar. Everywhere he went he insisted he was Solomon, but all
regarded him as a madman. During his wanderings he eventually
found work as the assistant to a blacksmith, whose son wanted to
be a goldsmith. Now Solomon, who knew many things, was himself a master goldsmith, and he taught the blacksmith's son, whose
skill so increased that he became the goldsmith for the king.

"One day Solomon asked the young goldsmith to be permitted
to make a gift for the king, and the goldsmith agreed and supplied
him with all that he needed. And when King Solomon had put his
hands to the gold to hammer it out, the divine dove concealed itself
inside the gold, and Solomon had only to hammer lightly against
the gold and it fell away, revealing the perfect dove beneath it.

"Soon afterward Solomon was amazed to discover that the
warmth of his hands was all that was needed to bring the dove to
life. It was also Solomon who, in his great wisdom, discovered how
the dove could become invisible. This came about when he took out
a mirror and held it before the golden dove. All at once the dove

vanished from his sight, although it could still be seen clearly in the mirror. That is when Solomon understood that the dove could be made invisible by capturing its image in a mirror. And how was it restored to this dimension? Simply by covering the mirror with a cloth. When the cloth was lifted the golden dove reappeared in the room, and the mirror ceased to reflect its presence.

"Now after the dove had fallen into his hands, Solomon was loathe to let it go. But because he had promised the goldsmith to use the gold to make a treasure for the king, he kept his word. For he knew that if he took the golden dove, the goldsmith would lose his life. Therefore Solomon gave it to the goldsmith, who gave it to the king.

"Now when the king received that dove from the goldsmith, he recognized at once that it was too skillfully crafted to have been made by his own servant, and he asked the goldsmith to tell him who, in truth, had created that astonishing treasure. The goldsmith then confessed that it was the work of Solomon, and the king had Solomon brought to him; in this way he was eventually set free from his exile. But that is another story. What concerns us is the golden dove.

"Now the cities of men that are built up out of the sand return to sand as well, and in time it happened that the king for whom Solomon had made the golden dove passed away, and before many generations had passed, the city was covered with sand, its existence unknown. So too was the golden dove lost beneath the sand, and there it lay until it was discovered one day by the traveler Rabbah bar bar Hannah, who had left a caravan and returned to the spot where it was buried to say the prayer after meals, which he had forgotten to say. But before returning there he told the others in the caravan that he was returning for a golden dove, so that they would not argue with him about his decision to turn back. And because in the eyes of God the prayers of man are equal to the most precious treasures, the Holy One had seen to it that the falsehood Rabbah had told was absolved, and the golden dove buried so long was at last rediscovered. For as Rabbah finished praying he looked down and saw an object buried in the sand that glittered in the moonlight. And when he dug it out he discovered, to his complete astonishment, that it was the golden dove.

"Then, as Rabbah held the golden dove in his hands, it began to stir, as if it were alive. Rabbah was so startled at this that he almost dropped the dove, but he accepted the miracle, for he felt as if he had entered an enchanted realm. Then the thought crossed his mind that perhaps the golden dove, which had been buried there so long, was cold, and needed the warmth of his hands. So he held it in his hands for a while, and when he opened them he saw that the golden dove was alive, and at that instant the dove flapped its wings and took flight.'"

Now when the king had heard the tale of Rabbah and the golden dove a shiver passed down his spine. For he had not forgotten his own dream in which he had returned to the oasis to recover the leaden cup and had instead discovered the golden dove. And in that moment he had a great revelation and recognized for the first time how clearly the hand of fate had determined all that had taken place.

Then the king came back to the present. He wondered why the golden dove had been revealed to him and longed to know what expectations fate had of him. He put this question to the sorcerer, who was still holding the dove. The sorcerer said, "You are right, sire, in assuming that the golden dove has been given to you for a purpose, for it is the messenger of destiny and never appears unless it is needed. Further, no one—not even a king—can ever possess the golden dove. It is a gift sent at the behest of the Holy One, remaining only as long as the blessing it brings is received. And such is the nature of this blessing that in order to be fully received it must be transmitted as well. And if it is refused the golden dove will be gone before another day has passed."

These words did not surprise the king, for he had sensed even from his own dream that the golden dove could be lost as suddenly as it had been found. As with Rabbah, the dove in his dream had flown away from him, and now that he had recovered it once more he considered himself blessed. From that moment on the king

knew he would be willing to undertake whatever task the golden
dove had brought him, for he knew he would be fulfilling his own
destiny. And the king said, "What then is the purpose for which I
have received the golden dove?" For now it was no longer merely
the mystery of the golden dove that was being revealed, but his
own fate as well. And the sorcerer said, "You have surely heard
that as a sign of the covenant between God and Noah the rainbow
was brought into being. It is little known, but that very rainbow,
the first of its kind, still exists, although it is invisible to all but the
truly righteous, who glimpse it from time to time. Until that rainbow was created, heaven and earth were separated, having become
severed as a consequence of the Fall. In each of the evil generations
that followed, heaven removed itself even further. At the same
time, the more removed heaven was, the more evil flourished on
earth, trying to fill the void made by the absence of good. And had
God not brought on the Flood, heaven would have become separated to such an extent that any possibility of having its earthly link
restored would have been lost forever. After the Flood, when the
waters began to subside, the absence of evil brought the heavens
closer to earth, and God created the rainbow so that heaven and
earth could be linked together once again. This immense rainbow
is attached to the earth in two places, in the Holy Land and in this
very kingdom which you rule. And the top of its arch is linked to
the world above and holds the heavens to the earth. The golden
dove has entered your life because the place where the top of the
rainbow is attached to the heavens has become frayed and torn in
several places and must be repaired, or else it will be severed, and
heaven and earth will be detached from each other for all time.
Ever since the destruction of the Temple in Jerusalem, it has not
been possible to reach the rainbow from the Holy Land. That is
why the golden dove has sought you out, for your help is needed
so that the rainbow can be repaired."

When he heard this, the king was staggered, for he had never
suspected that a mission of such great importance would come to
rest on his shoulders. As a king he was accustomed to great responsibility, of course, but never had the fate of the world been at

stake. Now, for the first time, the king grew afraid, for everything
had happened so suddenly, and his life had changed for all time;
there was no turning back. And he said, "What is it that I must
do?"

"You must see to it that the rainbow is repaired," said the
sorcerer. "Nothing more, nothing less."

This confirmed the king's own guess, and strengthened his
resolve. He said, "How can such a thing be done?"

The sorcerer replied: "The quest itself to repair the rainbow is
destined for another, but it is your responsibility to be certain that
the right one to undertake it is selected. For there is only one
person in the world capable of undertaking this mission." "But how
can this one ever be found among all the world?" asked the king.
"The one you must select already lives in this kingdom," said the
sorcerer, "for it was a part of his destiny to be born here. Further,
his profession is that of a weaver, for only a master weaver could
repair the fragile rays of the rainbow." "But there are a thousand
weavers in my kingdom," said the king. "How am I to know which
one to choose?" Then the sorcerer was quiet for a moment, while
he listened intently for the words of the golden dove as they rose
up in his soul and could be heard from within. And at last he said,
"You must announce a contest among all the master weavers in this
kingdom. Each must weave a rug which has as its primary design a
golden dove. And the one weaver whose work most closely resembles the true nature of the golden dove, as you have seen it
with your own eyes, is the one you must select."

Then the king wasted no time, but called in all of his royal
messengers and sent them to every corner of the kingdom to announce the contest. And he made it known that whoever succeeded
in weaving the winning rug would become the husband of his
daughter, the princess, and would inherit half his kingdom. For the
king knew that whoever was destined to serve on a quest of such
importance must be a very fine man indeed, and should make a
fine match for his daughter, as well as an eventual successor to the
throne.

Naturally every master weaver in the kingdom immediately

set out to create the most beautiful rug of all, and every one imagined the golden dove a little differently. Among them was one old
master weaver who had an apprentice, a lad who had worked
under him for almost a year. And when this young man saw all the
excitement about the contest of the king, he begged to be permitted
to weave a rug himself. The master laughed at this request, for the
boy had just learned how to use the loom and already wanted to
compete with the finest weavers of the kingdom. But since he was
certain the apprentice would make a fool of himself, he permitted
him to attempt to weave a rug of his own.

Then it happened that the golden dove appeared to this young
man in a dream, and when he awoke its image remained vivid in
his mind. He hurriedly made a sketch of the dove as he had seen it,
and sat down at the loom and started to weave—and he wove
without stopping for a day and a night as if in a trance and when
he finished he found that he had captured the very image of the
golden dove he had seen in his dream. And when the apprentice
showed the rug to his master, the weaver was astounded, for the
rug was the most stunning he had ever seen, and the golden dove
in it seemed as if it were alive. Then the master weaver burned his
own rug, which looked so poor in comparison, and took the rug of
the apprentice and entered it in the contest of the king as his own.

When all of the master weavers had delivered their rugs, the
king had them hung throughout the palace, so he could examine
each and every one. He knew that his most important task was to
select the right rug, and thus choose the right man to send on the
quest, and he was determined not to err. But imagine the king's
surprise when he came upon the rug woven by the apprentice,
submitted by the master weaver, which preserved the exact image
of the golden dove so well that at first he thought it was the dove
itself which was perched there. Then he knew without a doubt that
this rug was the right one, and he gave thanks that the decision had
been so clear. Then he sent for the weaver, for he was very curious
to know who he was.

But when the old weaver appeared, who had falsely claimed
the rug as his own, the king was distressed. Was this old man the

one who could repair the rainbow, marry his daughter, and someday succeed him as king? He could not believe that he was the one
fate had sent. Then something very strange happened as the old
weaver approached the rug—the image of the golden dove suddenly vanished, leaving only white thread showing its outline.
Both the king and weaver were startled when this happened, and
the king suddenly grew suspicious. He said to the weaver: "Are
you certain it was you who wove this rug? For the miracle that has
just occurred seems to suggest that you may not be telling the
truth." Then the weaver, who was terrified and feared for his life,
fell to his knees and confessed the rug had been woven by his
apprentice, a young man. Greatly relieved, the king said, "I will
not punish you for so disgracing yourself with this falsehood, as
long as you send for your apprentice at once and he confirms you
have finally told the truth." And in this way the young weaver was
called before the king.

Now ever since he had announced the contest, the king had
kept the golden dove in its invisible state, for he had been taught
the secret of how to make the dove invisible by the sorcerer, who
had recounted the tale of how King Solomon had discovered it. For
the king feared that someone might reveal the nature of the dove to
one of the weavers, and the wrong one might be chosen. In its
invisible state, the dove remained perched on the king's shoulder,
and he had grown used to its presence, which caused everything to
appear to him with much greater clarity. So the dove was invisible
when the young weaver was received by the king. And at the
moment the weaver entered the room, the king felt the invisible
dove fly from his shoulder. And at the same instant the young
weaver felt something land on his shoulder which felt exactly like a
bird, although there was nothing to be seen. For an instant he was
frightened, but since he was already terrified by being in the presence of the king, he acted as if nothing had happened. Then, as he
approached the throne, he felt a sudden breeze blowing across his
face, as if a bird were beating its wings nearby. He wondered
greatly at this, and thought that perhaps it was a natural phenome-
non in the courts of kings. Just then the king rose and greeted the

boy with a warm embrace, and as he did the king felt the gentle breeze created by the wings of the invisible dove, perched upon the shoulder of the boy. That is how the king learned where the dove had landed, which he had been very curious to know, and in this way the golden dove had confirmed his choice. So too was the king delighted that the young man was strong and handsome, and at that moment any doubts he may have harbored about the success of the quest disappeared and he felt more peaceful than he had in years.

Then, before he said anything to the young weaver, who had already begun to wonder at the king's silence, the king decided to surprise the young man. He motioned for him to follow him, and brought the young man to a full-length mirror surrounded with intricate gold trimming, that hung in that chamber. He had him stand in front of the mirror, and when he did the lad was astonished to see a golden bird perched on his shoulder, exactly like the one he had seen in his dream and woven into the rug. He quickly looked for it on his shoulder, but there was nothing to be seen, although he still sensed its presence. The boy was so startled that for an instant his heart stopped beating, and he suddenly broke into sobs. Then the king took out a cloth that had been folded in a golden chest next to the ornate mirror. He hung this cloth over the mirror for a moment, then pulled it away. And at that instant the young weaver saw that the golden bird in the mirror had vanished—only to reappear perched on his own shoulder. It was at that moment, for the first time, that the golden dove began to sing, and when the young man heard its song he was overcome with a sense of peace and certainty, and decided that everything happening to him must have been destined to take place, and he accepted it all, however strange and mysterious it might seem. And the king, hearing the song of the dove for the first time, saw the world in a new light and began to discern a Divine Presence that could be sensed behind all things. When the king looked again at the young weaver, he saw that he no longer had the appearance of a boy, but that of a man. And the king said, "Be seated, young man, and I will explain everything as best I can. For the golden dove perched on your shoulder, identical to that you wove into your rug, entered my life as suddenly as it did yours. I suspect the mysteries it represents are endless, but I also know it has come into our lives for a purpose. That is why it has brought us together, and confirmed by its presence on your shoulder that you are indeed destined to play an important role." The weaver greatly wondered what that role might be, but at the same time he felt certain he would agree to undertake it. And the king also sensed the young weaver's willingness to serve, and knew he would not turn away from this work of restoration, for that is what his calling as a weaver required.

It was then that the king had the sorcerer brought into the room, and while the king listened, the sorcerer repeated for the weaver the history of the golden dove he had learned while holding it in his hands and also revealed what they had discovered of its powers—its invisibility, its manner of replying by means of a sign or symbol, and its role as a messenger. Then the sorcerer told the young man the reason for the quest, to repair the rainbow so that the heavens should not be separated from the earth. And when he heard this, the weaver was truly astonished, and yet, strange to say, he accepted all that he heard as the truth, as impossible as that would have been even an hour before.

When the sorcerer had finished speaking, there was silence, and the young man knew they were waiting for his reply. Then he did not hesitate, but said, "Yes, I will willingly undertake this quest, and I will do all in my power to succeed. For even though I alone do not possess the power for such a mission, I sense how much the golden dove can enhance those powers with which I have been endowed. Only tell me all that you can about how I must proceed, for on such a quest there surely can be no room to err."

Then the king said, "Well spoken, young man. But as for the way to proceed, you must turn to the golden dove to learn that." "But how can this be done?" asked the weaver. And the king replied, "Simply take the dove in your two hands." And the weaver held out his hands and let the dove land upon them. When he closed his palms lightly around its feathers, he felt words rise up which seemed to be spoken from within. And those words assured him that he need only begin the quest and signs would be sent to guide him at every stage, for the golden dove had been sent from the world above to be his guide in this quest. The weaver told these things to the king and sorcerer, and when they heard this, they both felt certain the quest would ultimately succeed. Then the king ordered that the finest horse in the land be made ready for the weaver, and that supplies be prepared for his departure at dawn.

That night the young weaver slept deeply, and just before waking he dreamed he stood in the presence of Noah's rainbow, and was awestruck at its radiant beauty and how it stretched from one end of the world to the other. And in the dream he could see how the fabric which held the heavens to the earth had become unraveled, and he longed to see it repaired. But before he had time to begin the work of restoration, he awoke, and remembered all that had happened the night before, and the quest that lay before him. Just then the first rays of dawn illumined the sky, and the weaver quickly dressed and went out to the palace courtyard, where he met the king and the sorcerer, who had awakened in order to see him off on his journey. As he mounted his horse, the weaver also felt the invisible dove land on his shoulder, which greatly reassured him, and without further ado he set out on his quest.

Before he had ridden very far, the weaver came upon a young man sitting beneath a bare tree, with a wooden flute in his hands. The young man looked very sad, and his head sagged on his chest. "Why are you so sad?" asked the weaver. The young man looked up and said: "I am sad because there is no melody I cannot play on my flute except for one—and that is the one I long to play more than any other." "And what melody is it that so eludes you?" asked the weaver. "It is a melody I play in my dream, more beautiful than any other, that moves me to my very soul. But when I awake I cannot recall a single note." "And is it the same melody that you play in each of your dreams?" "Yes," said the musician, "of that I am certain."

Then the weaver, who had the invisible golden dove perched

on his shoulder, felt a breeze blow across his face, and knew that
the golden dove was flapping its wings. Knowing how inspiring
was its presence, the weaver said, "There is a melody I should like
you to play." "Yes, and what melody is that," said the musician,
"for I know a great many of them." "It is the dream melody of
which you have just spoken." "But I have just told you that I
cannot recall that melody!" cried the musician. "I know that," said
the weaver, "but I want to see it for myself. Just put the flute to
your lips and see what happens."

And although the musician felt foolish, he put the flute to his
lips, and at that instant he suddenly recalled a few notes of the
dream melody that had both haunted and eluded him for so long.
And when he began to play, he discovered that the dream melody
flowed forth as if he had known it all his life. And he was so
gratified and so relieved that tears began to roll down his cheeks,
and he recognized that the presence of the traveler had somehow
prompted him to recall what had been forgotten and had restored
what had been lost. And he said, "Who are you, for I sense that
you have somehow assisted me, although I do not know how." The
weaver replied, "It is not I who have inspired you to recall the lost
melody, but a spirit that guides me, which appears in the form of a
golden dove. This spirit is leading me on an important quest, for
something that has been broken must be repaired. And as I listened
to your dream melody, I sensed that it may possess remarkable
healing powers, and therefore you could be of great assistance to
me. Join me, and we will each contribute our abilities to achieve
the objective of this quest—to repair the rainbow."

Now when the musician learned what was the purpose of this
quest, he could barely believe his ears. Yet the miracle that had
just taken place, which had set free the imprisoned melody and
freed him of a heavy burden, had convinced him that the weaver
was possessed of great powers. And although he did not fully
understand all that was taking place, he decided then and there to
join the weaver and to assist him in his quest in any way he could.

As the weaver and the musician traveled together they passed
a man sitting beneath a tree, who appeared to be desolate. They

asked him why he seemed so sad, and he said: "I am a master potter. I can create the finest vessel of any shape or form, and I can repair any vessel which is broken. But there is one broken vessel which I cannot restore, and that is why I am so sad." "And what vessel is this?" they asked. "It is a vessel I have never seen, except in my dreams," said the potter. "I dream of it every night. It is a perfect vessel, a jar with a lid that fits so well it seems inseparable. And in the dream I lift that lid and a wonderful glowing light emerges from inside the vessel and fills the room with an aura that transforms everything into a vision of peace. But all at once a terrible thing happens, just before I awake: the vessel shatters, and its pieces are scattered everywhere. You cannot imagine how it pains me to see that vessel break. And when I awake I long to locate the broken pieces, that I might restore the vessel, and be in the presence of the aura of its light."

As the potter spoke these words, the weaver felt the gentle wind formed by the wings of the dove, which remained on his shoulder, invisible to all. Knowing that the golden dove was ready to bring its blessings to assist the potter in fulfilling his wish, the weaver said, "Tell me, have you ever searched for the fragments of the shattered vessel?" The potter said: "How would I know where to begin to look?" And the weaver said: "Let us begin to look here."

With that the weaver began to search for the pieces of the broken vessel, and the potter and the musician joined in the search. Just as they did, the potter saw something glowing beneath a log. He picked it up and found that it was the fragment of a broken vessel, to which clung a light that continued to glow as he held it in his hands. And without saying anything, they all knew that this must be one of the lost fragments for which they were searching. What they did not know was that it was the golden dove which had sought out that fragment and had hovered above it, flapping its invisible wings and causing the sparks that remained clinging to the fragment to glow brightly, making it visible.

So it was that the invisible dove led the three searchers through the forest, to one fragment after another it had caused to glow. And by the time they had come full circle, they found they had gathered ten pieces. The potter began at once to try to fit the pieces together. And lo and behold, his fingers moved so quickly that the vessel took form in no time, and every piece fit into the right place. When the last piece had been restored, they somehow fused into one another, so that the vessel showed no sign it had ever been broken. And to the amazement of everyone, once the vessel was restored the light began to glow from within, as if it had never ceased glowing at all. The potter wept tears of joy when he saw the perfect vessel, and the others marveled at its unearthly beauty. After that they told the potter of their quest to repair the rainbow, and asked him if he wished to join them, since he knew so much about restoration. And the potter gladly agreed to join them and to bring along the mysterious vessel, no longer broken.

So it was that the three young men traveled together through the forest. They reached a crossroads, and they did not know which way to choose. Since there were no indications, and the travelers had never been in that place before, they arbitrarily took the path to the left. But when they did, the weaver suddenly felt the golden dove fly away from his shoulder. He took this as an ominous sign, and said, "No, perhaps we should go the other way, to the right." And as soon as he spoke he felt the golden dove return to his shoulder, and knew it had confirmed the choice of the way.

After that the weaver let the golden dove lead them, since it knew far more of their destiny than they did. Before they had traveled very far on that path, they came upon a young man who seemed dejected, sitting beneath a tree. But when the three companions approached him, the man seemed startled and said, "Who are you?" "We are three travelers," said the weaver. "But please tell us, why do you seem to be so sad?" Then the young man replied, "I am a master jeweler. I have cut and polished the finest diamonds for emperors and kings. But there is one diamond I long to cut more than any other, and I am afraid I never will." "What diamond is this?" asked the potter. "It is a large, uncut diamond I continue to see in a recurring dream," said the jeweler. "In the dream I am

walking on a path in the desert when I come upon a cave. I go into
the cave, which is filled with light. I always become curious as to
the source of that remarkable light, which is purer and clearer than
any I have ever seen. I search in the cave, and sometimes the
dream ends before I find out its source, and sometimes the dream
lasts long enough for me to find that uncut stone, concealed in a
crevice. And each time I see it, I envision the perfect jewel it
would make if I cut and polished it; and this jewel appears to me
from inside the uncut stone, crying out in its perfection to be
brought into being. I am overcome with longing to complete this
task, but each time I wake up before I have time to undertake it.
Last night my dream lasted a little longer, and I held the uncut
jewel in my hand, and all at once the jewel appeared as it would
after it has been cut and polished, as if its uncut parts had fallen
away. And I held the jewel up to my eye, to see if I could discern
the source of the light within it." "And what did you see?" asked
the musician, who had followed this tale closely. "Why—I saw
myself talking to the three of you!" said the jeweler. "That is why I
was so startled to see you. I have already met you in a dream, and I
wonder at the meaning of this. But because I can never recover that
priceless jewel and cut it, I am so sad."

As the jeweler spoke, the weaver felt the wings of the invisible
dove beginning to beat, and he said: "Perhaps it is possible to find
the cave in which the jewel is hidden. Tell me, have you searched
for this cave?" "Of course!" replied the jeweler. "That is the first
thing I did. But it is nowhere to be found in this part of the
world." Still the wings of the dove fanned a light breeze on the face
of the weaver, and he said: "Let us not abandon the search yet. For
we would be happy to assist you in fulfilling your wish." But just
as the weaver finished speaking the jeweler yawned and his eyes
began to close. He said, "What is this? All of a sudden I have an
overwhelming urge to sleep. But I must not—for we shall search
together for the jewel." But no sooner had the jeweler spoken these
words, than he was sound asleep.

As soon as he slept, the jeweler began to dream. And in the
dream he found himself once again at the entrance of the cave filled

with light. In previous dreams, the dream had always started over, and he had no memory of prior dreams. But this time he remembered everything, and hurried into the cave, to the crevice in which the glowing jewel was concealed. There he found it, glowing brightly as ever. He took it in his hands, and was overcome with longing to take it with him from that place. He decided to try to bring it back with him, impossible as that might be. So he put the jewel inside the leather pouch at his side, and the instant he closed it, he awoke. At first he was confused, but then he remembered the dream and reached into his pouch. To his great disappointment, it was empty. The jeweler's eyes filled with tears, for he realized how difficult it would be to bring a jewel back from a dream. Then he told the dream to the others, and they found it encouraging, and told the jeweler not to abandon hope. After a brief silence the weaver said, "This gem of which you have dreamed must surely be precious—perhaps it is as old as the golden dove." "What golden dove?" asked the jeweler, since he did not know anything about it. "I will tell you about that later," said the weaver. "But let us think only of the miraculous jewel for now. Do not despair—perhaps you should return to that dream world, enter that cave, and attempt to bring back the jewel once again. But this time try to remain there long enough to fall asleep in the dream. This will be difficult to do, for it is very hard to remember to do things in a dream. But if you can remember to put the jewel into your pouch, and succeed in sleeping in the dream, you might awake with your treasure—for to sleep in that world is to awake in this one."

The jeweler considered these words, and although he was reluctant to raise his hopes again, so great was his longing that he decided to do as the weaver suggested. As soon as he closed his eyes, he found himself at the entrance of that cave once more. This time he hurried and put the jewel inside the pouch, and since he remembered everything they had said while he was awake he lay down in the cave next to that crevice and closed his eyes. And when he opened them he found himself sitting beside the three travelers. Then he put his hand inside the pouch and pulled out the glowing, uncut jewel. And even though it was uncut, it was more magnificent than any other jewel they had ever seen—and far more precious, since it had been taken from the Kingdom of Dreams!

Now that the jeweler had the jewel of his dreams in his possession, he wasted no time, but began to cut it. And no sooner had he just touched it with his tools than the outer stone fell away, revealing a perfect jewel, already polished. All were amazed when they saw that perfect jewel emerge in such a short time from the rough stone, and marveled at both its unparalleled beauty and the remarkable skill of the jeweler, whose dream had at last come true. And the light that burned within the jewel shone more brightly now than ever, illuminating the forest all around them. The jeweler brought it to his eye, as he had done before in his dream, to see the source of the light. But instead he viewed a rainbow of splendorous colors, arching high above them in the sky. He reported this to the others, and they each hurried to catch a glimpse of this luminous rainbow. The colors of this rainbow constantly shifted, moving so swiftly they seemed to be alive. And where they stood seemed to be directly beneath it.

The weaver was the first to realize what had happened—that the jewel had revealed the presence of the rainbow, which had been hidden from their eyes until then. Serving as a prism, it had evoked the hidden colors of the rainbow and made its presence known to them. And as they stared into the rainbow, the light reflected in the prism of the jewel was cast upon the ground, and suddenly a small flame began to burn. At that moment the golden dove began to beat its wings so strongly the weaver was afraid it might carry him aloft. Recognizing that the dove wanted to relay a message, but uncertain of what it was, the weaver took the dove into his hands as he had seen the sorcerer do, and as he had already done himself. Before long, the message of the dove rose up within him, and he turned to the musician and said, "Now is the time for you to play your dream song!" So the musician took out his wooden flute and began to play the song the weaver had helped restore to him, and each note seemed to beckon the flames to leap higher. Soon they discovered that as long as the musician continued to play, they did not need to feed the fire. But as soon as he stopped, whatever was burning was quickly consumed, and they had to toss other twigs onto the flames. After that the musician played the dream melody without pausing, and the weaver continued to listen for the words of the golden dove as they arose within. Soon the next message was sent and received, and the weaver turned to the jeweler and said: "Now it is time for you to cast your jewel into the fire!" And although the jeweler did not know the reason for this strange request, he did not hold back the precious jewel, but released it into the fire. In a few seconds the jewel split open in the flames like a seed and began to sprout roots and branches, and suddenly a great tree grew up in that place, reaching into heaven. As the four travelers stared at it in awe, the tree suddenly blossomed and bore fruit. And each fruit, as it grew ripe before their eyes, resembled the very vessel that the potter had restored, and just as it did, each of them had a light which glowed from within.

Then the weaver heard the command of the golden dove to ascend that tree. And lo and behold, the weaver looked up and saw that there were hundreds of rungs leading upward on the trunk of that tree, which rose all the way into the heavens. But the weaver could not take hold of the first rung, for it was slightly out of his reach. Just then the potter noticed that the tree was missing a single fruit exactly like the vessel of his dream. And he took the vessel and held it up to the one branch that was missing fruit, and as soon as it touched the branch it fused there and remained attached, as if it had grown from that very place. And at the very moment the missing vessel was restored to the tree, a rung appeared low enough for the weaver to reach. And he climbed upon that rung, accompanied by the golden dove, which remained perched on his shoulder. In this way he ascended all six hundred and thirteen rungs of that ladder, which reached from earth into heaven, until he reached the very juncture where the rainbow had begun to unravel. And there, in the uppermost branch of the tree so high in the heavens, was the nesting place of the golden dove. That nest seemed to be woven of light, and glowed as brightly as the moon itself. Now the golden dove had sought to return to its nest for very long, but it could only be reached by ascending those six hundred and thirteen rungs. But the tree that supports the rainbow withers and bursts into flames at the end of every generation, and all that remains of it in the ashes of those flames is the jewel, which is its only seed. That jewel must be recovered by a righteous man and cast into a fire, in order for the tree to take root and ascend anew. And because many generations had passed since the last righteous man had appeared to raise up the tree, the fabric of the rainbow had begun to unravel.

Now the golden dove was free to complete the quest. And while the weaver watched in amazement, it grasped in its beak one end of the straw of light that its nest consisted of, and flew off to the base of the rainbow in the Holy Land. And the unbroken thread of light it drew from its nest was never exhausted, for it unraveled from an eternal source. Soon the dove arrived at the holy city of Safed, which rests on the top of a mountain, where one pillar of the rainbow rises up from the place of the tomb of Rabbi Simeon bar Yohai, who had been steeped in the divine mysteries. Then the dove, with the thread in its beak, circled that end of the rainbow to reinforce it there. After that it reascended the arch weaving in and out of its warp and woof, faster than the eye could follow, stitching together the fabric of light which had become unraveled. Before long it had returned to its nest at the apex of the rainbow, where it reinforced the thread; then, descending the other side of the rainbow and circling the other base, it turned back to sew the next stitch. All in all, the dove stitched six hundred and thirteen rows of stitches, each reaching from one end of the rainbow to the other, until the fabric of the light was at last restored.

At the instant the dove completed the six hundred and thirteenth row of stitches the work was complete, the skies cleared all over the world, and for one hour everyone on earth gasped in awe as Noah's great rainbow was revealed once more in all its splendor. Even the ministering angels assembled before the rainbow's glory. And now the colors of the rainbow, which until then had changed a thousand times a minute, remained fixed, for now that the rainbow had been repaired, a new covenant had been made, and the order of the colors would remain unchanged for all time. The four travelers gave thanks for having completed their quest, and marveled at the rainbow in all its glory. And the king, standing with the sorcerer on the balcony of his palace, saw the glowing rainbow reaching across the heavens from one end of the world to the other, and rejoiced to know that the quest of the young weaver had been completed.

Here the *Shekhinah* finished telling the tale, and Reb Nachman returned from the land to which it had transported him. And when Reb Nachman saw that the tale had been told, words again rose up within him, and he said: "*Like the appearance of the rainbow in the clouds, so was the appearance of the brightness round about, which is the presence of the Glory of the Lord.*" And the *Shekhinah*'s final words were "*Shalom*, Nachman. Know that the rainbow is once more in need of repair. It is you who must restore it." And after speaking these words she suddenly became the golden dove again, and flew out of the open window. And Reb Nachman hurried to the window and watched the dove fly off until it was no larger than a star in the night sky. At that moment he awoke, lying in his bed, and realized that his meeting with the *Shekhinah* had taken place in a dream. And every word that she had spoken still burned in his memory as if it were written in flames. Then Reb Nachman noticed that the window in his room was open, although he was certain it had been closed when he had gone to sleep. And the light of the full moon that poured in through the open window shone upon his face.

Traveling with a Map

ONE Yom Kippur, Reb Nussan noticed that Reb Nachman was especially animated in his prayers, swaying back and forth while his eyes flew over the letters. As the long day proceeded, Reb Nachman seemed to become more and more remote. And Reb Nussan became frightened, for he did not know what it meant. But of course he did not approach Reb Nachman or interrupt his prayers.

The morning after, Reb Nussan told Reb Nachman of his fears, and Reb Nachman said, "Praying, Nussan, is like traveling with the aid of a map. The object is to understand how to read the map, in order to travel as far as possible in the time given. Because you, Nussan, kept looking up from the map to check my progress, you did not manage to travel very far, only to the shore of a dark sea. But I did not lift my eyes from the map, and in this way I managed to travel very far; in this way I came to pray at the *Kotel*, the Wailing Wall, which has witnessed all the griefs of the Exile. Thus it is that I have learned that this will be my last year in this world.

"On Erev Yom Kippur a seed of light is sown, and for those who travel far enough on the map it blossoms into a Tree of Light, that fills all the worlds, and its branches carry the light of knowledge to every corner of the world."

In all ways except one Reb Nussan was relieved to hear what Reb Nachman had said. But one sentence had stuck in his mind, and instead of being a seed of light, it was more like a seed of silence that took root inside a soft collapse. And he said: "But, Rebbe, how did you learn that this would be your last year—God forbid!" Reb Nachman said: "Every year, an old man, dressed in white and wrapped in white, prayed next to me there at the *Kotel* on Yom Kippur, and we always finished praying at the same time. But this year an old man dressed in black and wrapped in black joined me. He prayed beside me but he did not finish praying at the same time, and when I turned to go he was still *davening* at the Wall."

Not long after Yom Kippur, Reb Nachman took ill once more and did not live beyond that year.

The Decree

AFTER Reb Nachman had told, and Reb Nussan had recorded, the first six tales, Reb Nussan asked Reb Nachman if he wanted the tales to be published, for he felt that the world thirsted for the truths revealed in them.

"No," said Reb Nachman. "They must only be published after my death."

"If you care, Rebbe, tell me the reason for this," said Nussan.

"The reason," said Reb Nachman, "is that it was revealed to me that I would not hold the book of my tales in my lifetime. This was the decree. Therefore I do not wish to hurry the appearance of the book, which will appear after my death."

"There is a secret here, I know," said Reb Nussan, "but so far it has eluded me."

"Yes," said Reb Nachman, "the truth is that it was also decreed that the book would be the vessel by which my soul would remain among you. Every time you open the book and read at least one word, my spirit shall be called forth, and I shall be in your presence."

Reb Nussan and all the Hasidim were amazed to learn this, and they were speechless.

Then Reb Nachman said, "Now that I have revealed this secret to you, take note of my wish: See to it that a copy of the book of my tales reaches the Holy Land, so that my spirit may also emerge and wander there, for that is the place I have always longed to be."

The Yoke of Moses

for Charles Larson

REB Nussan had a dream in which the Rebbe gave a *D'var Torah*, and all of the Bratslav Hasidim, including Nussan, listened intently to his words. And Reb Nachman said, "When the Children of Israel were still slaves in Egypt, and Moses was a prince who was also their leader, the people saw Moses join the line of the slaves and receive a great yoke, tied to his back, which he bore to the top of the pyramids like all of the others. This seemed very strange to the people. On the one hand they greatly admired and respected Moses for sharing their suffering, but on the other hand Moses was very precious to them and they didn't want to lose him. They wondered about this, and came to him, saying, 'Moses, Moses, you are free from this. Why are you taking it upon yourself?' And Moses said, 'I'm carrying it for the great relief that will come the moment they cut away the yoke.' "

It was at this point that Reb Nussan awoke, with the dream still vivid to him. He picked up a pen and wrote down Reb Nachman's words at once, so that not a single one would be lost. For every word of his Rebbe was precious to him, whether he received it awake or asleep. But as Reb Nussan wrote, the full import of the dream became apparent to him, and he realized that Reb Nachman would not be in this world much longer. He became choked with emotion as he finished writing. But then he suddenly felt an unexpected sense of peace, for he knew his Rebbe would shortly experience the great relief of which he had spoken.

The Collector of Lost Souls

NEAR the end of his life, Reb Nachman dreamed that he had embarked on a long journey. In the dream he made his way through underground caverns that were also *kleippot*, empty shells that had ceased to serve as vessels. And in order to reach the next passage, it was necessary to break through the wall of each shell. There had been endless shells inside of shells for so long Reb Nachman had almost forgotten the purpose of his journey, and had almost abandoned hope of ever breaking through them. So it was that when the last wall gave way and he emerged into the light, so much the greater was his relief.

And what was the place he had finally reached, where every breath is drawn back and forth through countless stars? At first he did not know. It might have been an orchard or it might have been a garden. But when he saw the aura that surrounded it, he knew it must be a sacred place. He crossed the orchard and found a path there, which he followed. So far he had not seen anyone. He followed the path until it became a road, and the road led into a city. Still, no one was to be seen. But when at last he reached the center of the city, he saw that a great crowd had gathered there. All had formed a great circle, and were observing something that took place in the center of the circle, but from where Reb Nachman stood he could not see what it was.

Observing Reb Nachman's frustration, a man nearby took out a round mirror from beneath his garment and offered it to Reb Nachman, showing him how he could hold it above his head to see over the crowd. Reb Nachman gratefully took the mirror, and when he gazed into it he saw that the people were seated in ten concentric circles; in the innermost circle he saw an old man, who was seated on the ground. The old man was moving his lips, and all of those in the circle next to him moved their lips after him. Then those who sat behind them repeated the words as they heard them, and in this way his words were repeated until they reached the outermost circle.

Reb Nachman asked the man who had given him the mirror, "Who is the old man who sits in the center of the circle?" And the man replied, "His name is Reb Adam. In this world he is the Collector of Lost Souls. He takes what is given from above and translates it so that it can be understood here below. And those who sit around Reb Adam repeat his words to those closest to them, and they are repeated ten times, once for each circle of those who sit around him.

"And each letter of every word that Reb Adam speaks contains in it a lost soul, one of the six hundred thousand Jewish *neshamahs* that were present at Mount Sinai and have been searching for a way to return to this world. For when a soul first takes leave of a man's body it seeks to be remembered, but later it seeks to be reborn.

"And each time the words that Reb Adam speaks are repeated for the tenth time, that lost soul is set free from wandering in that realm between worlds and takes root in the womb of a woman, who brings forth an infant possessed of that soul. That is how the six hundred thousand *neshamahs* have remained present in each generation. And it is all due to that *Tzaddik*, who is the Collector of Lost Souls, that these same *neshamahs* have been able to be reborn."

Reb Nachman had often heard of the *Tzaddik* Reb Adam, who had transmitted the Book of Mysteries to the Baal Shem. Now that he too had read in that Book, he too had shared in the blessing that Reb Adam had made possible. And Reb Nachman wondered if this was the same Reb Adam. And he knew without asking that it must be. Then Reb Nachman said, "From where does Reb Adam get his words?" And the man replied: "They drop down to him from heaven. He receives them like a cistern that catches the rain. And when the level of the water has risen, the knowledge spills out of him, like a vessel that overflows."

And when he had heard this, Reb Nachman said, "Are the words of this *Tzaddik* altered when they are repeated?" And the man said: "Sometimes the words are repeated exactly as they were spoken, and sometimes they are repeated as they were heard. Those words repeated as spoken are perfectly preserved, while those repeated as they were heard are often clothed in a different garment, but the essence remains the same, for the heart of truth is eternal, and it is from this heart that the *Tzaddik* speaks."

Then Reb Nachman said, "It is this heart of truth that I have sought to reach all my life, but it is only now that I realize it is not an impossible quest."

And the man said, "In this world, Reb Nachman, one ascends the rungs of the ladder that reaches into heaven. For that is where the calling comes from. And whoever looks back loses his grip and falls back into the world of men."

Reb Nachman thanked the man for all that he had revealed, and after the crowd had departed, Reb Nachman approached Reb Adam, who still sat in the center of the circle. At first it appeared that the *Tzaddik* was asleep, for his eyes were closed. But without opening them he spoke first and said, "Tell me, Reb Nachman, what is it you would like to know?" And Reb Nachman understood at once that Reb Adam saw the world from within, and that is why he did not open his eyes. And Reb Nachman also understood that he had been granted one question to be answered, the question closest to his heart. And he did not have to think long to know what question that was, and he said: "How is it possible to distinguish truth from illusion?"

Then Reb Adam said, "I will answer your question, Reb Nachman. But first enter the palace before you and bring back a cup of water from the Well of Living Waters that can be found there, for I am thirsty." At that moment Reb Nachman looked up and saw the palace shimmering in the distance. And he did not hesitate, but approached it at once, so that he might fulfill Reb Adam's request.

But as soon as Reb Nachman stepped inside the gate of the palace he was astounded to find himself in a vast wilderness. The palace itself was nowhere to be seen. He turned to look for the gateway through which he had just entered, but the wilderness stretched dimly in every direction. What kind of palace was this?

Still, his goal was to bring back a cup of water from the Well of Living Waters. Since he did not know where this well was to be found, he was prepared to search in that place or any other. Therefore he strode into the dark wilderness unafraid, for so far fate had not led him astray.

Before he had walked very far, Reb Nachman met an old man who was planting a tree. He wondered why the man was doing this work at night, instead of during the day. Reb Nachman went over to the old man and said, "Is it so hot here during the day that the inhabitants work at night?" The old man looked up and replied, "It is never day in this place." "How can that be?" Nachman asked. And the old man answered, "Because the sun does not shine here." "But does not the sun shine everywhere in the world?" asked Nachman. And the old man replied, "That is true for the world of men, but not for this world." And Nachman said, "Is this not the world of men?" The old man answered, "No, it is not. It is one of the Four Worlds."

Now Reb Nachman had heard of the Four Worlds in the teachings of the Simeon bar Yohai and the Ari, but he had never fully understood what they were. And he wondered which of the Four Worlds he had entered. He asked the old man, who said, "This is the first of the Four Worlds, known as *Olam ha-Atzilut*, the World of Emanation. Here we plant in sorrow that which you reap in joy." "And what is the cause of this sorrow?" asked Reb Nachman. "It comes because we are never permitted to see the fruits of our labor. This tree, for example, which I am planting—the fruit it will bear will always be out of my reach." "And why is that?" asked Nachman. "Because it will grow ripe only in the Second World, *Olam ha-Beriah*, the World of Creation." "And are you condemned to this world for all time?" asked Nachman. "Those who inhabit this world are fated to spend different lengths of time here. We are all wandering spirits, without substance, and for some the stay may be very short, while for others it may last for eternity." "And on what does this fate depend?" asked Nachman. The old man replied, "It all depends on whether the fruit we plant becomes ripe and if it is picked at the proper moment between ripe and rotten. If not, it is too late." "And is most of the fruit so picked?" asked Nachman. "No," said the old man, with great sorrow. "Most of it is left to grow rotten on the branches. And it is this, above all, that breaks our hearts. For here we slave in the darkness in order to bring sustenance to another world beyond our reach. And when our effort succeeds yet remains unrecognized, it is a source of a terrible grief." Reb Nachman saw that this was a harsh world, in which one could not depend on harvesting what one had sown. Still, the planting had to take place anyway, in the darkness of that eternal night, and any reprieve depended on the inhabitants of another world. Then Reb Nachman vowed never to forget how the spirits of that world existed, and to do everything in his power to recognize the fruit once it had grown ripe and to pick it before it was too late. But he wondered what should be done with the fruit once it had been picked. He asked the old man, who said, "You are right. It is not enough that the fruit grow ripe and be picked at the right time. It must also be tasted. And not only tasted, but savored. For if it is not savored, it is the same as if it had never been picked at all." Reb Nachman considered these words, and recognized their wisdom. And he vowed to savor every fruit he tasted from that day forward. For never had he realized how much was at stake.

Then Reb Nachman told the old man he was searching for the Well of Living Waters, and asked if it could be found in that world. The old man replied, "No one can tell you where that well can be found, for every man must find it for himself. Yet I would help you, for I recognize that you are a true seeker." Then the old man broke off a branch of the tree he was planting. And as soon as he did this, another grew in its place, exactly like its predecessor, and Reb Nachman marveled at this. The old man said, "Take this branch with you, and use it as a staff." Reb Nachman thanked the old man for this gift and took his leave of him, and when he placed the staff upon the earth he discovered it was possible for him to move forward with great ease. Reb Nachman also found that with the staff in his hands he did not seem to grow tired, but became more refreshed.

In this way Reb Nachman proceeded a great distance, and passed many others planting trees in the darkness. For now that his eyes had grown accustomed to the dark, Reb Nachman perceived that this wilderness was filled with wandering spirits compelled to try to turn that wilderness into fertile land. Yet the truth was that despite their efforts most of the trees they planted withered before bearing fruit; of those which bore fruit, very few were picked before they grew rotten; of that which was picked, very little was tasted; and of that which was tasted, very little was savored. And only when the fruit was savored did the tree on which it grew flourish. Otherwise, it shrank until it was as small as a seedling, and then withered away until nothing at all was left. So Reb Nachman was all the more amazed when he reached a mighty tree, rich with fruit, that reached high into the heavens. He wondered what the secret was which made that tree so flourish, and he approached it, hoping to inquire about it, but there was no one to be seen tending it. Still, Reb Nachman was drawn even closer, so close that he leaned his forehead against the trunk, and when his eyes closed for an instant he saw a glowing light, as if there were a spark of the sun inside. Greatly mystified, Reb Nachman closed his eyes again, and once more he saw a point of light which resembled a glowing seed. When he opened his eyes, he saw an old woman approaching whose face shone with a light brighter than any he had seen in that world, except for that he had glimpsed when he leaned against the tree. And the old woman smiled and said, "You are Reb Nachman, are you not?" Now Reb Nachman was amazed that he should be recognized in that place, in a world that he had never entered before. He said, "Yes, I am Nachman, but how is it that you know me?" The old woman replied, "I have met you here many times before." "But how can that be?" asked Reb Nachman. "For I have never been in this world before." "You have merely forgotten," said the old woman. "For you have come to this place many times in your dreams. And each time you picked one of the fruits of this tree, and savored it all the night long. And that is why this tree has grown so high it reaches into heaven. For this is the dream tree that you yourself planted, Nachman, and which you

tended, and you are the only one who has tasted its fruit." Reb
Nachman could barely believe his ears, so unexpected were these
words. Yet as each word was spoken, Nachman's memory of it was
restored. And at last he recognized that tree of his dreams, which
had sustained him so often in the past. And he wondered what
world that was which he had returned to so often in his dreams.
He asked the old woman, who said, "This is the second of the Four
Worlds, the World of Creation, which you have reached." And
Reb Nachman marveled that he had traveled to another world,
even though he had not realized that he had left the first one.

It was then that Reb Nachman recalled the vision of the seed
of light he had seen when he had leaned against the tree and closed
his eyes. He told the old woman of this and asked her what it
meant. She said, "This tree of your dreams is not an ordinary tree,
Reb Nachman, but one grown with a sliver of the sun. It was you
who brought that sliver of light to this dark world and planted it
here, and that is what you saw glowing inside. Indeed, the inhabitants of this world are indebted to you, Nachman, for you have
brought to this world the only seed of light in many generations."

"All of what you say is most amazing and unexpected," said Reb
Nachman. "Yet I somehow know that every word is true. I do not
know what has guided me to this place, but I can see I was fated to
arrive here. Tell me, who are you, and how are you so familiar
with this tree created out of my dreams?" The old woman replied:
"My name is Asufit. I am the Collector of Lost Dreams. It has
been given to me to gather the scattered dreams left behind by a
multitude of dreamers and preserve them so they are not lost for
good, and can be reclaimed at the end of a person's life. For in the
moment a person departs from this life, I give them the basket of
their abandoned dreams as well as the basket of their merits. And
at that moment they learn how much was accomplished and how
much wasted in their lifetime. But the basket of your merits is
overflowing, Reb Nachman, while that of dreams abandoned is
almost empty because you have left so few behind. And because of
this you will be able to enter into the world-to-come as easily as a
person walks from one room to the next." Then Asufit handed Reb

Nachman a basket filled with his merits. And when Reb Nachman
saw that abundant basket, his eyes filled with tears, for he had so
often been in despair, and yet had somehow managed not to waste
the precious gifts he had been given; now he saw how rich was his
reward. And he greatly thanked Asufit, and told her of his quest to
reach the Well of Living Waters. And she said, "Fear not, Reb
Nachman, you will reach this well. For since you have reached
your own dream tree, be assured that you are on the right path."
And with these words Asufit turned away and was soon lost in the
darkness, which seemed much darker without her presence. But
Reb Nachman did not try to pierce that darkness. Instead, he
returned to his dream tree and leaned his forehead against the
trunk, touching his head to the very spot where he put the box of
the *tefillin*. And when he closed his eyes, he saw that sliver of the
sun once more, and let its seed of light take root inside him. When
he opened his eyes he found that most of the darkness had been
dispelled, and he was able to make out the world around him with
great clarity. He looked into the distance, and there he saw a vast
tent and decided to approach it, for he wondered what he might
find there. And as he came closer, Reb Nachman heard someone
shouting: "Collect all your merits and bring them to the tent." And
from every direction people were coming with baskets in their
hands, in which they had gathered their merits. Reb Nachman too
had such a basket on his arm, and he joined the others who entered
the tent and looked around. Inside he saw that a great crowd had
gathered and that an Ark had been set up in the Eastern portion of
the tent. The people lined up before it, bringing their merits with
them. As each one reached the pulpit, they either took their merits
out of the basket and threw them at the candle of the Eternal
Light, or else they approached the Ark and set down their merits
and supplicated there, before casting the merits into the flame.
And whenever the merits struck the flame, sparks flew out from
the candle and entered their mouths. And at that moment the
flame of the candle became a fountain, and the people drank of its
waters. And a moment later, as they opened their mouths to speak,
beings came forth from inside them, which were neither man nor

beast. And those beings which sprang forth from those who had cast their merits without supplication resembled grotesque demons, while those which came forth from those who first supplicated were very beautiful beings. Reb Nachman wondered greatly at this, and wondered what these creatures were. He turned to the man who stood in line before him and asked, and the man said, "These beings are brought into existence by a man's merits. If those merits are many, the creatures that come forth are very beautiful, but if they are few, the creatures that come forth are distorted and incomplete." "And what purpose do these creatures serve?" asked Reb Nachman. "They accompany their creators for all time," said the man. "Thus a person with many merits is accompanied by angelic beings, while one lacking such blessings must live in the presence of demonic beings. And this is what is meant when it is said that a man takes with him all that he has accomplished."

Soon it was Reb Nachman's turn in line, and he stood before the Ark. Then he put down his basket of merits and supplicated for a long time before the Holy Ark and the flame of the Eternal Light that burned there. At last he gently poured his merits onto the flame, and an immense number of sparks sprang forth and entered his mouth, so that he felt as if he were filled with light. And at that moment the flame of the candle turned into a river, not a fountain, and poured into the room, so that all who were assembled there were swept into the sea that had taken form. Some of them struggled in those waters, while others swam in them with ease. But when all of them had drunk of those waters, a peaceful expression came over every face. And Reb Nachman suddenly realized that he had brought a great thirst with him ever since he had entered that world. So he bent down to the waters and drank, and drank for a very long time. Nor was his thirst quenched, and he continued to drink until the sea had been reduced to a river, and the river to a well. Nor was there any danger that he might drain that well dry, for it was fed by a spring of living water that was inexhaustible.

Soon all those who had been drowning in that sea a moment before regained their composure and turned to Reb Nachman and regarded him with amazement. At last one of them said, "We have always expected that one would enter this world, *Olam ha-Yetsirah*, the World of Formation, whose merits would bring forth a river from the flame and not merely a fountain. But never did we imagine the sea of wisdom you have brought forth. Surely you are the *Tzaddik* of your generation, for only such a one could coax forth such a flood of water, and be able to consume those waters as well." And Reb Nachman asked what waters those were, but even as he asked he knew the reply. And the man said, "These waters flow forth from the Well of Living Waters, and sustain us in this World of Formation. For all who drink of this water share in the wisdom that sustains the world. And you who have brought forth a sea of wisdom must be blessed with a wonderful destiny indeed." And Reb Nachman felt filled with the wisdom of the ages, which had been transmitted to him in those waters. For upon tasting those waters he was transported to the fourth world, *Olam ha-Asiyyah*, the World of Making. There he was able to perceive all the worlds as they actually are. And so he realized that he had completed his quest to the Well of Living Waters, and took out the cup that Reb Adam had given him and filled it from the inexhaustible well. No sooner had he done so than Reb Nachman found himself standing outside the palace, and just before waking he heard the voice of Reb Adam, who said, "I see you have brought back the cup of water." When he awoke Reb Nachman found that long dream imprinted on his memory. And when he opened his eyes, the first thing he noticed was that the bowl on the table beside the bed, which had been empty, was now filled with water that glimmered in the light.

The Untold Tale

Now in addition to the teachings that Reb Nachman imparted to his Hasidim, he also wrote down some of his thoughts on the Torah. These writings he kept secret, and he warned his Hasidim not to look at these manuscripts, which he kept in a trunk. Before he departed from this world Reb Nachman announced to those Hasidim closest to him that he wanted the trunk of his writings burned after his death. Reb Nussan was grieved to hear this decree, for he longed to unlock his Rebbe's teachings to the world, and he did not doubt that the writings locked in the trunk could cast a great light in the darkness. So it was that Reb Nussan secretly hoped that the Rebbe might annul this decree; but Reb Nachman's health declined rapidly, and his passing came only a few weeks later.

Immediately after Reb Nachman's soul left his body, Reb Shimon hastened to the trunk, took out the hidden manuscripts, carried them to the stove, built a fire, and consigned them to the flames. All the while Reb Nussan followed after him in a daze, in order to sniff the sacred fumes of that awesome Torah, whose truths were thus denied to that and all subsequent generations.

There had been no time before the trunk was burned for Reb Nussan to read through it, nor did he think at the time that Reb Nachman would have wanted it. But for the rest of his life he regretted not having taken the opportunity to at least identify the papers that were to be burned. For all the rest of his life he was haunted by the notion that if he could have found even one tale of Reb Nachman's in that trunk which had not been told by the Rebbe in his lifetime, it was a great tragedy. And that untold tale haunted him, and became an obsession as he grew older.

Then it happened one night in his old age that Reb Nussan fell into a deep sleep, and dreamed that he was once more standing in Reb Nachman's study, as he had done for so many years. And

Reb Nachman's face seemed to glow, as it sometimes did before he told a tale. He invited Nussan to sit in his old chair, while Reb Nachman sat down on his fine wooden chair that so much resembled a throne. And in the dream Reb Nussan forgot that this chair had already been carved into pieces and smuggled from Poland to the holy city of Jerusalem, where it had been reassembled and placed next to the Ark.

In fact, Reb Nussan forgot that he was dreaming altogether. He only knew how natural it was to be seated there, in that room, with his Rebbe. And then he looked out the window, and he saw the full moon shining in the night, and the light of the moon illumined the tree outside the window, and Reb Nussan saw that it resembled a silver tree, its fruit the finest silver ornaments. And then Reb Nachman smiled and said: "You know, Nussan, you were right. If you had opened my trunk you would have found a tale, one that I left untold, one last tale I left for you to find. But Nussan, do not mourn over this. We cannot lose what really belongs to us, even if we throw it away. All that matters is that we remain true to God and to ourselves. Now, let me tell you the tale."

With that Reb Nachman proceeded to relate a long, involuted tale, a labyrinth full of twists and turns and tales within tales. And Reb Nussan followed every turn of the tale with awe, marveling at each episode as if he were crawling across an immense Persian carpet on which he encountered one intricate design after another. And when at last Reb Nachman came to the end of the tale, it was as if Reb Nussan had stood up and seen how all the figures in the carpet fit together to complete the pattern, and at that instant he came to understand a great secret, which cannot be repeated. And it was then that Reb Nachman arose and embraced his scribe, and Reb Nussan awoke and found it was still the middle of the night. This much is well known. But the fate of the untold tale is still very much a mystery. After all, the fact is that the tale is still untold. What happened to it? The Bratslav Hasidim hold four different opinions on the subject.

Among some of the Bratslavers it is held that although Reb Nussan remembered his meeting with Reb Nachman, he did not succeed in remembering the tale. Like so many other dreams, it was snatched away from him by Asmodeus, Prince of Demons, or by that sinister figure, the Destroyer of Books.

Others among the Hasidim feel certain that Reb Nussan recalled the dream in every detail, and that he was strongly tempted to write the tale down, but that on reflection he realized that the tale revealed such great secrets and mysteries it must be kept hidden. These Hasidim assume that since the tale remained untold during Reb Nachman's lifetime, the Rebbe did not feel that the world was ready to receive it, since those who understood might have found a way to bring the Messiah before his time. Therefore it remained untold. Among these Hasidim it is widely accepted that before or after Reb Nachman told Reb Nussan the untold tale, he also told him that he must not reveal it to the world, for the time had not yet come.

Still others among the Bratslav Hasidim are quite certain that Reb Nussan remembered only a small portion of the long tale upon waking, and so great was his despair at having retained only that fragment that he decided it would be better not to reveal any part of it at all, rather than present to the world only one jewel of a very precious crown. These Hasidim note that Reb Nussan did not live long after having had this dream, and attribute this fact to his distress at having failed to bring back from the other side the tale that had been entrusted to him.

Finally, there are those among the Bratslav Hasidim who are certain that Reb Nussan not only recalled the entire dream and tale upon waking in the night, but that he lost no time whatsoever in writing the tale down and preserving it with the perfection for which he was so well known. But they say that the next morning, upon rising and reaching for the pages on which he had written down the tale, he discovered, to his horror, that the letters had dissolved into a black powder and disappeared.

Burning the Scriptures

THE truth is that Reb Nussan never recovered from the burning of Reb Nachman's writings. For weeks afterward he had the taste of ashes in his mouth. What mystified him the most was why the Rebbe had ordered their destruction. At the same time he gave thanks that the manuscripts he himself had written from Reb Nachman's words had been spared this fate. And he understood with great clarity how important were those writings now, which were all that remained that could transmit to the world the greatness of the Rebbe.

The mystery of the manuscripts burned in the stove continued to haunt Reb Nussan, and then one night he had a dream in which he found himself in a cave, seated near a fire. When he looked up he saw that he was among many men dressed in white robes seated in a circle around it, and in the center of the circle next to the fire there was a man also wearing a white robe, whose back was turned to Reb Nussan. This man had a book in his hand, and while the others chanted and looked on, he tore out page after page of that book and threw it into the flames.

Now when Reb Nussan saw this, he wondered greatly what book it was they were burning. So he leaned forward to see if he could make out any of the words before they went up in flames. And by straining he was able to discern that the pages were written in Hebrew letters, and suddenly he recognized the handwriting—it was that of Reb Nachman, he was quite certain of it.

Greatly distressed, Nussan cried out in the dream, "Why are you burning those precious pages, which the Rebbe brought back from the worlds on high?" And as soon as he said this the chanting stopped and all grew silent. So too did the man in the center of the circle cease tearing out the pages of the book, and then he turned around, so that he stood face to face with Reb Nussan— and that is when Nussan saw that this was none other than Reb

Nachman himself. Face to face with his Rebbe, who had so recently departed this world, Reb Nussan was speechless and dazed. At last Reb Nachman broke the silence and said, "At a certain time, Nussan, we are called upon to burn these sacred scriptures. The time has returned, and we are repeating this ceremony, as did our fathers and their fathers before them. For when the words rise up in flames they are free to return to the divine realm of their origin, where they remain until they are called down once more by those living in the world of men. Do not imagine, though, that they no longer exist, only that the letters have flown from the page. For the time will come when someone who requires them will look closely enough at a blank page and bring them back into being."

It was then that Reb Nussan awoke, lying amazed on his bed. And he knew with a strange certainty that Reb Nachman's spirit was with him in that room, and that it was he who had planted the seed of that dream. What is more, he also knew that each letter of Reb Nachman's writing which had gone up in flames was such a seed, and that those seeds were now scattered all over the world like the sparks of the shattered vessels, waiting to be gathered so that the lost words could be restored.

Ashes

It happened as a sign and covenant on the first *yahrzeit* of the death of Reb Nachman that the unbound pages of the first edition of his tales reached Reb Nussan, his scribe. The night before the pages had arrived, Reb Nussan had dreamed they were already in his hands, and in the dream he was overjoyed to read them, the tales of his Rebbe, which it had been his great blessing to receive and transmit. And as he read the pages in the dream, the letters burned in his vision like fire.

For the next week he had read the pages over and over, taking care to be certain that every letter was firmly in its place. Then, on the eighth night, Reb Nussan could not sleep, and he got up and went into his study and there he read through the book yet one more time.

But that night, that one night, every word that he read turned to ashes. And Reb Nussan knew that somewhere in the *Yenne Velt*, the Other World, the spirit of Reb Nachman was grieving that very night. And when he realized this, Reb Nussan understood for the first time that a man takes his grief with him into the Other World, and even there on certain days the finest garments turn to rags. And Reb Nussan wept, for even though his Rebbe was in the *Yenne Velt*, he had seen fit to share his grief with his scribe, as he had always been willing to share his joy.

Reb Shlomo's Mission

WHEN Reb Nachman's tales were published, a copy was dispatched to the Holy Land at once, as was Reb Nachman's wish. The one who was chosen to carry out this mission was the eldest son of Reb Nussan, whose name was Reb Shlomo. In undertaking this journey Reb Shlomo was fulfilling the wishes of both Reb Nachman and of his father, Reb Nussan.

Now this Reb Shlomo was a deeply religious man, who drew his strength from the higher powers. He was a quiet and steady man, and a man who could be completely trusted. Above all he was a loving man, who was loved by all who knew him.

After Reb Shlomo had been entrusted with this mission, but before a ship departed to take him on the first leg of his journey, which would eventually reach the Holy Land, it happened that an army marched through Bratslav, burning and looting everything which stood in its path. Reb Shlomo and his family were among those driven from their homes, but it happened that by great good luck they were also among those who obtained passage on a ship that had as its destination the Holy Land.

Reb Shlomo carried with him no clothes for that journey, but in one hand he held his infant daughter, and in the other he carried his violin in a case, for he was a master of the violin. And in the violin case he had hidden his prayer book and the book of Reb Nachman's tales.

So it was that fate made it possible for Reb Shlomo to arrive in the Holy Land many months sooner than would have been possible. When Reb Shlomo stepped off the ship and onto the shore, the first thing he did was to kiss the earth of the Holy Land and offer a prayer of thanksgiving for having lived to reach that day. And the next thing he did was to take out Reb Nachman's book and read aloud the tale of the lost Princess and of the one who had sought to find her.

And as soon as Reb Shlomo read the first word of that tale he felt himself transformed, and saw that the land on which he stood was sacred; and he felt the presence of Reb Nachman in that place. Then he knew that he was like a plant whose roots, once cut, had started to grow again, and that what had been broken apart was about to be restored. And that plant soon grew extensive roots, which plunged deep into the sacred soil, and at last reached the springs of living water that bubble beneath the surface.

Why the Soul of Reb Nussan Cut the Silver Cord

ALL his life Reb Nussan's soul had sought to trace its way back to the Holy Land, as had happened once in his life on the day before the Sabbath. But no matter how hard his soul tried, it never again succeeded in being the first to reach the Promised Land. And Reb Nussan knew that this journey was identical to climbing up the ladder in his recurrent dream, in which he had always fallen back to the earth before reaching the final rung.

Yet it happened that one day, which fell on the day before the Sabbath in *Galut*, which is also the day of the Sabbath in the Holy Land, that the soul of Red Nussan once more flew ahead of every other soul that sought to reach Jerusalem, knowing that only one soul would be permitted beyond the gate.

But this time Reb Nussan did not permit himself to be called back before the sun had set and the *Havdalah* was performed. In fact, his soul did not come back at all, but having threaded its way to *Eretz Yisrael*, it decided never to take such a risk again, for reaching that place had been like climbing up the sheer side of a mountain. Instead of returning, Reb Nussan's soul cut the silver cord by which every man is attached to his soul, and there was no way to turn back.

And the sons and daughters of Reb Nussan who stood around his deathbed saw how his eyes had turned inward, and how, at the last moment, a luminous light passed through them, and a bright glow surrounded his face.

Reb Nachman's Chair

for Matti Megged

FOR four generations after the death of Reb Nussan of Nemerov, Reb Nachman's scribe, there were no scribes in his family. But in the fifth generation there was a young man whose name was Nathan, and this is the story of how he found his way back to Bratslav.

Now this Nathan was a Jew, of course, but he was unaware of the heritage of the Hasidim. Still, like many other Jews of his generation, he was drawn to the Holy Land, and made his home there for a year. One night in the winter, a night that was the *yahrzeit* of his ancestor, Reb Nussan, although he was not aware of this, Nathan dreamed a dream.

In the dream he was standing in a barren desert when he heard a voice calling out to him. And in the dream the voice was very familiar, but still he could not identify to whom it belonged. At last he caught sight of an old man, dressed in the black robes of the Hasidim, who was making his way through the desert to him. And this old man told Nathan that he had traveled a long way to reach him, and Nathan must come with him, for his help was sorely needed.

And Nathan followed this old man, who was his ancestor Reb Nussan, across the continents to Poland, from the heat of the desert to fields of snow, and they came to the city of Bratslav. And when they had reached that city, Reb Nussan led Nathan to a modest house there. He took Nathan into the study, and he showed him a finely crafted wooden chair, whose ornamental carv-

ings and velvet pillow made it closely resemble a throne. And Reb
Nussan told Nathan that his help was needed to carry this chair
back to the Holy Land. And Nathan did not hesitate in the dream,
but picked up the chair and placed it on his back. And though the
chair was very heavy, it seemed like a feather to Nathan; sometimes it almost seemed as if the chair were somehow carrying him
rather than the reverse. And the journey to the Holy Land took
place in the wink of an eye, and was much shorter than had been
the journey away from there. And when Nathan reached the Holy
Land his ancestor Reb Nussan embraced him and blessed him and
thanked him and took his leave. It was then that Nathan woke up
from the dream. And he clearly remembered the events of the
dream, but he did not know their meaning, and he let the dream
pass out of his mind like all of the other dreams that are only
fleetingly recalled.

Then, the next spring, on a night that was Reb Nachman's
yahrzeit, although Nathan did not know it, he went for a walk
through the religious section of Mea Shaarim in Jerusalem. And
when he observed all of the Hasidim in their dark and heavy robes,
he was reminded of Reb Nussan and his dream. And then it happened that he came upon the Bratslaver synagogue in that section
of Jerusalem, and he remembered the name of the city of Bratslav,
and he entered the synagogue.

Now it is the custom of the Bratslaver Hasidim to read the
tales of Reb Nachman on his *yahrzeit*. And so it was that when
Nathan entered the synagogue he found one of the Hasidim reading the tale of the lost Princess to the others, and all of the
Hasidim seemed lost in rapt contemplation of the tale. And when
Nathan heard this tale its truth spoke to him as if all ornament
had been discarded. Its form did not conceal its content, but
brought out its meaning to the full. And then Nathan looked up
and next to the Ark he saw a chair that resembled a throne, and
that was the very chair which he had carried from Poland in his
dream!

Then, after all the tales of Reb Nachman had been retold,
Nathan learned from the Hasidim the history of that chair. For

that chair was the chair of Reb Nachman; that chair was his throne. After the passing of Reb Nachman many of his Hasidim had made their way to the Holy Land. That is because they knew how much their Rebbe had loved the Land. And they were certain that if his spirit could be found anywhere in this world, it would be in the Holy City of Jerusalem; so that is where they established their synagogue. And about this they were right, for many of the Hasidim attested that they had encountered the wandering spirit of Reb Nachman there, especially in that place where his chair was to be found.

As for the chair, the Hasidim who had come from Bratslav had been forced to smuggle it out of Poland. To do this they had cut the chair into pieces, and each of them had been responsible for one piece. And in this way each and every piece of that chair had made its way to the Holy Land, where it had been reassembled and preserved in that place. And the Bratslaver Hasidim also told Nathan that those who said a prayer before that chair were often blessed and had their prayers answered, for the spirit of Reb Nachman would intercede in their behalf.

And so it was that Nathan prayed in that place, before the Ark and the chair. And as he left the Bratslaver synagogue that night, he encountered a vibrant wind as he descended the stairway that sent a long shiver through his soul—as if he had met and embraced a familiar spirit that had rushed up the stairs to greet him. And after this Nathan found what had been lost, and what had been taken away was at last restored.

The Tale of the Menorah

ONE year it happened that the *yahrzeit* of Rebbe Nachman of Bratslav fell on the Sabbath, and after a fine Sabbath meal and the singing of many songs, Reb Zalman of Zholkiew repeated to those present Rebbe Nachman's tale of the menorah. And this is the tale as Reb Zalman told it that night: "Once a young man left his home and traveled for several years. Afterward, when he returned home, he proudly told his father that he had become a master of making menorahs. He asked his father to call together all those who practiced this craft in that town, that he might demonstrate his unrivaled skill for them.

"That is what his father did, inviting them to their home. But when his son showed them the menorah he had made, not everyone found it pleasing in their sight. Then his father went to each and every one and begged them to tell him the truth about what they thought of it. And at last each one admitted that he had found a defect in the menorah.

"When the father reported this to his son, the young man asked to know what was the defect they had found, and it emerged that each of the guests had noted something different. What one craftsman had praised, another had found defective; nor did they agree on what was the defect in that menorah, and what was the most beautiful aspect of it.

"And the son said to his father: 'By this have I shown my great skill. For I have revealed to each one his own defect, since each of these defects was actually in him who perceived it. It was these defects that I incorporated into my creation, for I made this menorah only from defects. Now I will begin its restoration.' "

When Reb Zalman had retold this tale, he saw it was still taking root in the souls of his Hasidim. And he said, "I see that Reb Nachman's words still echo in this world, as well they should, since he brought them to us from on high. Since this night is his

231

yahrzeit, let all of us open ourselves to his spirit, which is surely present among us, and let us ask him if we might inquire further into the mystery of the menorah of defects." And no sooner had Reb Zalman said this, than each of his Hasidim discovered he could express his deepest understanding of Reb Nachman's tale.

Then Reb Zalman turned to Hayim Elya, his scribe, and bade him speak. And Hayim Elya said: "Surely this *maaseh* of Reb Nachman's illustrates a secret about the process of *tikkun*, of restoration and redemption. The purpose of that menorah, then, was to make the others aware of their defects, for only when this awareness has been attained can the process of *tikkun* begin."

Reb Zalman and the other Hasidim were pleased with this interpretation, and marveled at the skill of the craftsman who could capture the essence of another's defects. Then Reb Zalman turned to Reb Simcha, and bid him to speak. And Simcha said, "Surely the menorah represents the way a *Tzaddik* may serve his Hasidim— as a mirror to make them aware of their defects so that they may initiate the process of *tikkun*, as it is written in the Talmud: '*Anyone who finds a flaw finds his own flaw.*' " And this interpretation was also pleasing to the Hasidim, for it applied to Reb Zalman above all, who had served as a mirror in which they had been able to recognize their destiny, as well as their defects.

After this Reb Zalman turned to Reb Sholem, and asked him to reveal his understanding of the tale. And Reb Sholem said "Surely the model for that menorah existed before the creation of the world. Then each branch of it was a perfect vessel, unbroken and complete. But in order for creation to take place it was required that these vessels be broken, so that they could spill their sparks of light into the world. This is what we refer to as the Shattering of the Vessels. Thus the branches of that menorah were broken vessels, and that is why they appeared defective to the others. For it was necessary for them to first recognize that the vessels had been broken before they could begin their restoration." And when the others had heard Reb Sholem's commentary, they felt that it also rang true.

Then Reb Zalman turned to Reb Avraham ben Yitzhak, who

was also present that night, and bade him make known the meaning of the tale as he understood it. And Reb Avraham said, "Surely the craftsman who created this menorah is none other than the Holy One, blessed be He. Therefore the seven branches of the menorah represent the seven days of creation, and the light of the flames of the menorah represent the primordial light, which came into existence on the first day of creation, when God said, *Let there be light, and there was light*, while the menorah itself is this world. And why is it a menorah of defects? Because the defects are the defects of this world, since *God formed man out of the dust of the earth*." And the others marveled at these words, and understood how the tale might also be an allegory of the creation of the world.

Now the last of Reb Zalman's Hasidim who had not yet spoken was Reb Naftali, who was steeped in the mysteries of the *Kabbalah*. And when Reb Zalman turned to him, Reb Naftali said, "Surely the seven branches of the menorah represent the seven *Sefirot* that emanate in the world below, while the oil, the wick, and the flame of the branches represent the three *Sefirot* of the world above. And thus the menorah reveals how the worlds above and below may be drawn together, so that the light originating in the world above may also be reflected here below. That such a menorah would appear defective in the eyes of men is not surprising, for when the light of the *Shekhinah* is withdrawn, this world has no more substance than a shadow. But when the light of the *Shekhinah* illuminates our vision, we are able to perceive it from the perspective of the world above, where its perfection cannot be denied." And the words of Reb Naftali illuminated the understanding of everyone who heard them, and they began to recognize that the waters of meaning ran far deeper than they had first realized.

It was then that Reb Zalman spoke for the first time, and he said, "Surely this menorah can be likened to an opal. An opal's most distinguishing feature is the fire of its center, but this fire is also its flaw. When seen from one angle, the fire resembles nothing more than a crack, but from another perspective it is the most beautiful part. Thus what appears to some to be a defect in the menorah is what makes it unique and more beautiful.

"Now consider that the menorah in Reb Nachman's *maaseh* was actually *perfect* in every respect, and it was only the vision of those who beheld it that was flawed. When the *tikkun* had at last taken place and their eyes were opened, they saw that menorah in all its splendor, with each branch representing one of the seven heavens, which opened up before their eyes." And with these words each of those present were uplifted on one of the branches of that menorah into the celestial Paradise, and when they looked down from the heights they saw that the seven flames of the menorah all burned as a single flame, and that that flame illuminated the Bearer of every blessing. And there they also saw the spirit of Reb Nachman, which had been present among them all along, and they all understood that he was the one who had provided the clarity of their perceptions. At that moment they heard Reb Nachman's voice echo in their souls, saying, "Surely all that you have said about that menorah is true, for it is like an immense, many-faceted jewel; each of you has turned to gaze at a new facet, for the facets of the jewel are infinite. Yet it is but a single jewel you see, eternal and unchanging. It is the jewel in the crown of the King of Kings, who is none other than the craftsman who constructed this menorah so that the flames burning below might ascend on high, and all the world could be illumined by their light."

Reb Nachman's Tomb

for Moshe Shilge

Now in Jerusalem there was a wonderful violinist among the Bratslavers whose name was Reb Moshe. This Moshe was a *baal teshuvah*, one who has returned to the fold. Before he had come back to the ways of his fathers, he had played the violin with great skill, but now he dedicated his music to the Holy One, blessed be He, for when he played the violin he felt he was singing in praise of all that is sacred.

This Reb Moshe joined a group of Bratslavers on a pilgrimage to Reb Nachman's tomb in Uman, in Russia. For every Bratslaver Hasid seeks to go there once in his lifetime. That is because on his deathbed Reb Nachman had said that anyone who goes to his grave, gives charity to the poor, and says with *kavvanah* the ten psalms he always recited, in the proper order, which have a special quality of transforming the soul—that whoever does all this Reb Nachman will save from *Gehenna* if, God forbid, the Hasid should arrive there.

For in that old cemetery in Uman were buried in a mass grave thousands of martyrs who were killed in 1768 in the terrible pogrom that had taken place there. Reb Nachman had specifically asked to be buried there so that he could redeem the souls of the dead, much as the Baal Shem had once done in another town.

Now the journey to Reb Nachman's tomb was fraught with danger. For the Russian government threw many obstacles in the way of those who sought to reach the Rebbe's grave. And many were the Hasidim who were stopped and had to turn back, or were arrested and charged with being spies. In fact, not long before Reb Moshe planned to go to Uman, it was learned that another Hasid had been arrested while making the attempt. A considerable ransom was required in order to free him, and everyone contributed something for this purpose, no matter how poor they were. Al-

235

though this incident might have discouraged others from attempting to go, it did not discourage Reb Moshe.

So it was that before he departed Reb Moshe asked his wife for permission to set out on such a journey. And his wife did not hesitate, but gave him permission to go because she was certain that a messenger intent on performing a *mitzvah* would not be harmed. For Reb Moshe's wife shared his devotion for the study of the Torah and his love for Reb Nachman, whose spirit pervaded their lives.

So Reb Moshe took his beloved violin and set out on the long journey. The way brought him into contact with other Bratslavers, who were traveling from all over the world to complete this essential quest. The Bratslavers met in Europe and from there they traveled together. There were twenty-two of them in all. They arrived on the eve of Rosh Hashanah in Kiev, about a hundred miles from Uman. Reb Moshe felt that his heart was about to explode from his longing to reach the Rebbe's tomb—it was a storm in his heart that he had never known before. He felt as if he were being pulled there by a powerful magnet. Then he noticed that all of the others were the same—a special light shone from all of their faces, clear and bright. And Moshe was certain it was the presence of Reb Nachman's soul that had created this longing in them, which every moment seemed to increase.

So it was that all of the Hasidim were deeply disappointed when they were unable to reach the Rebbe's tomb by Rosh Hashanah. They remained in Kiev, and there they spent the days of the holiday and the Sabbath.

After the Sabbath they left Kiev before dawn and set out for Uman. On the way they stopped at a freshwater pond, and all immersed themselves in its waters. After this they prayed together under the sky. And at that moment, as their words rose in unison, so did their souls bind themselves into a single one, imprinting that moment in their memories for all the days of their lives. Then they continued the journey to Uman.

When they arrived at Uman, Reb Moshe felt the deep satisfaction of having fulfilled a long-standing desire. Once they entered the cemetery the Hasidim raced about, trying to find the Rebbe's tomb. A gentile woman who saw the Hasidim running pointed to show them the way.

When at last they reached the Rebbe's tomb they lay down at the foot of it, and for the moment Reb Moshe put aside his *tallis* and *tefillin* and the violin and cried in the great happiness and relief that he had been blessed to reach that place. After a while he put on the *tallis* and *tefillin* and said the ten psalms Reb Nachman had always repeated with great emotion, and understood them in that place as he had never done before.

Now Reb Moshe's father had passed away two months before his birth, and he was named after him. So there at the tomb he said the orphan's *Kaddish* with cries and tears. After this he took his violin and played the melody of his Rebbe. And as he played he felt a great calm and inner purity come over him, and he knew a closeness to God he had never experienced before in his life. He played quietly, simply, without flourishes but with a great deal of longing and desire. And there, surrounded by the other tombs and the great trees that grew there, the melodies of Reb Nachman rose in the air, pulling all of them up one rung after another, always ascending the stairway of the soul.

A Dialogue Among Disciples

WHEN the time of his death drew near, Reb Nachman gathered his disciples together and told them, "You will not need to choose a successor for me after my death. Even then I will still be your Rebbe." And after his death the Bratslaver Hasidim obeyed this behest, and to this day have never designated another as their Rebbe. For this reason they are sometimes known as the "Dead Hasidim," since their Rebbe is dead.

One day a hundred years later four of Reb Nachman's Hasidim were gathered in the Bratslaver synagogue in Mea Shaarim, not far from the chair of Reb Nachman that is set up beside the Ark. One of the disciples said, "Perhaps one of you could tell me why it was that Shimon, Reb Nachman's first disciple, was entrusted with the treasure of treasures, the Hidden Torah itself? Why did Reb Nachman not carry this jewel and Shimon carry the *Shofar*, instead of the reverse?"

A second disciple replied, "Reb Nachman was like a long blast blown on the *Shofar*. His spirit was so pure it could only thrive in the realm of the invisible, and music and story-telling are the only invisible arts."

The third disciple said, "Yes, you see, Reb Nachman was a direct descendent from the side of the Oral Law, and Reb Nussan, his scribe, was one of those descended from the side of the Written Law. And just as the Oral Law and the Written Law complement and complete each other, so too did Reb Nachman and Reb Nussan require each other in order to be complete. It was simply impossible for Reb Nachman, the man of the spoken word, to carry the flaming letters of the Hidden Torah across the River Sambatyon. Instead it fell to Shimon. Would that it had fallen to Reb Nussan himself—then the End of Days might already be with us. But it was not Nussan's fate; his destiny was to preserve the pearls that fell from Reb Nachman's lips, to be his scribe. Not to take part in any of the tales, but to be a witness to them."

The fourth disciple, who had listened with great attention to this discussion, then said, "The reason Reb Nachman was entrusted with the *Shofar* is that the *Shofar* did not depend on the Book as the Book depended on the *Shofar*. For without the Book, the *Shofar* was still permitted to set free the soul of the Messiah, while even if Shimon had brought the Book back, it meant nothing unless Reb Nachman also succeeded. This is because it is possible to offer up a prayer without words which the Holy One can comprehend without any explanation, while a spoken prayer offered without *kavvanah* is like a jug that has holes in it and cannot hold water."

Just then the disciples heard a voice which spoke in a whisper and seemed to emanate from Reb Nachman's chair: "Perhaps Shimon was chosen in the knowledge that he would not succeed—perhaps it was not yet time for the End of Days. Instead it was time to set free the soul of the Messiah to make way for another generation—perhaps your own—to complete the quest."

Glossary

All terms are Hebrew unless otherwise noted.

Adon Olam a hymn that has been part of the daily prayer book since the 15th century. It has been attributed to various medieval poets, particularly to Solomon Ibn Gabirol.

agunah a woman who is forbidden to remarry either because her husband has abandoned her without a divorce or because there is no proof of his death, even though he is believed dead.

Alenu the prayer recited as the closing prayer of the three daily services since the 13th century.

Aleph the first letter of the Hebrew alphabet.

aliyah lit. "to ascend." The term used for those who choose to live in Israel and also to denote the honor extended to a worshiper who ascends the *bimah* in the synagogue for the Torah-reading services.

Ari acronym for Rabbi Isaac Luria, who lived in Safed in the 16th century and is credited with having created the myth of the Shattering of the Vessels and the Gathering of the Sparks.

Asmodeus the king of demons, the nemesis of King Solomon, and a familiar figure in Jewish folklore.

Baal Shem Tov lit. "Master of the Good Name." The name given to Israel ben Eliezer, the founder of Hasidism, who lived in the 18th century. Earlier figures, such as Rabbi Adam, were also referred to as Baal Shems, implying their knowledge of God's secret Name and their attainment of extensive mystical powers.

baal teshuvah one who repents of his sins. The term is also used to refer to Jews who come to embrace Orthodox teachings for the first time in their lives.

bar mitzvah the occasion on which a boy of 13 is formally ushered into the adult Jewish community.

bat kol a heavenly voice.

Beit Knesset a house of prayer.

Beit Midrash a house of study, traditionally found next to the *Beit Knesset*.

Bereshith lit. "in the beginning." The first word of the Torah.

beshert Yiddish for pre-destined.

bimah the podium from which prayers are offered.

daven, davening Yiddish for "to pray." Refers especially to the intense prayers of the Hasidim, who, following the dictum of the Baal Shem Tov, attempt to *daven* with *kavvanah*, or spiritual intensity.

drash an interpretation of a passage in the Bible. Also, the third level of *Pardes*, the system of interpretation of sacred texts, representing allegory.

D'var Torah lit. "word of Torah." A concise lesson in Torah, interpreting a portion of the Bible or Talmud or another sacred text.

dybbuk the soul of one who has died that enters the body of one who is living, and remains until exorcised.

Eretz Yisrael the Land of Israel.

erev the eve of the Sabbath or a holy day, on which it begins.

Ein Sof lit. "endless" or "infinite." The highest, unknowable aspect of the Divinity.

gabbai an honorary synagogue officer.

Galut the forced exile of the Jewish people from the Land of Israel; the Diaspora.

Gan Eden the Garden of Eden; also a term for the Earthly Paradise, in conjunction with the Celestial Paradise.

Gehenna the place where the souls of the wicked are punished and purified, the equivalent of Hell in Jewish legend.

gematria a technique used by Jewish mystics to discern secret meanings in the Torah. In this system each Hebrew letter has a numerical value, and the commentator seeks out words or word combinations that have the same totals, which are then regarded as linked.

Hasid (pl. *Hasidim*) lit. a "pious one." A follower of Hasidism, a Jewish sect founded by the Baal Shem Tov. Hasidim are usually disciples of a religious master, known as a Rebbe.

Havdalah lit. "to distinguish" or "to separate." The ceremony performed at the end of the Sabbath, denoting the separation of the Sabbath from the rest of the week that follows.

Hayim Vital the primary disciple of the Ari and central transmitter of his teachings.

hazan a cantor.

Kabbalah lit. "to receive." The term designating the texts of Jewish mysticism. A *Kabbalist* is one who devotes himself to the study of those texts.

Kaddish an ancient prayer, written in Aramaic, and sanctifying the name of God, which is recited by mourners as a prayer for the dead.

kavvanah lit. "intention." Spiritual intensity, especially in prayer. A common saying among Hasidim is, "Prayer without *kavvanah* is like a body without a *neshamah* (soul)."

Kedushah lit. "Sanctification." Also name of a prayer restricted to congregational worship, requiring a *minyan*.

kleippot a *Kabbalistic* concept referring to empty shells that represent the concentrated forces of evil and obstruction.

Kotel lit. "wall." The retaining wall that is the only remaining section of the Holy Temple still standing in Jerusalem. It is also known as the Western Wall and the Wailing Wall.

Lamed-Vov, Lamed-Vov Tzaddikim according to the tradition, there are Thirty-Six (*lamed-vov* in Hebrew) Just Men in every generation, and the world continues to exist because of the righteousness of these *Lamed-Vov Tzaddikim*, as they are known.

Lilith Adam's first wife, in Jewish legend. Later she became identified as a night demoness who attempts to seduce men and strangle newborn infants.

Maaseh Bereshith the Work of Creation. The mystical doctrine of the secrets of creation.

mahzor a festival prayer book.

mehitzah a partition used in Orthodox synagogues separating men and women during public prayers.

menorah the seven-branched candelabrum described in the Bible and used in Temple days. The special menorah for Hanukkah has eight candlesticks, plus a ninth for the *shamash*.

Merkavah lit. "chariot." The *Merkavah* is the divine chariot in the vision of Ezekiel.

minyan the quorum of ten males over the age of 13 that is required for any congregational service.

mitzvah a divine commandment. There are 613 *mitzvot* listed in the Torah. The term has also come to mean a good deed.

nekevah lit. "female." The feminine aspect of man according to *Kabbalistic* doctrine, perhaps equivalent to the concept of the anima.

neshamah a soul.

Olam ha-Asiyyah the fourth of the Four Worlds, which includes both the whole system of the spheres and the terrestrial world.

Olam ha-Atzilut the first of the Four Worlds, the World of Emanation, linked with the *Kabbalistic* concept of the ten *Sefirot*.

Olam ha-Beriah the second of the Four Worlds, the World of Creation, linked with the Divine Throne and the *Merkavah*.

Olam ha-Yetsirah the third of the Four Worlds, the World of Formation, sometimes linked with the angels, especially Metatron.

Pargod lit. "curtain." In Jewish mysticism it refers to the Curtain that is said to hang before the Throne of Glory.

pardes lit. "orchard," and also a root word for "Paradise." Also an acronym for a system of textual exegesis based on four levels of interpretation: *peshat* (literal), *remez* (symbolical), *drash* (allegorical), and *sod* (mystical).

parasha a sub-section of the weekly *sidrah*. Sometimes used interchangeably with *sidrah*.

Reb (Yiddish) an honorific term used among Jews in addressing a man who is a scholar. It is also used among Hasidim to address each other.

Reb Adam a legendary medieval sorcerer, identified as a Baal Shem, who gave the seminal Book of Mysteries to the Baal Shem Tov, according to Hasidic legend.

Rebbe (Yiddish) the term used for Hasidic leaders and masters.

Rosh Hashanah the Jewish New Year, which takes place on the first day of Tishri. Tradition says that the world was created on Rosh Hashanah.

Sefer Torah the scroll of the Torah.

Sefer Yetsirah lit. "The Book of Creation." Widely regarded as the earliest *Kabbalistic* text, deriving from the 8th century, and containing mystical numerical formulas.

Shahareis the morning prayer service.

Shekhinah lit. "to dwell." The Divine Presence, usually identified as a feminine aspect of Divinity, which evolved into an independent mythic figure in the *Kabbalistic* period. Also identified as the Bride of God and the Sabbath Queen.

Shema the central prayer of Judaism: *Shema Yisrael, Adonai Elohanu, Adonai Ehad*—Hear O Israel, the Lord our God, the Lord is One. It is based on Deut. 6:4–9.

Simeon bar Yohai a talmudic sage of the 3rd century who spent 13 years in a cave while hiding from the Romans. Tradition holds that he authored the *Zohar* during that period, although it is now believed that Moshe de Leon was the true author.

shofar a ram's horn used by the ancient Hebrews in battle as a trumpet. It is sounded as part of some high religious observances.

siddur prayer book.

sidrah the weekly portion of the Torah which is read.

Simhat Torah the concluding day of the festival of Sukkot on which the cycle of readings from the Torah is concluded and begun again.

Sofer a scribe, whose duties include copying and repairing the *Sefer Torah*, and, among the Hasidim, recording the teachings of their Rebbes.

tallis a four-cornered prayer shawl with fringes at the corners, worn by men during the morning prayer services.

tefillin phylacteries worn at the morning services (except on the Sabbath) by men and boys over the age of thirteen.

tikkun restoration and redemption.

Tisha B'Av the ninth of Av, traditionally the day on which the first and second Temples were destroyed. It is a day of mourning on which disasters have recurred among the Jewish people.

Torah the Five Books of Moses. In a broader sense the term refers to the whole Bible and the Oral Law. And in the broadest sense it refers to all of Jewish culture and teaching.

Tu B'shvat the 15th of the month of Shvat, when it is customary to plant tree saplings in Israel. It is the day the almond blossoms are said to first appear.

Tzaddik (pl. *Tzaddikim*) an unusually righteous and spiritually pure person. Hasidim believed their Rebbes to be *Tzaddikim*. A *Tzaddik ha-Dor* is the leading *Tzaddik* of his generation, sometimes identified with Messiah ben Joseph, who, if the time is right, will pave the way for the coming of Messiah ben David.

Tzohar the illuminating stone of Jewish legend, which Noah is said to have hung in the ark as a source of light at night.

yahrzeit Yiddish term for the anniversary of the death of a close relative.

Yenne Velt Yiddish term for the Other World, inhabited by spirits and demons.

yeshivah school for talmudic and rabbinic studies.

Yetzer Hara the Evil Impulse.

Yom Kippur the most solemn day of the Jewish religious year, spent in fasting and prayer. It is regarded as the Day of Judgment, on which God decides whether or not a person will be inscribed in the Book of Life for the coming year.

Zohar lit. "illumination" or "splendor." The central text of *Kabbalah*, written in the 13th century by Moshe de Leon, but attributed to the talmudic sage Simeon bar Yohai.